# ABSOLUTE POWER

Baron Alexander

Wilderwick Press

Forest Row, UK

**Baron Alexander/Wilderwick Press**
**Unit 4 Ashdown Court**
**Forest Row, RH18 5EZ (United Kingdom)**
**www.baronalexanderbooks.com**

Publisher's Note: This is a work of fiction. Names, characters, places, and incidents are a product of the author's imagination. Locales and public names are sometimes used for atmospheric purposes. Any resemblance to actual people, living or dead, or to businesses, companies, events, institutions, or locales is completely coincidental.

**Absolute Power/ Baron Alexander**. -- 1st ed.

Dedicated to Joe

# CONTENTS

# CHAPTER ONE

# Berlin 1880

"This way."

"Here?"

"No. There."

"All the way down?"

"All the way down." She said it with a smile as she watched yet another man sweat with excitement at his first time. He looked at her with wild eyes. His hair was disheveled and suit crumpled. She could see that he was a powerful man, whatever it was he did, but here, she was in charge. She had seen even the most powerful men shake and cry with uncontrolled joy.

He paused before doing what she knew he had to do, but instead did something unexpected. He closed his eyes, slowed his breathing, and fixed his suit. He used his hands to flatten his hair, probably blown wild by his drive over, and straightened his tie. "I'm sorry but I can't think straight. You need to show me." He took her hand and started walking in the direction she had pointed.

She felt his warm hand envelop hers. The touch was electric and short circuited any remonstrance. It was against hospital policy for her to leave her post. It was also against policy for her to have such inappropriate contact with the public, but the power of his personality overwhelmed her and she found herself quickening her step to stay ahead of him. There was no reason for him to be holding her hand and, in any other circumstance, she would have released herself immediately. The touch was completely innocent, solely intent on getting him to where he needed to be. She was a tool for him, like the switch that turns on a light. She was there to bring him to his newborn son.

"Have you been working here long?"

"Pardon me, sir?" The question, like his touch, was unexpected and she wasn't sure she heard correctly.

"You look too young to be a matron. I was wondering how long you've been working here."

She blushed. "I'm not the matron but I am in charge when she steps out. In fact, I'm going to get in trouble for taking you to your son."

"Tell her it was my fault. If you have any problems, I'll speak to her and explain." He seemed to notice he was still holding her hand and let it go, slowly releasing his fingers. It was another moment before he felt her fingers let go of his.

"He's just around the corner. Do you want to see your son or wife first?"

His look told her and she opened the doors to another identical hall, pristine in order and cleanliness. On one side, half way down, a window replaced the wall and overlooked a room of babies, each ensconced in their little cots.

His pace slowed and he stopped at the edge of the glass, not wanting to miss a thing. His hands involuntarily raised to feel the barrier. "Which one is mine?" He began to sidestep along the length of the window, never altering his expression of wonder and searching each little face for recognition.

"You aren't allowed into the room. I'll go inside and bring him next to the glass. I'll be able to bring your baby to you and your wife shortly." Seeing his face, she added, "It's hospital policy. There's nothing wrong with your son; simply administrative procedure."

He nodded and saw her disappear through a door and reappear on the other side of the glass. He heard only the pushing of a broom or mop somewhere in the corridor, but he ignored it. He expected to see screaming red-faced babies but they were calm and each looked like an angel.

When the nurse brought his son to the window, he could feel his body change. It was as though all his molecules rearranged themselves and he evolved from a man into a father. His son's eyes were closed and his skin was darker than he would have imagined. He was wrapped in blue with a little blue cap. Holding him, the nurse beamed. It was the first time he had noticed her as something more than the conduit to his son.

She was pretty and young, with perfect teeth and large blue eyes. Her skin glowed as though she had just given birth herself and his son was hers. She held him in front of the window with such pride that he needed to shake himself from the thoughts that threatened to creep into his mind. On her left forearm, he noticed a birthmark where her sleeve fell back. It could have been a heart in someone's imagination, but to him it looked like a map of Africa.

"Beautiful," he mouthed. "Thank you."

She nodded slightly, eyes closing in the process, and mouthed, "You're welcome." She returned the bundle to his cot and returned to him moments later.

"You'll be wanting to see your wife," she said. Something in her voice was hard to place, but he noticed she wasn't in a hurry to return to her station.

"Yes, thank you. And thank you again for this." He waved at the room full of babies.

"It was my pleasure. I can see you are a proud father. Your son and wife are very lucky." She lowered her head and began walking. "Your wife is not far from here."

"Wait." He put his hand on her shoulder, lightly, barely touching her. "What is your name?"

She turned and opened her eyes. "Anna."

"Thank you, Anna. You have been very kind and gentle with me. I'm Meyer Hildebrandt. My wife's name is Siegrun."

"I know your wife. I was assigned to her when she came in."

"Then you know how difficult it has been." He was a tall man, large across the shoulders. He filled his suit as only the truly affluent do. But, as he said this, he seemed to shrink and his shoulders droop.

"Everything is fine, sir. Your son and wife are doing well. We are keeping her in for a couple of days just as a precaution."

"Please, call me Meyer."

She blushed. "I don't think that would be appropriate. I don't want people talking."

"Nonsense. I choose with whom I am to be familiar, not others. Remember that. You are in charge of you, no one else." His suit filled out again and she caught a glimpse of the power he wielded outside of those walls.

"Yes, sir. I mean, Meyer."

He smiled and put his hand on her shoulder again. "Let's get me to Siegrun before she starts wondering where I disappeared to."

Anna's shoulder felt warm for the duration of their walk. She could feel his hand through her starched white uniform as though it had never left. She walked slightly ahead of him and became aware of the way her feet met the floor and her body moved. She dared not look back or make any conversation. She was a professional and took care of women at the most profound moment of their lives. She loved what she did. But she had never met a man like Meyer before. No one had ever had this effect on her. She was the one who watched other men become tongue tied and awkward around her. She was the one who was used to every eye being lifted to watch her walk into a room. *Get control of yourself, Anna,* she thought.

"Your wife is here," she said. "In this room."

"Thank you. It was a pleasure to be in your company, Anna. Now, if you'll excuse me…"

"Meyer?"

He turned to look at Anna. He saw her eyes darting around his face. "Yes?"

"Are you forgetting something?"

Meyer's eyes moved from corner to corner as if searching his brain. "I don't think so."

"Flowers? Something special?" Anna immediately regretted it. Meyer was not a young man, perhaps old enough to be her father. He wouldn't want to be belittled.

His reaction was that of a man frustrated by his own impatience. He clenched his fists and shook his head but recovered quickly. "You shame me, Anna, and you're right. I've been so distracted by fear that I forgot to have joy." He hung his head. "Do you know where I can find something nice in short order?"

Anna's face lit up with her easy smile. "I do. Follow me. It'll only take a few minutes." She took him by the hand and pulled him away from Siegrun's door. They stopped outside of an empty room.

"What's this?"

"Mrs. Schultz left earlier today. She had so many flowers and gifts that she gave them to the staff. As I am part of the staff, it would be my pleasure to give them to you. Take your pick."

Meyer eyed the bed surrounded by flowers and boxes of what he presumed to be candy or chocolate. Every surface was covered. His eye fell on a small potted plant with white flowers. "Is that what I think it is?"

"In the small pot? It's edelweiss, my favorite of all of them." She retrieved the gift and put it in Meyer's hands.

"It is beautiful," he said. He turned the small pot around and lifted it to the sunlight. He turned to Anna to find her looking at him already. "You know, there's been talk of a new technology that will change the way we live in ways we can't even begin to imagine."

She laughed. "Looking at a flower makes you think about technology?"

"I'm thinking about light as I look at this beautiful specimen. Then I am reminded of an American inventor who has made light from electricity. I've seen it. It is remarkable. It is already being fitted in all the best homes and I have no doubt we'll see them in hospitals before long. No more gas."

"Edison?" She had read about it in the papers. Everyone had. It was the biggest news of the decade.

"That's him. I met him recently. Cantankerous character, but brilliant. He'll become rich from this invention, though. Mark my words."

"We have some lights already in our surgical rooms. I'm told the entire hospital will convert as soon as practical."

"And every lightbulb will make Edison richer. It is a wonderful thing, to own a patent." Meyer drifted into his thoughts once again, alternating his gaze from the potted flower, to Anna, to the windows in the hallway.

"Siegrun?"

"Excuse me?"

"I don't wish to be rude, Meyer, but your wife probably would like to see you?"

He snapped back into the present and grasped his gift. "I'm sorry. I get wrapped up with all of the wonders of the world. We live in such a magical time. My baby's healthy and life is wonderful."

Anna let him babble. He was becoming the new father that she had seen when he first arrived at her desk, out of breath and terrified of missing the moment. "Follow me. I'm sure the two of you have lots to talk about." They walked in silence and she opened the door to his wife's room.

It was identical to the one that held the flowers, except that the bed was occupied. Siegrun's long dark hair was matted with sweat and lay splayed across her pillow. Her face was serene with an expression just shy of a smile. Her body was tired and lay motionless on the bed with three thin blankets on top. Next to the bed was a large chair with thin arms and a side table with a small clock, a pitcher of water, and a glass. On the wall above the bed was a crucifix.

"I'm sorry I missed it."

"That's okay." Her voice was tired and resigned, yet happy. "Did you get to see him?"

"I did. He's beautiful. You're beautiful."

"Don't. I'm hideous."

"You're the mother of my son. You'll never be hideous."

They sat in silence for a while, his hand holding hers. She liked the way his hands made hers feel so small, the way he made her feel safe in his arms. The strength of his will made everything okay.

"It almost makes everything else feel less hard." Her eyes became glassy with tears as soon as she said it.

"Shhh. Let's not talk about that."

"It's why I haven't named him yet. I wanted you to be here. I wanted it to be real before I…" She stopped again as her body shook softly and tears began to run down her cheeks.

"He's strong and beautiful, just like you."

"He is gorgeous, isn't he?"

"He'll want for nothing and he'll change the world."

"No pressure then," she said. Her face was smiling again and she wiped her tears with the back of her free hand.

"Can you sit up? That's it, slowly. Good. Now have some water. Can you eat?"

"I'd rather see our son."

"Anna is bringing him to us."

"Anna?"

"The nurse?"

"I know. I didn't think you knew."

"I was a mess when I arrived and she helped me." He turned to where he left the little pot and handed it to Siegrun. "Here. Isn't it beautiful?"

She ran her fingers along the furry petals and smiled faraway thoughts. "It's magical and perfect. Thank you." She lifted his hand to her lips and kissed them. Meyer inwardly thanked Anna.

"Have you thought about a name?"

There was a pause again as emotion washed over her. "Each of our…" she couldn't finish the sentence at first. "…other children were named before they were born. I didn't want to tempt the fates."

Meyer held her hand firmly. His own emotions were rising as he could still feel the fear and panic as he pushed through the hospital doors. Each time, he was met with the cold hand of death. Each child, a complication that the staff couldn't deal with. He steeled himself, knowing that his pain was still a fraction of his wife's.

"Let's meet our son and see what name fits him," he suggested.

"Seeing this edelweiss, I want to call him that but I can't think of any boys called Edel. If she was a girl, we would have her name."

Meyer kissed her hand and leaned in to kiss her softly on her lips. He stroked her hair and waited for Anna to arrive. He didn't have to wait long.

"Who do we have here?" she said, talking to the baby. Anna held the blue bundle gently against her chest, her hand expertly cradling the head. She looked flushed and happy. She entered Siegrun's room and placed the precious child into her arms.

At first, Siegrun cried and held her baby, all birthing pain forgotten. She moved sideways slightly with her body and her head continued the pendulum as she danced with the life that was given to them. She kissed his cheeks and let Meyer do the same. Anna looked on, hypnotized by the love in the room. It was the reason she enjoyed her job so much.

"Isn't he the most beautiful baby ever born?" Siegrun's face was all happiness.

"He is," Meyer replied. He was stroking the swaddling, wanting to feel his son's little hands and feet but deferring to his wife's needs first.

"Anna, what name would you say matches our little boy?"

Anna was still standing transfixed in happiness over the bed. She reached out and touched the little boy's face with her hand and looked into his eyes. "Joseph, like in the Bible. It is a strong name. An honorable name for a good family." She looked at Siegrun and nodded. When she looked at Meyer, she found him already looking at her. She could feel the heat of the flush rise on her neck. "But I should get going and leave the three of you alone." She lowered her eyes and left the room.

"I like Joseph," Siegrun said. "And Adel. I've been thinking. It is close to Edelweiss and it means someone noble."

"Sounds fine to me," Meyer said. He was still absorbing the electricity from Anna's glance.

"Joseph Adel Hildebrandt. I think that's your new name! Meyer, meet your son Joseph."

He took the bundle from her and moved up and down as he held the baby next to him. "You are going to bestride the world when you grow up," he whispered in his son's ear. He stood and danced with his boy when the sound began. It was the clear, beautiful sound of a healthy baby crying. It made Meyer weep with joy. "I think our son is hungry." He passed Joseph back to Siegrun and sat down. *Life is grand*, he thought.

∞

"Everything okay with Mrs. Hildebrandt?"

"Everything is fine, thanks." Meyer barely broke his stride as he opened the door and went to his usual chair. The room was full of cigar smoke and ten other men. "Sorry about the interruption."

"Nonsense, Mr. Hildebrandt. Why else would we do this if it wasn't for family?" Mr. Rock stood and walked towards Meyer, intercepting him with an outstretched hand. "Congratulations. Boy or girl?"

"Boy. Healthy and strong."

"Good man."

Each of the other members shook his hand and clasped him on the back. It was the first time Meyer had seen such an outburst of affection from these men.

"What did I miss?" He wanted to bring things back to business. The total membership rarely met and each man was a titan in his own industry.

"Mr. Rhodes has outlined his expansion plans and we are all in accord. Mr. Rock has set out his objectives for his industry and has agreed to direct funds from those enterprises into the membership at some future date. The Very Reverend Mr. Peter Beckx has condoned Bismarck's latest actions and we have all agreed that no recourse is needed."

Meyer was mentally checking the points as they were raised and then recorded into the memories of the eleven men. Nothing was written down and no man would ever repeat what was said here. This group helped Meyer become the man he was. As the owner of industries and railroads across Europe, he ensured that his backing brought the right men into power—and that they would protect him once there.

"And my proposal for an expansion of my railways? Any objection?" Meyer tried to be as nonchalant as possible. He had not known of a request to be refused; if it was, it would represent a loss of trust in him. And trust was all he had.

"None whatsoever," Mr. Roth said. "My banks will ensure you have all the monies you need."

"Then this year will mark the best period of my life so far," Meyer said. "My son, my business, and my family. What more can a man want?"

"You speak the truth, Mr. Hildebrandt," said Mr. Roth. "And that can only come with peace. That has always been the purpose of this Order, as it was for our predecessor."

"They were more interested in enlightenment," another said. "Peace is its practical application."

"Yes," Mr. Roth continued. "And peace does not necessarily mean a lack of discord. I have been especially fond of Bismarck's ability to bring together the German states with minimal bloodshed. But blood will continue to be shed for the cause of peace. There are many out there who do everything they can to derail order and create nothing. Between ourselves, we create and control over a quarter of North American and European wealth. We must use our strength, our influence, and our determination to keep the course. Peace can be achieved. But we may have been too short-sighted. It may need to be solved at the global level. The world has become much smaller and we need to become more proactive."

"With our money?" Mr. Rock said.

"Yes, and with our influence. Someday, the world may outgrow our brute financial strength, but influence will steer the ship. The soft power, the intelligence, and the ability to shape a leader's willpower will allow us to create the peace we all desire."

"Hear, hear." All voices agreed.

"What do you propose?" asked Meyer.

"The world looks pretty good from where we are sitting, but when sailing a ship, one must always look to the horizon for clues of an impending storm. We must reinforce our relationships, build new ones, and keep our eye on our objective."

"In other words," said Meyer, "let's enjoy the good times because they won't last. We'll prepare for the worst and continue to hope for the best."

"I couldn't have said it better."

The room relaxed as each titan settled into his chair. The room itself was set off and reserved for the opera house's directors and special guests. It was spacious, with enough room for fifty seated men. Its ceilings were more than thirty feet high with gilded flourishes. The height absorbed the smoke without it becoming uncomfortable, and the soaring windows were built for gods to peer in on their creations. At Mr. Aguado's urging, all talk of business ceased and the servants were let in to tend to their needs. The best wine from Mr. Roth's vineyards flowed beside the brandy from Mr. Aguado's estates.

∞

"Have the prince contact Bismarck and see if we can sit down for dinner in the next couple of weeks. Thank you. No, Mrs. Hildebrandt will deal with the domestic matters. Yes, Joseph will be coming home shortly. Yes, he is the blood that flows in my veins and the breath that wakes me at dawn. No, I don't have time for that; let Mr. Horst see to it." The conversations rang in Meyer's head as he made his way into his study.

When Siegrun arrived, he noted the noise and excitement of the house but stayed firmly behind his desk. The niceties of the servants always annoyed him. *If I could run a respectable household without them, I would,* he thought.

"Can I come in?" It was Siegrun.

"Of course. I'll be right there."

As he opened the door, his chest began to pound and his palms sweat. He kissed his wife and took Joseph in his arms, partly to provide a barrier between himself and Anna. Her presence shook him as her eyes searched his face. He nodded to her and looked questioningly at Siegrun.

"It was my idea. You never get along with anyone so I wanted to ensure that our new nanny would be someone both you and Joseph could like." She was still beaming and the world could do no wrong. She was twenty-six years old and had been warned against marrying such an old man as Meyer, but she was content. He had given her a beautiful boy, a safe home, and status in society none of her other suitors could match.

Her parents reluctantly accepted his proposal and came to like and respect him. Three still-births later, they remained happy with each other but were both firmly aware of the harsh realities of life. Romance and fairies were something for operas and fiction writers. They lived resolutely in the real world.

"Hello, Mr. Hildebrandt, sir." Anna extended her hand.

He looked down briefly at her elongated fingers and then back to her face. "Meyer, please. I wasn't kidding." He found himself in a difficult position of having a staff member calling him by his Christian name. In ordinary circumstances, he rarely had contact with the staff and left the running of the house to Siegrun. No one in the house called him anything other than 'sir' or 'Mr. Hildebrandt'. Yet, he had extended the offer to her and now it was a point of honor to retain that relationship.

"I'm sorry, Meyer, sir. I mean, Meyer." She looked straight at him.

He could feel her hand in his again, the second time in as many weeks. Her fingers were warm and left a lingering sensation on his palm as she withdrew them. In his other arm was Joseph and Meyer stood dumbstruck for the briefest of moments while he took in the scene before him. He would revisit that moment later, he knew. He forced himself to return to the exchange of pleasantries and the joy of his boy.

"Meyer?" said Siegrun with genuine surprise. "I'm convinced more than ever that I made the right decision." His face held an empty smile that Siegrun interpreted as she wanted, namely of his pleasure with her choice of nannies. Anna excused herself and he was able to walk Joseph into his study. Siegrun watched as her husband held their precious boy. She knew she had chosen him as her husband for this, not the wealth or power he wielded.

"Do you see all of the fancy books? Look at the lovely yellow colors. Yes, I know you do. You're such a lovely boy. Soon, you'll be reading here with me. They look big and scary at your size but soon you'll learn to love them. They hold the secrets of the universe and I'll show you the key to unlocking all of them. Sounds exciting, doesn't it?" His moustache tickled Joseph as he whispered the words. To Siegrun, it looked like he was gurgling in their son's ear, but Meyer was parting with his most intimate hopes and dreams. "You will bestride the world, little Joseph. I will show you the way. Just be strong and healthy and everything will be okay."

His walk around the paneled study took a further four minutes as he slowly made his way amongst the furniture and took Joseph's hand in his and touched the books. Each step contained a little bounce to please Joseph. In return, his eyes opened and he gave his father a gummy smile. Then a yawn and he fell asleep. Careful to not wake him, he handed the bundle back to

Siegrun. The two smiled at each other, eyes brimming with joy. Siegrun turned to seek out Anna and Meyer returned to his desk, content. His house had finally become a home.

The leather of his seat and the top of his desk was in oxblood red. He had his desk customized when he finished his first hundred kilometers of railway line. He commissioned his mansion when he finished his thousandth kilometer. He was invited into the Order when he finished his two thousandth kilometer. Chancellor Otto Von Bismarck's mini wars inadvertently helped Meyer secure his position as top industrialist in the new Germany with steel mills, coal mines and political access second only to the Kaiser himself. As with all industrialists, he looked eastwards past the safety of Prussia's spheres of influence into Russia and its unlimited need for railways. As a realist, he restricted himself to the new worlds controlled by England, France and Germany. Their colonies absorbed everything he could throw at them. He became partners in materiel or finance (as Mr. Roth's front man) in over half of all railways in the United States. He kept his name out of the papers and out of the history books with shares that didn't cause offence or concern. He was happy with less than five percent and a seat on the board. He would let others take the glory. He was there for the money.

All of his accumulated money and power came at a cost. It was one of the reasons he waited so long to get married. He was forty-four years old when he met Siegrun. She had just turned twenty and many were beginning to talk of her becoming a spinster. She was the most beautiful woman he had ever met with a mind that could challenge him and keep him interested in her. They would have beautiful, smart and strong children, he thought, and proposed after only three months of courtship.

"No, please, I don't wish to be interrupted." His concentration was broken as his butler knocked softly on his study's door. He enjoyed reliving his successes. *And today is my greatest triumph,* he thought. *Finally, a successor. Someone I can teach and give everything to. Immortality.*

"I'm sorry, sir, but Mrs. Hildebrandt has retired to her room and the new girl wishes to have a word with you."

"Excuse me? What has she to do with me? Please deal with her for me."

"I'm sorry, sir, but she is insisting that she must speak with you." He waited expectantly for some guidance.

Meyer looked at his desk for a moment before nodding his head. "OK, bring her in."

The door closed and then reopened with Anna framed by the heavy dark oak, her hand resting lightly on the handle. Her hair was down and she wore the uniform of the house. She looked like an angel to Meyer.

"Hello Anna. Is everything OK?" He was torn between standing and remaining seated. As they were on familiar terms, he decided to stand when she entered the room.

"Not really," she said as she released the door. It closed on its own as she walked towards his desk. She had the grace of an athlete and trained dancer. Her body was always balanced between steps and her torso remained immobile. When it did move, it did so in order to ensure that her head and eyes remained fixed on their subject, like a cat on the hunt.

"Shouldn't this be something you take up with Siegrun? I generally don't deal with household matters and I can't see what has happened…" he fell silent as she walked closer towards him. The desk remained between them and she took a sideways step to get even closer. She stopped when there was no furniture between them.

"I needed to talk to you, alone." Her head tilted up and caused her hair to fall away from her face. Her eyes were fixed on his and her hands hung by her side, not moving.

Meyer's mouth was dry and his body began to warm. "What do you need to talk about?" His chest involuntarily puffed out. *Why is she affecting me so much? I deal with the Kaiser and Bismarck and world leaders. She's just a girl.*

"I may be a spinster but I'm not blind Meyer."

"Blind to what?"

"You're uncomfortable with me being your nanny. Your wife can't see it because she's in another world. But I need to live here and I don't want to feel I can't talk to you or her or anyone."

"Do you always talk to your employers this way?"

She smiled. The furrows between her eyebrows disappeared and her white teeth made her lips even more noticeable. "I've been told before that I'm a little too forward."

He was surprised at himself as he laughed. "You're just fine. I like women who have a mind of their own." When he saw her blush, he quickly corrected himself. "I mean, I like everyone in the household to feel comfortable enough to talk to either myself or my wife frankly."

"I'll remember that, Meyer." She dropped her eyes.

Each time she said his name, he could feel a bolt of warmth in his torso. "You don't have to worry about me. I thought you were super at the hospital when I arrived like a fool and you helped Siegrun through some very tough days. This whole process has been tough on her."

"I know," she said as she put her hand on his arm. "She told me everything. I felt like I knew you before we ever met. The way she described you, I didn't think they made men like that anymore." She let her hand drop when she realized what she did.

Meyer was as lost as a schoolboy with his first crush. "Well, don't believe everything. I'm sure she exaggerated." He took a step backwards, away from her, and started looking through a stack of post he needed to attend to.

"I'm sure she didn't," she said in a soft voice. She turned and began walking towards the door.

"Anna?"

"Yes?" she turned to face him, half-way to the door. Her face was once more illuminated.

"You're welcome to come and see me anytime. But, if the door is closed, it means I'm not to be disturbed. Understood?"

"Understood." She said it as much to herself as him. Her eyes closed as she nodded farewell and then left him alone.

∞

Time passes slowly and quickly as a parent. The long nights when the baby can't sleep and cries non-stop. The feeding schedule when the baby doesn't cooperate. But equally, the clothes that the baby outgrows. The first crawl, first step, first word.

"I can take Joseph at nights so you can sleep," Anna said.

"And miss my baby's tears?" Siegrun was fiddling with his clothes, the third change of the day after a diaper malfunction. "I want the cries as well as the laughter."

"You're a good mother. But if it gets too much, let me know and I'll take him gladly. He's such a bonnie little boy."

"I still can't believe it. He fills me with such joy I can't put it into words." After a moment, she added, "How are you with Meyer? I know he hasn't been around much but he does appreciate all of the work you do with Joseph."

"Meyer's been very kind to me. I can't complain."

"Have you ever thought about marriage?" Siegrun couldn't believe she asked the question. Anna didn't seem to mind.

"Yes and no. If I could find a prince like yours, yes. Most men are fine but I am not sure whether I am prepared to be a wife. You still live like a free person with Meyer. Most women don't." She spoke freely and it was one of the things Siegrun liked most about her. She needed someone to connect mentally with.

"And you don't mind not having children?"

"That's the hardest part. I love children, especially after working in the hospital and, now, working here. They are pure innocence. All they want is love, food, and sleep."

"Would you be prepared to meet someone if they were the right person?"

Anna began to imagine Meyer and then nodded. "Yes, of course."

Siegrun became more excited. "I have someone I'd like you to meet. He's Prussian, an officer with an income and inheritance, educated, and thirty years old. He's got a good family and would be perfect for you."

She held Joseph but it was only her and Anna in the room. "What do you think?"

"Ah, well, I don't know. I'm probably too old for him by now anyway."

"Don't talk nonsense. You're the same age as me and prettier by far. He'd be a fool not to snap you up."

"You're too kind, but I know men a little better than you think I do. They don't want someone old like me. They want someone fresh. Fourteen, sixteen, eighteen at the oldest."

"I won't have it. I am inviting him to tea next week Wednesday. We'll find someone to take care of Joseph and you will join me in the salon. If you like him, we can take it from there." She wasn't going to take no for an answer.

Anna laughed. "All right, but no promises."

"Life is all about broken promises. Our role is dealing with the fallout."

They returned to Joseph and made sure he was loved, fed, and rested. The hours and days accelerated and Wednesday was upon them before they knew it.

Siegrun took the seat of honor in the salon with Anna to her right. They each wore dresses that were tight around the waist now that Siegrun had her figure back. They opted for a small hoop that always reminded Anna of a peacock strutting with its feathers behind. The cut was low enough to entice any red-blooded man, with frills along the seams, arms, and wrists. Anna was in red with white accents while

Siegrun wore a more demure blue. Around them gathered society's grandest women, none of whom knew who Anna was or what she did. If they had, they would not have talked to her.

"We're in for a treat. Bismarck is meeting with Meyer afterwards and he has accepted my invitation to drop in. As has Alex von Trippen, the prince I told you about." She noticed with delight Anna's little squirm. "There will be the usual gentlemen who call in, I'm sure, but you need to concentrate on Trippen."

It wasn't long before Anna leaned towards Siegrun. "I think there's someone there who might match your description."

"Yes, that's him. Isn't he dapper? His moustache is perfect, and he's groomed like an Adonis."

Anna looked over at her. "Are you sure he's for me or you?"

They laughed and waited for him to come over.

"Good afternoon, Mrs. Hildebrandt. You have a lovely home and thank you for inviting me."

"Your Serene Highness is too kind."

"Please, we're amongst friends. Call me Alex."

"Certainly. Please call me Siegrun."

"The pleasure is all mine."

Siegrun blushed slightly as he lifted her hand to his lips. "And let me introduce you to my great friend, Miss Anna Voigt."

Alex stood straight, clicked his heels, and bowed deeply to Anna. The action was graceful and well-practiced, but its effect on Anna was profound. It was as though the concussion of his heels was felt through her chest and her eyes became larger than normal. She stared directly into his eyes, causing him to stare back. For a moment, the salon ceased to exist for them both, falling away into a blur of colors and sounds.

"It is my greatest pleasure, Miss Voigt."

"Please, Anna."

"And you must call me Alex. May I sit near you?" He was already bending and had reached the seat by the time she assented.

"I'll leave you two alone for a moment," Siegrun said. "I need to talk to Meyer about something. Please excuse me." When she stood, all the men in the room stopped their conversations and stood. "Oh, please be seated. I'll just be a moment." Knowing that her behavior would be gossiped about for months, she continued walking until she left the salon, ostensibly in search of her husband.

"I think we'll need to be finding a new nanny," she said to Meyer when she found him.

"Sorry to hear about that. What's happened?"

"Nothing, other than the way Prince Alex von Trippen just about fell over when he was introduced to Anna, and she him."

The news brought a pang to Meyer. While he had no intention of acting on his feelings, the thought of a rival hurt. He felt a weakening of his body as a result. "That's great news for her, but does he know who she is?"

"Of course not."

"Don't you think this will cause a scandal?"

"We need a good scandal once in a while to keep things interesting." She smiled with a glint in her eye.

"Siegrun Hildebrandt, I would never have thought it. You are a subversive deep down." He was smiling and pulled her towards her. They were alone and he snuck a quick kiss. "I'm sure we'll weather whatever happens. I'm more concerned about Anna. There's no guarantee that Alex will take her once he is aware of all the facts."

"True, but who are we to stand in the way of true love?"

"Alex can't afford true love. No one in his position can. They need to marry well and be mindful of their strategic importance in Europe."

"You're about as fun as a bucket of cold water," she said. She was smiling so he took it as it was meant.

"I only mean for you to be careful. Anna isn't an experiment or a diversion to keep you busy."

"We can always have another baby," she said, coming closer.

"I'm doing everything I can in that department," he said. "The rest is up to God."

"Then I'll mention Anna in my prayers for us as well."

Meyer shook his head and let her fantasize. There was nothing he could do to change her mind, but the thought of Anna with another man caused something to stir within him.

∞

"You knew this would happen," she said. Her face was flush and she tried to gather as much air as her corset would allow. "He was never going to be allowed to love me. Me, a lowly nurse. A servant." She slumped in the corner, the hoop pressing against her back. It hurt, but strangely made her feel better to have a pain other than the one tearing at her shame.

"I had no idea Mrs. Kohler would open her big trap. And she wouldn't have known had it not been for her maid."

"But why did she have to embarrass me like she did? I wasn't hurting anyone."

"I know, Anna, and it's wrong. It's probably my mistake. I wanted you to meet the prince and you hit it off. I thought he would salvage the situation in due course but it was too soon to expect him to do anything other than distance himself from you. I wanted him to spend more time with you to be as enchanted as are we."

"You two are not the norm. People are mean. And you wonder why I'm still a spinster."

"It's because you are looking to the sky when there are diamonds all around you. But the heart wants what the heart wants. I just hope you find your prince some-day." She got up and gave her hand to Anna to help her out of the corner. "In the meantime, let's get cleaned up and see our men. Joseph is always happy to see us and Meyer may have time, depending on how his session goes today. Sometimes he and the chancellor can spend all afternoon and evening together. I wonder what they talk about so much."

"Meyer is very intelligent," Anna said. "Maybe the chancellor is picking his brain."

"You have a very high esteem of my husband."

"Of both of you. But it's a man's world and your husband becomes our champion by default."

Siegrun look carefully at Anna. "You're very intelligent yourself. How come you are here and not at a university or doing something with your brain?"

"I tried university, then nursing, now being a nanny. My parents have some money but that was never my interest. I want to follow my heart, and it led me here."

Siegrun smiled and hugged her. "You are my diamond. I don't need to look at the skies any longer. But it doesn't mean I'll stop looking for a man for you. You deserve it."

"You're incorrigible."

"I like to think so."

# CHAPTER TWO

# Best Friends

"It's early days." Siegrun's face was excited and slightly oily. Joseph had learned to walk early and the two of them chased after him in the garden.

"That's wonderful news. Does your husband know?" Anna took Siegrun's hand and stopped walking. They watched Joseph out of the corner of their eyes as they looked at each other.

"Not yet. I wanted to make sure first. You know, with all of the problems in the past, I didn't want to disappoint him."

"Don't talk like that. You could never disappoint him. I know he loves you."

Siegrun grew quiet. *I know he loves me, but he doesn't look at me the way he looks at you anymore,* she thought. "Joseph! Come here. That's a good boy." Their conversation would have to wait. "Not so close to the pond."

Anna got to him first and scooped him up. He squealed as she kissed his tummy. "Let me carry him. From now on, you're not to lift him unless absolutely necessary. We need to protect you." Her smile was genuine and Siegrun couldn't suppress hers.

"Then let's get out of this sun. It's wearing me down."

"Sounds wonderful." Anna had become more of a friend than a nanny. "Shall we put our little prince to bed first?" Joseph's eyes were already closing, the effect of his efforts taking its toll. They put Joseph to bed and instructed a servant to watch over him as they went for their walk.

From a distance, the two women looked like sisters, one blonde and the other dark. Their ivory dresses hovered above the grass as the two figures floated towards the main house. It sat on almost one hundred acres, with a landscape inspired by Casper Friedrich. Its design elicited no interest in either woman. Their preference was the pond at the bottom of the grounds where they could feed the ducks and hold hands with Joseph. As the ground fell away, they could make the house disappear, touching the bark of the Lebanon cypress tree as they passed. No follies cluttered this part of the grounds and the two women felt free.

The first time Anna asked her, Siegrun grew red with embarrassment. "Swim? Here? It's not done."

"Who's going to say anything? Who's going to see us?"

"The gardeners, passing dignitaries. It's not right. I wouldn't do that to Meyer."

"But you want to?"

The summer's heat was unbearable and the high ceilings of the house weren't enough when the wind was non-existent. "I'm not a girl anymore, and I'm pregnant. I can't risk it."

"There's a place just here that is sheltered and no one passes. We have been here countless of times and I have never seen a soul."

Siegrun looked at the cool water. Its liquid was held by the long grass and clay soil and was overlooked by the willow tree. The translucent green leaves provided further shade and she could see a run of fish in the shallows. She imagined them surrounding her, kissing her body as she lowered herself into the water. She could see herself stretching and floating on her back, oblivious to the world. As her head cleared, she realized Anna was already in the water. Her head looked away but her eyes stared.

"Anna, what are you doing?"

"I'm luxuriating."

"I can see through your clothing." Siegrun whispered it loudly, afraid someone might hear. She looked over to her left and then right and spun in a circle to ensure there wasn't someone behind her as well.

"Come in. It's cool. We can dry off in the sun together."

"I can't do it."

"Just dip your toe in. Let your feet feel this." Her eyes were fixed on Siegrun as she floated on her back. The wet clothing clung to her, hugging her legs and torso. Siegrun looked at her smile, but her eyes registered every inch of Anna's nakedness.

She found herself undoing the intricate laces of her boots. She put them aside, careful not to get them dirtier than necessary. She saw the pile of Anna's clothes and began to step out of her own dress. It was as though she was outside of her body, her hands not her own, as the buttons were unfastened, hooks unclasped, and stockings removed. When she was done, her hands tried to cover herself, though she was still covered with white cotton. Anna had stopped coaxing and crouched in the shallows. She watched as Siegrun took her first step into the water.

"It's wonderful," she said. "Step aside, I want to go in further." She felt the vegetation change under her feet as she went deeper. The soft mud squeezed between her toes and the water rose above her waist. "No, just wait. I want to go until my head is under water." She felt the ground steepen as the pond became deep and she was forced to swim. The water surrounded her and the fire inside her began to cool. She began to imagine the fish swimming with her, brushing the inside of her legs and keeping her afloat.

She put her head under the water. When she broke the surface, Anna was floating next to her. She felt her fingers reaching out to her and they held hands as they floated in the sun, then shade, under the willow tree.

"I could stay like this forever," Anna said.

"Me too. I can't remember swimming feeling so good."

Forever lasted almost an hour before their bodies needed the shore. They went towards the shallows, feeling heavier with each step.

"You look like you jumped in with a bedsheet," laughed Siegrun.

"And you? Do you think you look any different?" She continued walking slowly up the shore, then turned back. "Are you okay? What happened?"

"I'm okay."

"You don't look it. Is it my comment? You know I didn't mean it."

"No, it's just that I will not look like this ever again." She was touching her belly and looking at Anna.

She put her hand on Siegrun's belly. "You're beautiful. You know that. You'll recover again, you'll see."

"I'm not as beautiful as you. I've seen Meyer looking at you. You couldn't have missed it as a woman."

Anna's hands traced Siegrun's belly in silence and she allowed her. She took Siegrun's hands and put them on her waist, one at a time. She let her. Anna continued to trace her body, never breaking the lock on her eyes. Time stopped and Siegrun felt her body inch towards Anna's. When their bodies finally touched, she felt a familiar fire and her insides became soft. She felt herself being led up the shallows before Anna knelt, still in the water. Siegrun followed suit, ignoring the moss and grass at the water's edge. When Anna kissed her, Siegrun felt flashes behind her eyes as though she had never been kissed before. Her body began to tremble with adrenaline and she reclined, allowing the fish to swim with her, kissing her body all over.

∞

"I know you're not fit to receive anyone, but can you please ensure everything is perfect for this evening?" Meyer hit full stride by the time he reached his clothes, already set out on a mannequin by his valet. Contrary to many men of his station, he shared his bed and bedroom with his wife, and preferred to dress himself.

"This belly makes me look grotesque. I love giving you another child, but why must I put myself through this?"

"Don't worry about tonight. I'll talk to Horst to sort everything out."

"I can barely walk up and down the stairs. Sometimes I think the baby will just drop out, it's so huge."

"Are you sure this is okay? Look at it, I don't want to seem to be trying too hard."

"Don't worry, Anna will take care of me. She's been so supportive. I don't know what I'd do without her."

"That's a good idea. Now all I need to do is figure out how to get Bismarck to be civil to the kaiser's son.

It can't be healthy, having divisions in a family like that."

"Do you mind if I just lie in bed? Can you open a window? I need the cold air on me."

"What? Sorry, I've been busy with this convention and I need to push some people together and some apart. If people weren't so damn bull-headed and actually listened, the world would be a better place."

"Don't worry, I'll do it myself." She swung her legs off the bed and slid down until her feet landed on the thick carpet. She felt the blood flowing downwards and immediately wanted to crawl back into bed. There was no pain, other than her lower back, but her body wanted rid of the baby and all she could do was wait. It would come when it was ready.

"That's a good idea. Here, let me help you with the window."

"Thanks."

"Now get back in bed. I can't believe you got out for something as silly as that. I wish you'd just tell me what you want and I'll do it."

"Maybe we should go to the hospital. I'm not feeling great and the baby was due last week."

"If you think it's best, but we have Anna and she'll be able to give you better treatment than any hospital. People go to hospitals to die. I wouldn't want to wish that on our new son or you." He came over to kiss her, his trousers open and shirt hanging loose.

"Maybe ask Anna to come when you're done?"

"Certainly. I'll get her to make sure you're right as rain. Everything will be fine, sweetheart."

"Thanks." He was putting the final touches on his tie and had just put his hand on his jacket. "And Meyer?"

"Yes, my love?"

"Don't get too worked up over those monkeys. They need you more than you need them."

"Only my money. I need their souls!" He smiled at his joke. "You remember Wagner's Dr. Faustus?"

"Yes, darling. Very funny. Just don't forget."

"I won't. I'll be back late. If things go well, I may bring back some of the squeaky wheels to apply some grease."

"Good luck."

"Good night, my love."

The door clicked as he closed it gently behind him. Three minutes later, it opened again, this time with Anna. She closed the door behind her before coming to the bed. In silence, she put her hand in Siegrun's.

Siegrun closed her eyes and nodded.

"Are you staying in bed or getting up?"

"Staying in bed. I can't face people."

"Then I'll stay with you." She kissed her softly on her lips before lifting the clothing that covered her belly. The lotion felt cool against Seigrun's hot skin before Anna's hands began to rub it in.

"That feels wonderful."

Anna nodded silently, letting her hands move from Siegrun's belly to her legs. The covers were thrown back to allow her legs to soak up the oils. Anna spent most of her time on Siegrun's feet, repeatedly rubbing as deep and as hard as she could. Occasionally, she would hit some point that caused Siegrun to cry out. "Sorry," Anna would say, head still down, all energies focused on oiling her body. When she was done, Siegrun lay naked on her back, glistening from the treatment. Anna removed herself to the adjoining room to clean her hands. She came back smelling of perfume.

"It doesn't matter how often I use it, I love indoor plumbing." She was smiling as she climbed onto the bed. It was massive and the two of them barely covered half of it.

They lay in silence. The room was far enough away from the household activity so as not to hear anything and the closest neighbors were across the estate. It was as though they were the only two living souls on earth. They closed their eyes as they interlaced their fingers, and fell asleep.

It was almost dawn before Meyer arrived. The door opened and closed and he undressed onto the floor. After a quick visit to the water closet, he put himself under the covers and snuggled next to his wife. His body was much larger than hers and his drinking caused his belly to expand like her own.

"You feel wonderful," he said. His hands traced her naked body, feeling the smoothness of the oils. He felt her body respond, stretching and pushing against him. In a dreamlike state, he felt his body unite with hers. His eyes, closed from the beer and the familiarity between them, saw her in his mind. He remembered the first time he saw her. She was the most striking woman he had ever met. Tall in a short body, proud, and smart. Where most men shunned intelligence, he embraced it. Her body felt as it did on their wedding night, firm and supple but without the hesitancy. He felt her shudder and then kiss him deeply. Her hands scratched him on his chest. She was different than before, more aggressive and certain of herself, and he liked it. He found himself on his back looking at her in the darkness, his hands reaching for her. The light began to change but not quickly enough. When he finished, his eyes closed tighter and he fell into a deep sleep.

Siegrun couldn't sleep at all.

∞

The morning air was glorious, fog rising graciously from the ground. Siegrun had slipped out shortly after first light. Meyer wouldn't notice, as his arm was still around Anna. *Anna, whom she loved; who swam between her legs like the fish in the pond, who opened her eyes. Those same eyes that could not now be closed. And they saw more clearly than ever before.*

Barefoot and draped in her robe, she walked down the stairs. The cold stone, then carpet, then tile left their brand on her feet. The wet dew, disturbed, clung to her feet as they shuffled past.

Her mind no longer saw the joy of her children, born and unborn. It had become black from the image of Anna's betrayal against her. She sought out happiness in her despair. It came into sight as it always did, making the house invisible.

Into that world she walked, then waded, then drowned.

∞

*Was I her Hamlet that she became my Ophelia?* He stood over her lifeless body as it lay in the grand salon. Doctor Christoph had left and the unpleasantries of death lay ahead. Meyer's large body shook as grief overtook him. No further thoughts could break the torrent of images that flooded his mind. The worst was the image in front of him now—her waxen skin, lifeless limbs, and a still heart.

He felt a hand slip into his and he gripped it tight. He could smell the perfume before he saw her. Despite his grief, which had numbed him moments before, he felt his body ignite as their eyes met. She nodded briefly and let go of his hand. He felt her presence leave and the numbness returned. He would seek her out later.

Later happened that same night. Within three months, they were married. Six months later, their first child was born. Elizabeth Siegrun Hildebrandt became the light of Meyer's existence.

He had wealth, power, and love. He was complete. He was also suspicious of the rest of the world and trusted no one with his money, which he divided into four parts. Three would form anonymous structures with no ties back to him. While not strictly legal, the jurisdictions in which he formed them allowed him to leave everything to the son of his grandson. In the event no such person existed, the remaining living relative of his grandson (from either Joseph or Elizabeth) would get everything. The fourth part he kept visible in Germany to allow them to live in the lifestyle to which they were accustomed—and to keep the authorities placated. He died satisfied he had done everything he could in his life. Fortunately for Meyer, he died in 1913, before his beloved Germany went mad.

Joseph was married and had a son in 1905, and together, they would inherit everything. Elizabeth was given a dowry sufficiently large to attract a wealthy American and they had a child before Joseph, in 1899. Anna would survive Meyer to see his great grandson born in 1931.

# CHAPTER THREE

# Absolutely Powerless

"It's an outrage. Meyer was one of us."

"Yes, twenty years ago. Before the Great War and before this madman, Herr Hitler."

"Herr Hitler won't listen. He never did. His existence is a reminder of why we need to persevere in our efforts. He is why we exist—to take the edges off history."

"Yet here we are, as impotent as a eunuch in a whorehouse." If Mr. Taylor thought he'd elicit a chuckle or grin from the ten other men, he was wrong.

"We must be able to assist the family. We all know Anna. We can't let her end her days like that."

"We don't involve ourselves in these matters," snapped Mr. Roth. "When have they come to help us? If they had the chance, we'd all be hanging from our necks. No, I vote against it. Germany may have taken temporary leave of its senses, but it is still our most valuable asset outside of England and its colonies."

"Especially since Lenin and Stalin took away Russia. We need to think bigger. Let's fight and prepare for the next war, not this one."

The Order took a vote. It was unanimous. Anna, Joseph, and Elizabeth would be on their own.

"May God protect you," said Mr. Roth to no one in particular.

∞

"It's not so bad," Anna said. "We'll get to the bottom of this and I'm sure everything will be fine. We have powerful friends."

"I hope you're right, Mutti," Elizabeth said.

"The trial was a farce," Joseph said, still fuming and picking at a thread that stuck out where his front button once was. "How could they call us Jews?"

"Or homosexuals?" Elizabeth was smoothing her wool skirt as they settled into their train carriage. "I'm just relieved little Joe and Teddy didn't have to go through this."

"How are they?"

"I received a telegram saying that Joe's fever from the measles has broken."

"Thank God for that," said Anna. She forgot where she was when her great-grandson was discussed. "And Teddy?"

"He's watching over the business and making sure Joe is okay. He's the most wonderful husband I could have hoped for."

"And your daughter-in-law?"

"Missing. No one knows. Last I heard, she was trying to get back to America from Hamburg."

"Maybe we should have gone too," Joseph said. "Germany is losing its mind."

"Germany is the greatest nation on Earth," Anna said. She sat taller when she said it. "Your father laid these tracks and much of our fortune is still in them."

"And they're taking us to some concentration camp in Sachsenhausen."

"A work camp," she corrected him. "Many political prisoners are sent there. I've spoken to our advocate and he will see if our friends can get us out before long. You'll see. Everything will be okay."

"I don't know how you can remain so calm, Mutti. Lizzy, have you seen my son?"

"Otto's talking to the guards. They were in the same regiment together."

"That's a good sign. Maybe we'll get out of here after all."

The door to their compartment was left open for Otto to return. The entire compartment was full of the Hildebrandt family—Anna, Elizabeth, Joseph, and Otto—and their luggage. Each sat with the haughtiness of one enduring an underling's abuse of power. Otto returned and the four sat in relative silence for the duration of the one-hour journey. Berlin passed through the windows, its familiar shops and people going about their everyday business. Nothing had changed except for this ridiculous court ruling. Their advocate appealed and, pending the outcome, they were to be held at Sachsenhausen.

"When are you going to settle down and give me another great-grandchild to obsess over?" Anna asked Otto. She was determined to normalize the day.

He flushed. "I am waiting for the right woman, Nana."

Anna looked at his fair skin, almost like porcelain without a hint of facial hair. He looked like a boy and not the thirty-one year old man he was. "Then find a woman you can tolerate and make some children. You must be one of the most eligible bachelors in Germany, if not Europe. They must be banging down your door."

His eyes looked to the floor as the red traced his neck and up his cheeks. "I am trying."

"Leave him alone," Joseph said. He put his arm around his son and pulled him towards him. Otto teetered and then righted himself as the arm was removed. "He's young. He wants to spend time playing football and drinking with the boys. There's plenty of time for him to get tied down and have children."

"For him, but not for me," Anna said. "I'm not getting any younger and shenanigans like this court hearing are not doing me any good."

The train exited a tunnel with a woof and they were in the countryside. It was harvest season and the golden fields were covered with workers. Fruit trees required extensive pruning after the picking was done and the evergreen trees stood solemnly, watching on. All was as it should be. The only thing out of place was the plume of coal smoke that trailed the extent of the carriages. Its snake-like body writhed from Berlin to Sachsenhausen without emotion, without slowing, and without mercy.

When it did begin to slow, their heads turned to see what was coming.

"This doesn't look so bad," Anna said. "It looks like any other train station."

"And the town looks nice," said Otto. His eyes took in the orderly houses and clean streets. "Maybe you're right."

"Of course I'm right. They know with whom they are dealing. Germany owes our family a debt of gratitude for the industry, jobs, and prosperity we have provided."

Elizabeth looked at Joseph knowingly. *We've heard this all before.* But they were silent.

"Everybody out!" the conductor yelled. It was reinforced by the troops who supervised the disembarking prisoners. The four got up, gathered their luggage, and joined the rest of the political prisoners on the station platform.

"Can I speak to the person in charge, please?" Anna asked one of the officers with the lightning bolts on his uniform's lapel. "There seems to have been a mistake…"

"You can take it up with the commandant when you get to your barracks. Now back in line." He was polite but firm. She didn't see him turn and smile to his fellow officers.

"See," she said when she had returned to her children. "Everything will be fine. We'll talk to the commanding officer and sort everything out."

"Let me carry that," Otto said. "I think we are walking to wherever we're going."

"Walking? That's preposterous."

"I mean this in the most polite way, Mother, but please be quiet. These aren't police. They are SS." Each of them looked closely at their minders and saw the increasingly familiar lightning bolts on their lapels.

"Why should I be afraid? I haven't done anything wrong. I'll speak my mind whenever I want to."

A large young man stepped briskly up to her and clicked his heels together. "I'm sorry for the confusion Mrs. Hildebrandt. Please, come with me. The others as well." He gestured with his hand at Joseph, Elizabeth, and Otto. His eyes rested on Otto briefly before he turned, arm out to assist Anna, and escorted them to large black car. Anna looked at them smugly.

Their journey was brief but they took the longer route. While the other prisoners walked through town, the young man drove them over the bridge and around the nearby lake, ensuring they had the most scenic views. He stopped outside of the heavy metal gates. They were inscribed "Arbeit macht Frei"; Work will set you free.

"What are they expecting us to do in there?" Anna asked her new friend.

"Whatever you are best suited for."

"But I'm not suited for anything," she said. Joseph squirmed forcefully in his seat. "Are you okay, Joseph?"

"Fine, Mother."

"You will find all the help you need on the other side of those gates," the young man said. He was smiling and waved them off as though they were entering a steamship cruise.

"What a lovely young man. It goes to show you that manners will out in the ..."

"Put down your luggage. Men to the right. Women to the left. *Schnell*!"

Anna hesitated and found the small handbag she carried taken away. "Hey!" she cried involuntarily. She received a gloved slap in reply from the officer.

Joseph rushed to help her but was held back by four other guards who were waiting for the walking prisoners. Otto stood watching in disbelief. He had never seen anyone say a cross word to Nana before. He couldn't imagine her being hit like this. It created a burning pang that went vertically down his sternum and he felt his throat close up.

"I'm okay. I'll do what you say. I was told to speak to the commandant and I'd like to do that, please."

The officer who hit her stopped himself from hitting her again, hand mid-air. He began to smile. "You want to see the commandant," he repeated. He began to laugh. "She wants to see the commandant!" He repeated it and all the men laughed. "I will show you the way, Mrs. Hildebrandt."

H*e knows me yet he hit me?* Her thoughts became jumbled. The hit threw her off balance, physically and mentally. Her body absorbed the blow but her untouchability was shattered. *I'm no beauty anymore; no charms or beguiling smile to wrap them around my finger*, she thought. *But I am rich and powerful. That still counts when it comes down to it.*

The commandant's office was spartan but held the key symbols of power: The picture of Chancellor Hitler on the wall, a large swastika hanging next to it, and a shelf full of books and fine art. Next to that, on a side table, was an assortment of yellow alcohols. The cut crystal had a gray lackluster finish.

The commandant was a tall man, around sixty years old, she thought, with a well-tailored uniform. He had kind eyes. He stood when she entered and came around his desk. Clicking his heels together, he provided her with a brief nod and then extended his hand to shake hers.

"Thank you, sir. You are very kind."

"I heard that you and your family were arriving today. I just wanted to say what an honor it is to have you here under my command."

Anna could feel a swell in her bosom as a faint smile crept into her face. The sting of the leather glove had subsided. Even the pain in her joints was gone. "You may have known my husband?"

"Meyer Hildebrandt? No, I would have been too young, I'm afraid. Your husband was connected at the highest levels, being the personal friend of Chancellor Bismarck, the kaiser, and all the international powers. We studied how he expanded his railway empire across Europe. The military has courses named after him in appreciation of how he approached his business. We felt that the military could learn from him—as we learn from all things. Don't you agree?"

"Absolutely," said Anna. "If we don't learn from history, we're doomed to repeat it."

"Exactly," said the commandant. He walked around his desk and sat down. There was no chair for Anna to sit on except at the far end of his office. She chose to stand.

"I would like to ask your indulgence, sir, as it is clearly a mistake that we are here. And when we are out, I will be able to repay your favor tenfold."

The commandant nodded silently, a smile growing on his face. When he stood, the smile had disappeared.

"Just like you Jews and homosexuals to bribe an officer the second you put foot in a place you dislike."

Anna was shocked and a cold trickle trekked down from her shoulders across her chest and into her legs. They began to weaken. She opened her mouth but nothing came out.

"I wanted to disbelieve the stories, the rumors, and the lies. How could such a great man as Meyer be married to a whore like yourself? You lied about not being Jewish. You lied about not being homosexual. You lied about hiding your fortune. And now you come to bribe me?" He had come within six inches of Anna and towered over her. She could feel his energy and rage. His neck strained at the collar of his uniform. His face changed to a blotchy purple. Spit formed at the sides of his mouth and sprayed her face.

"I didn't think it was a bribe, ju…"

"Silence. From now on, I'll treat you like the dogs you are. All of you. Corporal!" The door opened and a young man of twenty-five quick-stepped next to Anna.

"Yes, sir?"

"Take this prisoner to where we put the Christmas tree."

The corporal looked quizzical but then understood. He marched her out of the office, through the front gates, and towards the barracks. They stopped in what looked like a parade square or, more accurately, a parade semi-circle. In the middle of this area was an elevated structure with a trap door. Anna's insides became cold, then liquid, as she realized where she was and what might happen.

The siren sounded and the cadence of hundreds of feet entered the compound. They were separated into men and women. All luggage was confiscated and they were directed to stand in the parade area. The corporal remained standing next to Anna when the commandant arrived.

He strolled in as though he was taking his favorite dog for a walk.

"I will make this short and as painless as it can be. You are here because you have been found guilty of crimes against the Fatherland. I am not here to re-try or grant you favors." He looked pointedly at Ann before continuing. "I am here to make you work. When you have worked enough, you will be set free. You will make shoes, toys, furniture, whatever we give you to make. You will not complain. You will not argue. You will not fight. You will not escape. If you do, you will be punished." He looked around to ensure everyone had heard him.

"You all know about the famous Hildebrandts. There is one in front of you now. Mrs. Hildebrandt, please turn around and take a bow. There, that's good. She has been tried and convicted of crimes that can't be tolerated in an open and free society like ours. She, and you, will be given identification patches. You must wear them at all times. If not, you will be punished.

"You will be assigned a barrack. Learn from those around you. Learn from the guard assigned to you. They are here to help you." He stopped abruptly, looked at the sea of eyes, turned, and left. When he was gone, the uniformed guards of the camp waded into the masses and assigned each man, woman, and child a place. When the crowd dispersed, Anna remained alone with the corporal next to the gallows.

"What am I supposed to do now?"

"You do what is told of you."

"Which is?"

"Stand here."

"How long?"

"Until the commandant tells you otherwise."

"I will do that gladly."

"Don't leave before you are dismissed. Otherwise, there will be trouble and I will not be able to help you."

"Thank you. You have been kind."

The guard looked sideways at her and watched her lift her chin as he returned to his barracks.

∞

The next day, Anna saw her children and grandchild through different eyes, and they her. Gone were the fur trims, diamond broaches, and delicate pearl necklaces. Gone were the lovingly prepared shoes that caressed their aristocratic feet. In their place were black and white striped outfits with a designation sewn onto the upper left part of their torso. On Anna's were two triangles sewn on top of each other to form a star. One was pink and upside down, the other was yellow. Otto wore a single upside down pink triangle. Elizabeth wore one yellow upside down triangle, as did her brother Joseph.

"I am so sorry I didn't grab all of you and leave Germany when we had a chance," Anna sobbed when she saw them. "Me and my damn pride."

"We could have gone ourselves, Mutti." Joseph could see the strain on her and didn't want to add to it. "We are all too foolish. It is a new world and we are no longer wanted in it."

"Don't talk nonsense," she snapped. Her fire was reignited momentarily. "We will always have a place in society."

The others let the comment go, opting to take in their surroundings. The camp was recently built and the prisoners' first jobs were to build more barracks and factories. It looked, apart from their garb, more like a construction site than a prison. Everyone in stripes was walking, working, and carrying something while under the supervision of their assigned guards.

"Why does Nana have a star, you have yellow triangles, and I have a pink triangle?" Otto asked.

"Because you're a queer," an officer answered as he walked by. "And you'll be given specific duties to cleanse your dirty habits."

"And the others?," Otto was too naïve to keep quiet.

The officer's arm twitched, as though he wanted to do something with the small whip that was tucked into his belt. "The purple and red triangles are for political prisoners. Yellow is for Jews. You are the first Jews to join Sachsenhausen."

"But we're not Jews," Elizabeth said, her hand tracing the fabric above where her heart would be.

"A court says you are. We are not here to argue the law, just enforce it." He walked away.

"What are we supposed to do now?" Elizabeth turned to Anna, seeking guidance from the head of the family.

"We listen, keep our heads down, and wait for this madness to pass." She was uncharacteristically resigned and it disturbed the others more than seeing her hit the previous day.

A whistle indicated that they were to rearrange themselves according to barracks. Otto and Joseph were in barrack 52, while Anna and Elizabeth were in barrack 23. As they separated, they tried to keep within sight of each other as long as possible before the barracks themselves barred their sight.

"Do any of you have any crafts or trades?" The guard overseeing barrack 52 began his interrogation of the new inmates. "Especially engraving of metal or wood?"

There was silence and then Otto raised his hand slowly. "I have some basic understanding, but only at an intellectual level. I…"

"Enough from you. You will report to factory C. You should hope they find you useful," he said with a smile. "Otherwise, your kind tends to do badly in places like this." Despite the threat, his eyes looked Otto up and down and settled on his face for a moment too long.

"The rest of you will be doing construction. The completion of this facility is scheduled for two months from now. Look to your neighbor, see what he is doing. Ask him what is expected of you. We are all trying to get along here. If you make our lives easy, we'll make your lives easier."

There were no questions or movements from the prisoners and the guard left.

"This place doesn't sound so bad," Otto said.

"Let's hope it stays relatively civil. I've seen some of the other prisoners. They don't look too healthy."

"This isn't a resort, you know. It's supposed to be a punishment."

"Whose side are you on?" Joseph asked.

"Ours. Germany's. If we don't have discipline, things fall apart," Otto said. "They'll figure out we don't belong here and everything will be fine."

"I hope so, son. I hope so."

In barrack 23, the women were introduced to Ilse Koch and Anna Klein, the female guards in charge. They were answerable only to Commandant Michael Lippert himself.

"We will not tolerate attitudes or airs. You will do what we say, when we say, and you will work like you've never worked before." Koch walked to within an inch of Anna and looked her up and down before continuing. "We don't care who you think you were outside of these walls. Here, you are prisoners. You have a duty to wash your evil from yourself or die trying."

This was taken as hyperbole by one of the new prisoners and Klein saw the giggle.

"Do you think this is funny?" She was in the petite woman's face and glanced down at the red triangle on her jacket. "Communist bitch!" She raised her whip and brought it down with all her force on the prisoner's face. The giggling woman managed to turn her head in time and took the blow across her ear and neck. She fell to the ground. "Are you giggling now? Is there anything funny? Have I missed the punch line?" She kicked the woman as hard as she could in the belly. The woman curled into a ball on the floor. No one moved. "How about now? Anyone else find your situation funny?" She put her boot on the neck of the woman and watched the legs straighten and arms grab for her boot. She put her entire weight on the neck and walked over the woman as though she was using a stone to cross a stream.

"She'll live," said Koch. "Just remember." The two guards left.

Outside, Klein was flush with excitement. "I'm going to see if the commandant is free." She smiled at Koch. Her blonde hair fell out of place from the exertions and her cheeks were reddening. No more than twenty-five years old, she enjoyed her job almost as much as she enjoyed her free time. She walked briskly, turning right once outside the gates. The commandant's quarter was straight ahead and she closed the distance as quickly as her marching would take her. As she knocked on his door, she held her breath.

"Come in."

"It's me," she said with a girlish smile. Lippert put down what he was doing and walked over to her. She stood in the doorway, waiting. When he reached her, he locked the door behind her before grabbing her in his arms.

∞

Otto walked to factory C, expecting to see a workshop of some sort. Instead, he discovered an immaculate workspace with artisans and machinists bent over their craft. "What is it I am supposed to do here?"

"You will take your position and work."

"Doing what?"

"Preparation."

Otto looked at the metal plates. They featured what looked like a framed Grecian goddess holding something in her hands, and the rest was a fine pattern with ornate writing. It took a moment for him to understand. "We've become counterfeiters?"

The reply was a punch to the head by a gloved fist. "Your next outburst will take you to the brickworks instead. *Verstehst?*"

Otto understood and sat down in a space between two older men with bushy mustaches and three day's stubble on their faces. They were in a world of their own, concentrating on the carving of the plates and replicating the artistry of the paper in front of them. Otto was familiar with the process of making plates because of Hans. He struggled to remember the finer points and the only memories that came to him were that of him hunched over his work aided by his mounted magnifying glass and instruments in hand. His own hands would trace the man's body, feeling the muscle and bones held together so sensuously under the fabric of his shirt. It was his job to distract him until he turned around. They played the game so well that Otto began to become interested in what Hans did. He was a willing student under a willing teacher who rewarded him in ways that accelerated the absorption of his skills.

It was not a surprise for him to find the pink triangle on the left side of his jacket and right side of his trousers. He knew what he was even if his father was blind to it. His grandmother seemed to know but played along in her own way, teasing him about grandchildren. It provided good cover.

"Pick up your tools and pretend you know what you're doing," a voice whispered to him.

He did so.

"Now look carefully at the five pound sterling note in front of you and pretend to be studying it." The same voice spoke but no one was turned towards him. He realized it was the man to his right. He laughed to himself as he looked exactly as he imagined Pinocchio's creator, Geppetto, to have looked like.

Otto nodded, adjusted the magnifying glass as Hans had done, and hunched over his work. He imagined himself looking like Hans or Geppetto and it brought a warmth of happiness to him. As he picked up his instruments, he could feel the naked flesh of Hans against his and the world became full of joy. The courtroom, the spitting, and the jeers all faded; the shame as they were escorted under guard from their mansion to be tried and convicted of crimes that put them in here. Everything fell away and he was able to feast on his moveable memories. He almost smiled at the familiar smell of stressed metal, oils, and ink. *This will not be so bad at all,* he thought.

∞

Anna looked at the work expected of her. Timber, stone, earth, all being moved by younger bodies. All straining under the labor. And this was only her third day. The first day she was forced to stand for hours on end before she was allowed to go to her barracks. The second saw her witness the brutal assault by one of the guards on a fellow prisoner. She thought better of complaining after looking at the eyes of her daughter.

"You can do this, Mom."

"I don't think I can." She felt at the double triangle she was forced to sew onto her jacket and trousers.

A voice interrupted them. "You, come here." It was the guard who beat the other prisoner. Klein.

"Yes, Fräulein." Anna walked towards the guard, never breaking her stare.

Klein bristled, growing enraged with each successive step. Anna stopped within an arm's length of Klein without being told. "Follow me," Klein barked. Anna did.

Elizabeth watched her mother walk behind Klein and around the corner of one of the barracks. Her eyes begin to fill as the reality of the situation bore down on her.

When Klein finished walking, they stood outside a building set aside from the others but otherwise identical in appearance. Inside, a doctor in a white lab coat looked up.

"She's too old," he said.

"Not for your experiments, Doctor. For any help you may need."

"She's too old," he repeated. He returned to his papers. Anna was able to see what looked like animals hanging in the other room alongside a stainless steel metal table. As Klein turned to go, Anna looked again and then vomited against the door.

"Damnit, woman! Clean that up!" The doctor got up from behind his desk and looked at the mess. "Use this." He threw a rag at her and pointed to the operation room to get some water.

"I'm sorry, Doctor."

She received no reply as she looked at the room that caused her reaction. There was a smell of something foreign in the air, like a cleansing agent but different. She couldn't place it. It was covering some other smell that she also couldn't place. She got up, noticing the tiled finishes. Everything was either polished concrete or tile. The next room held a steel table along one wall. There was a cabinet, from floor to ceiling, with bottles and samples. She noticed a second steel table and a basin.

Her foot trembled, not from feeling her seventy-eight years but from avoiding the sight of those four figures that caused her to vomit. Despite herself, her peripheral vision drew her attention to the blackened, naked bodies hung by hooks behind their ears. Her mind envisioned the curved metal that held the skull.

She found a small bowl and poured water into it. Almost half the water spilled as she returned to the place where she had her accident. There was no more conversation as the guard watched and the doctor continued his reading, ignoring the scene.

Anna realized her vomit lacked any substance. The food she had been eating since her arrival consisted of bread, soup, and a little meat. It was enough to live on and she would not starve from it, but it was not the fare her body was used to.

"You are shocked?" The doctor raised his head when she was done.

She nodded. "I'm sorry. I've never seen a dead body like that before."

"It is difficult at first," he said, suddenly kind. "Many in my class found it too difficult to deal with the death in life. But it is a reality."

"And me?"

"You, me, even Fräulein Klein will die eventually."He smiled. He was skeletal and the action pulled his thin skin tight against his face, creating a ghastly visage. "But don't be fearful. Those poor souls were dead already. I was conducting a post mortem on them to determine the cause of death."

Anna's body relaxed; the explanation soothed her nerves. She returned the bowl and rag to the two-tabled room and stood next to the door. "Is there anything you need from me?"

"No, I'll let you know if that changes. Thank you, Fräulein Klein."

The door opened and the sweet smell of free air hit Anna. She was visibly shaken as her body struggled with the distances between her feet and the ground. Everything seemed foreign to her lungs and eyes. In an odd way, she felt reborn.

Klein looked at the pathetic woman in front of her. With all her advantages, all her money, she was now hers to command. She didn't want it to end quickly. She would enjoy this. *I wonder whether any of the boys would like to have a go at her*, she thought. She felt a thrill of excitement at the images her mind conjured.

# CHAPTER FOUR

# Despair

"No one's coming for us," Elizabeth whispered to her mother. They each slept on the bottom berth in their barrack.

"I am starting to believe you."

"It's been too long, Mutti. We're not getting out."

"It's hard, I know. But this is the world we live in. What can we do?"

"I know I've asked this so many times, but how could this have happened? I can't believe anyone would do this while Papa was alive."

"They wouldn't have dared, but we have been living on his money for so long without doing anything with it. Perhaps his enemies saw a chance to finish us off. You know what they say, revenge is a dish best served cold." She smiled ruefully. Her teeth were still all hers but her eyes no longer danced and her body had become hard with exercise and work. She was thankful not to have a mirror; she didn't want to see her sagging skin and unkempt hair.

"Ice cold, I would say. And to classify us as Jews. Jews? How is that possible?"

"Don't ask silly questions, Lizzy. They wanted what was ours and couldn't take it. We didn't have political protection, relying on our money to keep us safe. In today's world, politics can redefine who you are with a stroke of a pen. Someone, somewhere, did just that. Jews' property was to be confiscated, and here we are. Simple. When rules are in place, all they needed was to reclassify us to fit them. The rest was legal and all the mechanisms of the state worked against us."

"But we're not Jewish. Doesn't that matter? We were all baptized Catholic, we all went to Catholic schools, and are all buried in Catholic cemeteries."

"I don't think they can be confused or deterred with facts. Once the designation had been made, there was nothing that could be done."

"Then we are truly doomed."

"Until something changes. Something always changes. Chancellor Hitler will not always be in power." Anna was resigned to her fate. It was a long way from her nursing station when she first met Meyer. She smiled at the memory.

"What do you find funny?"

"Not funny, just memories. I was thinking about the first time I met your father. He was a great man."

Elizabeth was silent. Her mother was drifting into that memory more often recently. The present was becoming further away and less relevant to her with every day. She understood and did not wish to seem disrespectful.

"Do you hear that?"

"There must be new prisoners arriving," Elizabeth said.

"Not that, the music."

"I think it's disgusting. They imprison our country's best musicians on the grounds that they are homosexuals, then make them play upbeat music when the prisoners arrive."

"I don't care about their cruelty anymore. I just want to listen to the music." Anna's eyes were closed and she was transported to her salon where Chancellor Bismarck would attend, even after he was fired. She could imagine his old face lighting up if he had lived long enough to be told that Joseph's only son was named after him. She could feel Meyer's arms around her, slightly unsteady by old age near the end, and they would dance slowly to the gramophone. It wasn't as good as live music, but they could listen to it over and over again.

"We need to go out or we'll be in trouble."

"Let them come and get me. I'm tired of doing their nonsense work."

Elizabeth looked around. "You can't talk like that, Mutti. Stay strong. They can't keep us here forever."

"You're right about that. Eventually we'll die." She said it with resigned satisfaction, almost anticipation.

"Not if I can help it. Now get up. Good. Start walking. There. Out the door. Keep going. Let's go to see the orchestra."

Since war was declared, the number of prisoners increased. Many, including Elizabeth, commented on the reduction of rations and that some prisoners were beginning to look more gaunt than usual. As the new set arrived, they were ordered to march in tune to the upbeat music and clap. Singing was encouraged where the music allowed. They sounded terrible but their clapping was in time. The guards thoroughly enjoyed the entertainment.

"Can you see Joseph? He's over there." She pointed to her son. She waved but he didn't see her.

"He's looking healthy. The work is doing him some good. It's getting all that extra weight off him and putting some muscle on his bones."

"Mutti! Don't talk like that. We're not in a spa."

"Hush. We are where we are in our mind. Never forget that. The closer I get to the end, the more I imagine it as a beginning." She smoothed her wrinkled jacket. "I wish it would finally happen."

Elizabeth watched as her mother's hands, once manicured and beautiful, fussed over her clothes. Her skin hung along her jawline and neck, and her eyes never fully closed. Her hair, white and thinning, needed to be washed. It was covered with a rag tied around her chin.

"I wish I had skills like Otto. Have you seen him? He goes to his factory like nothing has happened. I think he even likes it. We three are worked like common laborers."

"We have no skills other than spending money and ordering people around." Anna's face smiled at the image.

"I have skills," Elizabeth countered.

"We all have skills, *mine schatz*. Sometimes life is kind enough to match our skills with our circumstances." She looked away, watching Joseph stand at attention, admiring his fine figure. She began to drift back to her university days, her nursing days, and her days with Siegrun. Her suicide was the greatest shock of her life and she never fully recovered. When Meyer married her, she ensured she kept her private life separate from him and everyone else. *How did they find out?* She thought. *If I were young and beautiful, even like Elizabeth, I wouldn't work. I'd make that commandant scream with pleasure. Failing that, I'd make Fräulein Klein beg me to be hers. I'd survive. As it is,* she looked down at her body, *I don't think I want to survive.*

She closed her eyes and began to sway to the music. She put her arms in Siegrun's and began to move towards the orchestra. The other prisoners didn't notice her at first. Then they made room for her, allowing her to glide to the area in front of the musicians. There, to the delight of the guards and the prisoners, they watched the wife of one of the richest men in Europe dance like a woman in love. They swayed in silence as they felt her passion, transcended from their current lives to a time within, where love and hope existed. The music played on. When it stopped, she opened her eyes and remembered where she was. She bowed to cover her embarrassment and returned to her barrack. The next morning, Elizabeth found her dead.

∞

1941

"They want us to build a crematorium to help process the dead bodies. I guess it's better than letting them rot." Joseph had resigned himself to his fate long ago. As they had all survived nearly six years already, he was beginning to think it was just a matter of time before they let him go. He had heard of a few prisoners who were discharged after working for a few years.

"To make it easier for them to kill us," Elizabeth said. They had discovered a way to meet up and talk. It was not safe, but they needed to exchange information and feel as though their family unit still existed. "You've seen the way they beat the prisoners. Now that the Jews have arrived, I've seen them shot in the head for no reason at all."

"But those are Jews. What can you do about them? They have done worse to us, believe me. You haven't heard half the stories."

"And the others? Russians? Poets?"

"Communists and queers. They deserve to die."

Elizabeth held her tongue. They didn't have the luxury of arguing moot cases. Nor for her to point out the pink triangle his son wore.

"You think I don't know what you're thinking? About Otto? It's as true as them calling our mother a Jew and a homosexual. It's the most ridiculous thing I've heard. She was married and had children. How could she be a queer?"

"Joseph, let's not disagree. Let's build what they want us to build. If we live or die, it is not in our hands. If we don't have a choice, why worry about it?"

"How did you become so wise?" Joseph held his hand to Elizabeth's face.

"How did you become so thin? Have you seen yourself? You're becoming all skin and bones."

"It's a special diet. If we get out, I'll tell you about it." He laughed but noticed that his sister was not as gaunt as he was. They parted ways, him to his worksite, and her to Klein's barrack.

When she arrived, Klein was already there. She was holding the negligée that she had taken from a prisoner's luggage. It was white, and she was wearing something similar in red. Her blonde hair was undone and had spread itself across her shoulders and down her back. Her muscular legs were bent at the knee as she brought one of her heels to her calf to practice her poses.

"What do you think?" she asked. "Just what the doctor ordered?"

"You look like a movie star," Elizabeth said. She began taking off her prisoner's uniform as she closed the door.

"Come, quickly. They'll be here soon." She began helping Elizabeth remove her clothes until she was completely naked. They looked at each other as their bodies closed the distance. Klein's hands caressed Elizabeth's curves, kissing her neck and allowing hers to be kissed. "We have to be quick. They'll be here any moment." She was breathing heavily and had lowered Elizabeth to her bed. As their bodies entwined, the door flew open and the new commandant stood in its place.

He stared at the two naked bodies and they stared back, frozen. He closed the door and they heard the sound of metal on metal as the bolt slid shut. Saying nothing, he walked, heel to toe, from the door to the edge of the bed. When Klein or Elizabeth looked like they were going to move, he held up a hand to freeze them where they were. He took his whip out slowly and traced Elizabeth's body. He gave her bottom a slight tap but was otherwise gentle. He did the same to Klein. Elizabeth noticed that the fear was gone from Klein's eyes and was replaced with excitement that she could include a new partner in her pleasures. The moment was electric and Elizabeth's lips parted, barely able to breath. Klein moved slowly at first, like a cat stalking its prey, fearful of any quick movements. She slowly raised her head, looking at the recently appointed commandant, and began to unbuckle his belt. The moment of crisis was upon them and their fate would be decided by his next action. When he closed his eyes, they knew they were safe.

∞

Otto had found a protector within his first month. It was the same guard who had escorted them by automobile from the train station. Eric Rödel had served in the Luftwaffe and had been a paratrooper in Spain. He had moved up the ranks sufficiently to receive a safer job closer to his home town of Berlin.

"If I hadn't taken a safe job, I'd never have met you." Eric shared some boiled beef on rye with Otto. "Try some mustard on it. It brings it alive."

"You haven't tried the rations they feed us here," Otto said. "Everything is alive in comparison." He devoured the half sandwich and licked the mustard off his cheeks and fingers.

"You are a hungry boy. Any room for desert?" He had begun to take off his uniform. They were able to meet once a week like this when the camp was quiet. Otto was ordered to report for duty and the rest of the prisoners felt sorry for him, blaming his excessive work regime on him being a queer. No one said anything and everyone avoided his gaze. Joseph tried to intervene but Otto convinced him to stay quiet and safe.

"I came for the desert; the meal was a bonus." Otto had already taken off his prisoner's stripes and looked like a man again. Eric feasted his eyes on his next meal.

When they were finished, Eric was quieter than usual, savoring his cigarette. "I've been promoted." The smoke came out of his mouth as he spoke.

"Where?"

"I don't know yet. I only know they can't afford to have a trained paratrooper babysitting skeletons."

"I'm no skeleton."

"Many of you are. Have you taken a look recently?"

"I haven't noticed. We're all a lot thinner than before, but what can you expect with the workloads?"

"I want to take care of you but I can't get you out of here. I've tried. Someone wants you all here and to never get out."

"I figured that. Our family has enemies. I wish I knew who they were. It might make this whole thing bearable. You know, to understand why we are being punished."

"Whoever they are, be careful. With your money and power, I would have thought you could have purchased anything you wanted."

"Not now that they classified us as Jews."

"They should have done a closer inspection," Eric laughed. "They'd never believe you were Jews. Definitely not you."

Otto found the closest thing and threw it at him. It was his prisoner's jacket. "Don't kid. One of the first things I did was drop my pants and showed them. They still didn't believe me."

"Then, my friend, you need to become religious. Pray. I can't do anything more for you." He got up, dressed, and left. It was the last time Otto ever saw Eric.

∞

Christmas 1941 saw a tree placed in the gallows, as was the custom. There were no lights on it but the orchestra was allowed to play and the singers sang. Everyone else huddled to stay warm.

"I don't know if it is colder than usual, but it seems worse than I ever remember." Elizabeth shared Klein's bed more often, as much for the food as the warmth. She enjoyed the warmth of Klein's thighs and allowed herself to be snuggled into her breasts. She no longer thought about her husband or child, as though they belonged to a different life. She could no longer live that way and refused to delude herself or cause herself pain by remembering. Her life was in the hands of Anna Klein, a sadistic bitch who loved sex as much as she loved being mean. She wanted men, women, and both at the same time, but it was Elizabeth who soothed her inner rage the best and who received the favors of food and warmth in return.

"It's cold outside," Klein mumbled.

"More people will die this winter."

"They always die. Some sooner than others."

"And the rest?"

"Why all the questions?"

"I don't know how we'll feed everyone. More people arrive every day."

Klein propped herself up on her arm. "Don't worry about it."

"I don't, but others do. And they are talking."

"Let them talk. What are they going to do?"

"Nothing. I was just saying."

"Don't say. Go to sleep. Unless you want to sleep in your barrack?"

Elizabeth fell silent and tried to go to sleep. She noticed the new crematorium Joseph had been working on was now operational. The white smoke was a constant companion, as was the dust it created on a windless day. She knew the bodies needed to be dealt with, if only for hygienic reasons, but she also saw the increase in brutality as new guards were brought in. Last week, she saw Klein execute a woman for looking at her the wrong way. It made her blood run cold but, when Klein touched her, her body responded with an excitement she couldn't explain. *Am I becoming a monster like her?*

A week later, she had her answer.

A new commandant had taken charge of the camp a few months earlier. Fresh prisoners were arriving by foot from the train station and he was inspecting his guards as well as the condition of the camp. Everything proceeded as expected until he reached the counterfeiting factory. On the steps, one of the old artisans had collapsed, blocking his way.

"Who is this?"

"No one, *mein Commandant*. Just a prisoner. Probably passed out."

"I don't care if he's dead, passed out, drunk, or all three. He is in my way and I will not move for some rubbish communist prisoner. Not on my watch."

"Of course, sir." The officer pointed at Otto to drag the old man away.

Otto ran to the spot. The commandant remained stationary and was becoming increasingly irate. Otto looked at the face of the old man and saw it to be Geppetto, the man who gave him the advice on his first day. He cradled the man's head, stroking his hair, and talked to him. "It'll be okay, Peter. You need to stand up now." His last word was drowned out by a gunshot. Otto's face was splattered with blood but the bullet's target was between his hands. Geppetto's face went blank as blood began to flow from the hole. The rest of his body jolted and fell still.

"I didn't ask you to sing him a lullaby," said the commandant. "I wanted him out of my way. The next bullet is in your head if that carcass is not gone in two seconds." He paused. "One second."

Otto dragged the dead body as quickly as he could. The old man should have been as light as a feather but

Otto no longer had the strength to pull him. After slipping twice, he looked up at the commandant to see the pistol pointed right at him. It was the last thing he saw as the bullet ripped through his skull.

"Now I have two bodies in my path. If they are not moved within fifteen seconds, I will continue to execute discipline on these grounds until someone listens."

Five prisoners ran to the bodies and pulled them to the side. They stood at attention as he passed. He did not look at them. One of those prisoners was Elizabeth and she mourned her soul as much as the loss of her brother's.

"Schweinhund!"

The commandant and his aide stopped walking, their faces registering disbelief. Klein's head turned in slow motion to see her lover denounce the commandant. The two men turned to look at Elizabeth. She saw his hand return to his Luger sidearm but then pause as he took in her body.

"Take her," he instructed the officer next to him. "Have her taken to the mess hall, and tell the men what they will be having for desert this evening."

"Yes, Commandant." The officer nodded to another guard, who grabbed Elizabeth by the hair and began to drag her. She held onto his hands to reduce the pain and managed to stand and stumble behind him. She saw Klein look away as she passed.

That evening, she was raped first by the commandant, then each officer took a turn. When they had all satisfied themselves, the guards were let in. She lay on the ground, bloodied and beaten, when she saw Klein arrive. She wept as Klein helped her to her feet and walked her towards her quarters. When they passed the usual turn, Elizabeth looked up at Klein without speaking. Without looking at her, Klein pushed her into the electrified fence. The current passed through her body, causing her hands to grip the barbed wires and extending the agony until there was no more life and her corpse fell backwards onto the New Year's snow. Klein lit a cigarette and inhaled deeply as she gazed at her broken lover, then turned and left.

It was a week before Joseph learned of his sister's death. Her body had been removed and burned at first light. It was assumed she had tried to escape and it generated no news in the camp. It was her absence at their weekly rendezvous that caused him to worry.

"I didn't ask questions when my boy still looked healthy and the rest of us became skeletons. I didn't ask about Lizzy either. They were surviving." He spoke to himself as well as anyone who would listen to him in the barrack. His eyes watered, trying to make tears, but there wasn't enough liquid in him to spare such luxuries.

"Maybe they're better off," a voice said.

"Maybe, but it doesn't make it easier." He rolled over on his side, numb from the shock that wouldn't pass. "We're never getting out of here."

"You just figured that out now?" It was the same voice. There was no humor in it.

"I want to die but something stops me from killing myself. I want to walk into those wires or punch the commandant. I want to do something before I die to remind the world that I once lived."

"Perhaps you never did," the same voice said.

Joseph was too tired to turn or to argue. *Perhaps I never did*, he thought, more depressed than ever.

But death never came. Joseph watched the camp convert from a concentration camp where its prisoners were worked until exhaustion, but still were fed and housed, into a death camp where people were processed and burned. All semblance of social graces between guards and inmates disappeared. In August of the previous year, 1941, almost sixty thousand Russian prisoners of war were brought into the camp and summarily shot. He thought that was why they needed the crematorium, but those soldiers were buried.

The crematorium was built to process those who died of exhaustion or, later, were gassed. Most prisoners unable to work were simply shipped away. Joseph did what he was told and, somehow, survived.

"What's your secret?" one prisoner asked him upon hearing that Joseph was the longest serving resident of the camp.

"I don't know. I get beatings, like the rest. I barely eat, like the rest. Either God or the commandant doesn't want me dead."

"You can barely tell the difference in here," the man said.

"My brother was shot by the previous commandant and one of the guards threw my sister into the electric fence, although they say it was suicide. I don't know how long ago that was. It feels like yesterday but it could have been three years ago."

"I arrived in September of '44 from Warsaw. I'm just glad they didn't send me to one of the other camps."

"I don't know anything about anywhere else." Joseph wanted to know, but equally it would not serve him well.

"The Germans have these camps everywhere. They're burning the Jews, gypsies, and anyone who is sent there. Entire villages have been emptied. Undesirables across the Nazi empire are being sucked into…"

"Stop. I don't want to hear about it. Those are probably lies anyway."

"Look at me, Joseph. I'm a Jew from Warsaw. I know what I've seen. I know what I've done. And I'd do it again. These are not people, they are animals."

"They are my countrymen and I don't accept that they could have done this. It is a lie and you're probably spying on us for them, waiting for us to say something against them. Well, I won't. I love my country. I disagree with the way we got here, but I love the Fatherland. Now stop asking me questions and leave me alone."

The Jew from Warsaw was gassed the next day.

∞

"Everyone up, up, up." A guard burst into the barracks as the siren wailed. "Inspection on the square, now."

There was a mass of movement as men lowered their fragile frames from the bunk beds and stumbled to the square. Every prisoner knew it was a semi-circle, but no one dared comment. People died for less.

"I can't move," Joseph said. No one took notice. Each had barely enough energy for themselves. "If they ask, tell them I can't move."

"I wouldn't draw attention to myself, Joseph. Keep quiet or they'll ship you out."

Joseph nodded. He had felt queasy the night before but he had stopped thinking about what his body experienced. The constant smell of bodies being burned or worse, decaying, was edged out by the smell of hundreds of men living in quarters designed for forty. In nine years, he had never felt as poorly as he did today. His body refused to move. He lay in silence as the bodies passed and the door closed. Even the siren stopped.

The men never returned. The next day, he was able to move his head and legs. As he went to the door of his barrack, he heard shouting. He turned to hear better.

"Over here. I think there's another one over here!" It was in a different language, not English or French. Maybe something Slavic.

Joseph saw a large man walking briskly, followed by three other soldiers. When they saw him, they stopped. They put their hands out, as if approaching a dog, saying something softly. Each of them stared, not saying a word. Occasionally, they would turn to each other and make some expression but kept coming. When they realized he couldn't understand anything they were saying, one turned and ran, yelling something at the top of his voice. Another man returned with him, again stopping the moment he saw Joseph. They walked as though they were in a church—or a cemetery.

"Hello. My name is Sergie and we are Russian. Do you understand me?" He was speaking in German slowly.

Joseph nodded, looking for any sign of the guards. "Yes."

"Do you know where everyone is?"

Joseph shook his head. "No. Everyone was here yesterday."

The soldiers turned and talked amongst themselves. "You are free. We, on behalf of the Union of Soviet Socialist Republics, have liberated Sachsenhausen. You are free to go."

The words registered but he felt nothing. "I don't understand."

"We have taken this from the German forces. It is only a matter of time before all of Germany is defeated."

The idea of Germany being defeated was too much for Joseph. He had to sit down. Tears, unavailable for his brother or sister, flowed down his cheeks.

∞

The Russians liberated Sachsenhausen on 22 April, 1945. German forces surrendered in the west on 7 May, 1945, and in the east on 9 May, 1945. Joseph found himself being photographed with soldiers as they began to document the horrors of the camps. He was still being cared for in a make-shift Russian hospital when a uniformed man came to see him.

"Mr. Hildebrandt?" The voice was carrying a clipboard and was wearing an American officer's uniform.

"Yes?"

"I assume you speak English?"

*How American*, Joseph thought. "Yes. How may I help you?" His body seemed to ache more now than in the camp. His bed was too soft and his body was rejecting the rich food being given to him. There was a drip of something tied into his arm but at least it didn't stink, and there were pretty nurses who talked to him and bent over him when they fluffed up his pillow. He hadn't felt a woman's touch in almost ten years. It felt like he was in heaven.

"You are Joseph Hildebrandt, son of Meyer and Anna Hildebrandt?"

"Son of Meyer and Siegrun Hildebrandt. Anna was my step-mother."

"Of course. Apologies. You were in Sachsenhausen with your son Otto, sister Elizabeth, and step-mother Anna. Is that correct?

Joseph hesitated, but decided there was nothing this fancy man in a suit could do to him the Nazis hadn't already done. "Yes."

"Then I've been instructed to give you this." He reached into his pocket and pulled out a syringe. He used his weight to hold Joseph down and then put the needle in his neck. The whole process lasted less than five seconds. He pocketed the syringe and watched Joseph.

"Why? What could you hope to achieve?"

"I'm not here to answer questions. I have a job and I'm just waiting to see that it is done. Don't worry, you won't feel a…"

Joseph's eyes looked at the fancy man in the American suit but he saw nothing. He heard nothing. He was dead.

# CHAPTER FIVE

# Max

Max Harding's birth certificate said that he was born on 29 February, 1931. For his whole life, he didn't know whether to have his birthday party on 28 February or 1 March. It was only years later he realized that 1931 was not a leap year. At the time, he never thought anything of it.

He didn't know his father as much as he'd liked. He had remarried and Max was an awkward situation for him. It was the year the Star Spangled Banner was adopted as the national anthem of the United States, Ferdinand Porsche started his automobile company in Stuttgart, and the Empire State building was completed in New York. Coincidentally, it was also the year the British Empire abandoned the gold standard. None of this mattered for Max, as the result was the same. He didn't see his father after his fifth birthday.

He was five when he was told his mother died crossing the Atlantic. He never learned more about it and, not knowing anything different, grew up with his nannies and classmates. He knew his mother loved him. His nanny told him that every day. Over time, he went to a prestigious boarding school that set him on the path to an Ivy League education. He always found school easy and was advanced to grade eight by the time he had reached the age of eight. He graduated from MIT with honors at the age of fourteen and received his PhD at sixteen.

The Massachusetts Institute for Technology embraced its role within the military industrial complex of the United States and promising students were earmarked for research and military duty. When Colonel Blake first met Max, he knew he wanted him on his team.

"Where will I be stationed?" Max asked.

"We need to get you through basic training first but you will be where the action is hottest," Blake said.

"Korea?"

"I think so, unless the war ends before you're ready. It's 1952 and no one's sure how it's going to play out."

"Do you think I'll see action on the front line?"

Blake laughed. "Son, you'd better not! I need you to crack codes, hear what the enemy is saying. I need your brain, not your body."

"But I'll be in Korea?"

"Yes, son, if you sign up now I'll have you in Korea as fast as they'll allow me."

"Good," Max said.

The transport plane was the first time Max had flown. It was scary but there were men around him more scared than he was. That made him feel better. His rank as an officer meant he didn't get too much trouble from the troops. He made an effort to make friends with everyone.

"First time on a plane?" a voice asked.

"Yes, sir."

"Don't worry. If you need to vomit, go ahead. The crew would like you to use a bag, though." The man handed him a bag.

"Thank you, sir."

"Chris Stammer." He held out his hand.

"Harding." They shook. It provided a distraction to the noise and movement.

"Not a big fan of rollercoasters?"

"What?"

"Don't like the bumps and dips?"

"No. To tell you the truth, it's making me think twice about all this," Max said.

"Too late now," Chris said. "Besides, you must be important for them to fly you all the way there. Most get shipped out like a parcel of post."

"I guess so. I hope so. I'll try, sir." Max's stomach was tight. He ground his teeth and felt the sweat from his tense muscles.

"You know you don't need to keep calling me sir every time? You're an officer too, from what I can gather." Chris wasn't much older but he had four younger brothers. He felt sorry for Max.

"Sorry, sir. I mean, thanks." Max flushed. "I'm pretty new."

"I gathered that. Are you even old enough to fight?"

"I just turned twenty-one and I have a PhD from MIT. Colonel Blake recruited me from the research department." Max wondered whether this information should be shared. *It's already out*, he thought. *No sense worrying about it.*

"Hmmm. Wunderkind." Chris pursed his lips. "I can guess why they want you."

"Radio comm," Max said.

"That's for the others. I know why you're here."

"That makes one of us," Max said. He tried to smile but ended up looking constipated. They hit some turbulence and he could feel the flesh on his face shaking. He saw Chris' body straining at the harness and realized he may not get to the bag in time.

∞

When they finally landed at Pusan West K-1 Air Base in South Korea, Max had given up hope of living. He just wanted his feet on solid ground. He stumbled out with his pack. Chris followed. The cargo plane was being unloaded.

"Next time, when they tell you you're going to be flying somewhere, check to see what type of plane it is!" Chris slapped Max on the shoulder and smiled. He seemed to know where he was going, so Max followed.

"Want something to eat?" Chris asked. "You couldn't have much in you right now."

"Uh, yeah. I think I'll just have a Coke."

"Suit yourself. I'm off to the officer's mess. Get yourself checked in and join me there."

"Thanks, Chris. See you."

The first thing that struck Max was the lack of women. He expected things to be tough—it was war—but the idea of not having women around unsettled him. The base itself was functional, and the landing strip and endless tarmac surrounded them like black fields.

"Take a good look, my friend, because that's as good as it will ever get."

Max saw the man watching him. He even saw his mouth moving but the words never reached him.

"Excuse me?"

"They just finished tarmacking it. Compliments of the new heavy bodies that joined our efforts." He nodded in the direction of the massive bomber planes nearby.

"You mean the runways weren't paved?"

"They had something but nothing as beautiful as this. I think some contractor must be eyeing things for when the war is over."

"I thought we're still fighting."

"Sure, but both sides have bulked up. We're not going to get the Commies or the Chinese to back down and they don't want a nuclear retaliation from America if they kill us all." He was smiling. "That's not official, just my take on things. Name's Bull. Tim Bull."

Max shook his hand and nodded. The noise of the area and the violence of his journey made him want to get inside. "Max Harding."

"Don't worry. We're too far from any real action. We're here for support."

Max raised his eyebrows.

"We're the brains, they're the brawn. I can see you're with comms. That means you're with me."

Max glanced at the insignia on Bull's left arm. It matched his.

"Are you able to tell me what we're doing all the way out here? I want to see action, not act as a glorified phone operator."

Bull laughed. "I'm going to like you, Harding. The colonel will fill you in on the official line and I'll do the rest later. Just check yourself in and get your things sorted." He saw Max's apprehension. "And relax. Everything'll be fine." He gave a quick salute and left.

Max saluted in reflex, wondering how he forgot the courtesy earlier. He settled in before meeting with his officer in charge.

"Is everything in order, Harding?"

"Yes, sir. Better than I expected."

Colonel Frank Wells looked slightly amused. "Care to expand on that?"

"I was expecting tents, the way people back home talked. So I was pleased to see wooden barracks and running water."

"We try, Harding. I see you've just completed your basic training. You're some type of hotshot head case?"

"Sir?"

"I'm trying to determine whether you are going to be trouble or an asset."

"An asset, sir. I'm here to serve."

Max's gung-ho attitude impressed Wells and he smiled. "That's good to hear. Your mission here is top secret. You are not to talk about it to your girlfriend or mates, or even God. Understood?"

"Understood."

"Here. This will give you an idea of what we are up against." He gave him a dossier enclosed with a file marked Eyes Only. "Become familiar with that. It is not to leave this room."

Max opened it to see aerial photos of what he understood to be enemy positions and strengths. "Sir?"

"It sets out what we're up against. The Reds are too strong and they have an endless supply of bodies. It is up to us to convince them that it isn't worth their bloodshed to retake south of the 38th."

"How do we do that?"

"Read the file. The essence is a series of demoralizing smash and grabs, sabotage, and counter-intelligence against the enemy. We can only assume they'll be doing the same to us so we need to factor that in as well."

"But I don't have the language."

"We need what's between your ears. Ever heard of Alan Turing? No? Neither has the rest of the world. People like him, like you, win wars. We need an edge, a way of thinking that hasn't been utilized. We need a group of young bright patriotic minds able to analyze and advise us fossils."

Max wasn't sure whether to trust Wells. He was being too friendly, too open. "I'll do what is expected of me, sir."

"Good. When you've read that, the work begins. I want you with the rest of your company tomorrow at 0600."

"Sir, yes sir."

∞

Max enjoyed his fellow members of Company Bravo Two Nine, especially Bull. Their company was independent of JACK, the Joint Advisory Commission, Korea, headquartered at Tongnae in the south-east. They were based less than eighty miles from the shores of Japan where General Douglas MacArthur had just granted the nation independence after occupying it since their defeat in 1945. The United States was the only foreign power to occupy Japan in its entire history.

"Last month, our artillery fired over two million rounds into the Reds. Mao has ordered that the Chinese forces assist North Korea and Russia in destroying the United Nation's efforts. President Truman has ordered American blood to be spilled in order that this doesn't happen. You are here to find out how to win this war apart from brute strength." Chief Warrant Officer Hague was short, around 5'5" and thick, approaching fat. His hair was graying and cut to regulation, his burned scalp visible to the fourteen members in the room.

"In front of you is the key information we believe you need to know. Shipping, air routes, military lines of supply. If you need anything else, let me know and I'll put in a request. You will be assigned a listening station and you will monitor the airwaves for anything that resembles a pattern. You will listen to our own people to ensure no breaches have occurred. Most importantly, you will learn to hear when things are in code and just plain bullshit meant to confuse us. If the Brits were able to crack the Enigma, then we can crack whatever Stalin and Mao are using."

Max didn't bother asking the question. He understood how code was produced and disseminated. The language of either side was secondary. The team could handle this assignment.

The world of cryptography in the US Army was surprisingly similar to university research, except he had to learn how to recognize rank, salute, and wear a tidy uniform. The army fed him, clothed him, and gave him accommodation. *As good as tenure*, he thought with a smile. He didn't have any budget constraints, as his department was considered vital. *I think I'm going to like it here.*

"Up for drinks afterwards?" Bull had positioned himself next to Max's station.

"Sure. Where?"

"Secret. You'll like it."

"I'm in."

A voice boomed in the room. "Are we in kindergarten, gentlemen, or are we fighting a war? Stop passing notes and get to work."

Max smiled inwardly but turned to face his listening device. *I am a glorified phone operator*, he thought. *This won't help us win the war. It's just some general's idea of looking clever. Think Max, think.*

His thinking took a break that evening.

"Harding, I'd like to introduce you to a little place I like to call paradise." As he opened the door, Max saw drunken men with women draped over them. The music was loud, the air smoky, and the light low.

"Thanks Bull, but this isn't my scene. I'd like to talk to my dates."

"Why talk? I always thought that was the worst part of a date." He smiled but followed Max out. "There is another place, much more sedate, where the MASH nurses hang out. They're American but were stationed in Japan until recently. They may be a bit too much for your young blood to handle."

"I think I'll take my chances. How far?"

"In a car, nothing's far." They hopped in and Max hung on as they slammed into every pothole on the way.

"I think you missed a couple holes back there."

"Just checking to see if you were watching, my friend."

"Much farther?"

"We're here."

"Where?" Max looked across the barren landscape devoid of lights. Nothing came into focus.

"Just here." The road turned and the familiar barbed wire and guards came into view.

"Sirs." The guards stood taller and saluted.

Max and Tim saluted back. "I'm just showing a new officer around the camps. We're from Bravo Two Nine in Pusan, a detachment of JACK. Mind if we enter?"

The guards lifted the barrier bar. *Jack-offs*, they muttered when out of ear-shot.

The camp was not as developed as Pusan but it had one thing their base lacked: nurses, and lots of them. The Army Nurse Corps was originally stationed in occupied Japan but came onshore to Korea following the troops. They arrived in Pusan and followed the American troops up to and past the 38th parallel in MASH units—Mobile Army Surgical Hospitals. This camp was a permanent hospital for long-term care and allowed the nurses to mingle with other officers on their leave days.

The building was barely better than a barracks but had the benefits of tables, chairs, music, and American nurses.

"I don't think I've ever seen anything more wonderful in my life," Max said.

"Hang on, Harding, you've barely left stateside. Imagine what I'm going through."

"You've been here so long, nothing works anymore. Just accept that you're a casualty of war."

"We'll see about that."

"Calm down. I'm going to get a drink and see if that one with red hair wants to dance."

"Fine. I've got the rest."

Max wiped his hands on his pants as he approached her. She was talking to three other women but he got the sense they saw him and were tracking his movements from the moment he walked in the door. "Hello, my name's Max. Would you care to dance with me?" He didn't hesitate, didn't greet any of the other women, and looked her dead in the eye. The others excused themselves.

The moment she lifted her head and looked at him, he knew there was no one else in the room he wanted to be with. She put her glass down demurely and placed her hand in his. As they moved into the center of the room, Frankie Laine's voice warbled the famous *Ballad of High Noon* through the radio and she put her head on his shoulder. Max saw Bull dancing with a tall blonde nurse, and when Bull caught his eye, he winked. Ali Martino was next with *Here in My Heart*. Max couldn't believe his good fortune. All the girls melted for Martino and this one was no exception. Even he felt the emotional tug of the words on his heart as he floated away from the unreal war he was part of. At the end of the song, she pulled away gently and he saw her blushing.

"Shall we grab a drink?" The air was hot and humid at the best of times. He could feel the sweat forming under his shirt and saw a sheen on her forehead.

"That sounds perfect."

"What's your name?"

"Sarnecky." She paused. "Sophia."

"How long you've been with the Army Nurse Corps?"

She took a slow drink before answering. "I'm not Army."

"I didn't know they allowed tourists in here."

"I'm not a tourist either."

"Is it a secret?"

"It may be. Let's see how the evening goes." She smiled, her teeth chewing on the plastic straw.

Max felt a shooting heat fill his torso as he watched her ordinary movements. Her hair was long and curly, reaching well past her shoulders. It was more rusty than red and her face had a band of freckles that started at her ear and went straight across her face, over the bridge of her nose, to her other ear. Green eyes and full lips hypnotized him as he sipped his beer. His only thought was not blowing it. *Stay cool*, he thought. *Talk about her, not yourself.*

"And what do you do?" She beat him to the punch.

"Radio comms with Bravo Two Nine in Pusan. Nothing exciting. Or at least, nothing that'll get me killed."

"Do you want to get killed?"

"I don't think so." His answer surprised him. "I mean, I'm not afraid to die but I think there's more I can do alive."

Sophia laughed and that was the final piece in the puzzle for Max. It transfixed him. "That's the silliest thing I've ever heard. Of course you can do more alive." She said the words but he only felt her hand as it briefly touched his chest before covering her laugh.

"I mean, you know what I mean. I'm here to do my duty."

"And what's that? Spy on the enemy—or us?"

"Are you sure you're not comms yourself?"

"Just an observation. But you don't need to worry. I know what you do."

"Really? I barely know myself."

"Let's dance some more. We can talk shop later."

Max was led back to the dancefloor. They danced until two in the morning, neither of them tired. He felt her whole body dance with him as Ella Fitzgerald and Mario Lanza sang through the speakers. Jo Stafford's *You Belong to Me* came close, but it was Nat King Cole's third song of the evening, *When I Fall in Love*, that saw them kiss for the first time.

"I'd have signed up just to meet you," Max said as they were ushered out. Bull had struck out and was waiting impatiently in the jeep. "Can I see you again?"

"I'd be angry if you didn't," she said. She gave him a long, slow kiss that made Bull look away.

"How can I get in touch?"

"I know where you are. I'll find a way to reach you." She smiled and gave a little wave as he got in the car.

Max lifted his arm in the dark as the jeep jerked forward.

"Didn't I tell you? Was that a great evening or what?" Bull was defiant, despite striking out with the ladies.

"I just met the mother of my children," Max said in a faraway voice. He slumped back in his seat and allowed the night air to wash over him.

"Let's not get ahead of ourselves," Bull said. "She's a nice girl and all, but there's plenty more fish in the sea."

"I'll leave them for you. I've caught the one I want."

"Okay, we'll see how that works out for you."

The next day, Max was floating on air. Even his cold gray equipment looked cheerful to him. His mood would become anxious when he realized he had no way of contacting Sophia, but he reconciled this against the fact she must love him as much as he did her. When he did see her again, it didn't go as planned.

"Harding, how's it hanging?" Bull could see Max's spirits were lower than usual and his best medicine was collegial hassling.

"Low and a little to the left, thanks."

No longer interested in the banter, Bull moved to his point. "I have a solution to your blues, my friend."

"I doubt it."

"I know where she is."

Max perked up. "Why didn't you tell me sooner?"

"I figure you needed to suffer a bit longer, but the guys and I are fed up with seeing you moping around. It's time."

"You knew before this?"

"I can't say."

"Can't or won't?"

"Neither."

"I don't care. Take me to her."

"She's here. Your appointment is in five minutes."

Max hit him. "Sometimes you can be a real asshole."

"Don't forget to salute, my friend."

"Huh?"

Bull was already on to his next victim of torment, arm around his shoulder and rubbing him on the head.

Max disregarded the bravado and went towards the door Bull had indicated.

Behind the desk sat Sophia, in uniform, looking better than he remembered. Her shyness was gone and she was all army. He glanced at her rank and noticed it was the same as his, major. *She must have come in on the same program I did,* he thought.

"Harding, please have a seat."

Max was trying to understand the change of circumstances. She barely acknowledged him.

"You may be wondering what's been going on and I wouldn't blame you." She got up and walked around the desk. "Whatever happens going forward, we start with a clean slate, understood?"

"Yes, ma'am."

She looked at him for a second, trying to see something in his character she missed the other night. "People far above our pay grade have been looking at you and would like you to join our team."

"Aren't we all on the same team?"

"Of course, but some of us are in the stands, some are on the field, and others are on the sidelines coaching and coercing. We are the ones who recon the field and stands before anyone arrives, making sure it is safe to play. No one sees us or even knows we exist."

"So no team jackets?"

"You get plenty of goodies with the job."

"You?"

"I'm not a goody."

"Where do you fit in?"

"Same place as you."

"Are we stationed together?"

"I believe so."

"Then I'm in."

That was too much for Sophia. She finally allowed herself to smile. "Be careful, Harding. This is a serious operation. You may not like what you see when you get to know me better."

"That's as good a reason as any to join. I told you the other day I'd have joined the army to meet you. I meant it. I'll join whatever team you say if it means I serve with you."

Sophia was sitting on the edge of her desk and got up, smoothing her government-issued dress, and walked the perimeter of the room. Max followed her with his eyes, turning his body to face her.

"This isn't some high school crush or silly game. Let me make this a little clearer, as you are obviously muddled in the head. We are not army."

Max sat back. "Then who are you?"

"We are part of a new department, set up in '47, called the Central Intelligence Agency. Our department is a subset of the CIA. Our designation is G29 and not even the director of the CIA knows who we are or what we do."

"Why are you telling me this?"

"Because you are going to volunteer to join the G29 on the recommendation of myself and another officer."

"Why would I want to do that?"

"For love." She pursed her lips and he caught a glint in her eye. "Of your country."

Max was quiet. He was always on the outside growing up, without parents. He was always the youngest in his class, never able to socialize with all the rest of the students. He always felt like he was different from everyone else. Joining an inner club would mean belonging to something. The whole idea was attractive.

"Can I think about it?"

"I thought you said you would go anywhere I was."

"But you said we are starting with a clean slate. That means I can't assume anything."

"Then perhaps we should change that."

Max ignored the invitation. "Who's in charge?"

"I don't know. There is a chain of command. We would report to the designated CO and that would be the extent of our knowledge. Everything is based on deniability."

"Which means we are disposable."

"I think the word you are looking for is 'expendable'."

"Cannon fodder."

"No. We may be many things, but we are not cannon fodder. We are the specialists who prepare the battleground before the first shot is fired. We work on wars decades before they start. We make things go away that are deemed a security risk."

"Assassins?"

"I told you that you may not like me when you know what I do."

"Not at all. I just need to know what I'm signing up for."

"Effective defense of our nation. We don't get carried away with bureaucratic niceties. We have objectives. We receive cover and support from Langley—CIA HQ—but we are left to our own devices. If we get caught, they deny having any connection to us."

"Not much cover then," Max said. He imagined himself being tortured by the North Koreans or Chinese.

"We get funding, intelligence, and objectives. The rest is up to us. In some ways, it's a good life."

"I've heard about the CIA but why would they want or need someone like me? I'm a square. I'm usually stuck in a lab or library, not some cloak and dagger enterprise."

"The CIA was set up primarily in response to the attacks at Pearl Harbor. We realize that we have enemies and we need to take action before our troops and citizens suffer from our incompetence. Pearl Harbor could have been prevented by someone like you."

Max wasn't sure about that, but he wasn't going to ignore a compliment from Sophia. He no longer saw the uniform. Her hair was tied up, showing off her freckles and green eyes. Her movements were graceful, reminding him of her body next to his as they danced those hours away. Her lips were kissing him, not talking, and he could see their children on the swings in the back yard. He shook his head and he was back in the Pusan air base with Major Sarnecky.

Max opened his mouth then closed it. He stood up and saluted Sophia. "When do I start?"

# CHAPTER SIX

# G29

"In case none of you have been keeping up with the news, I want to fill you in on the success we have had so far this year. Last month, our group managed its first major political assassination. You would have read about it as a drunken Stalin dying of a stroke. In fact, it represented years of ground work with the people around him, gaining their trust, and influencing their thinking." Colonel Smith eyed his fourteen recruits from the crypto-division, waiting for the information to sink in. When no one interjected, he continued.

"It is our stated mission to get the job done. This means targeted assassinations, inciting overthrow of governments, and making America safe. I am not mincing words here, gentlemen; we are the sharp end of the spear. We are not large in number for a reason. We have the total resources of the US military to bear if need be, but the smart action is in remaining invisible."

"How was it done? Stalin, I mean," asked Sophia.

"That's classified. What you need to take from it is that it can be done in a way that helps America. We have been closely involved with the coterie of men around Stalin and there are more shared goals than we had initially anticipated. We leveraged those goals, playing against their fears, and made our objective a reality. If this is handled correctly, we will have invaluable intel from those sources, which goes all the way to the top of the communist hierarchy."

Smith strutted the length of the blackboard, then turned and strutted back. "You will all learn to keep your mouths shut. We do not need to sound clever or right or anything outside of this room. Out there, you will act like nobodies. We will ensure a suitable cover." He glared at them, catching every eye before continuing. "We are not playing games. You have been chosen because of your abilities. You will perform or you will fail. There is no quitting. If you look at our CIA base in Seoul, there are two hundred agents but not one of them speaks Korean. Yes, Harding?"

"How do we overcome the language then?"

"You figure it out. You find an asset and you make him sweat. Just beware of those gooks; there are more double agents amongst them than our entire force. They are on their home turf. They have all the advantages. You have one, maybe two: your anonymity and our resources. Stay sharp. Your missions will be given to you after this briefing along with a contact CO. You will report only to him. You will trust no one else amongst yourselves or anyone else once you receive your mission. Until you are successful or receive new orders, you are to focus only on achieving your mission. Understood? Good." Smith turned, not taking any further questions, and left.

"Sounds like a piece of cake," Max said. Sophia and Tim Bull sat next to him.

"I like it for one reason, my friend," Bull said. "The clarity. So much of this," he waved his arm in a circle, "is bullshit. This whole war is bullshit. How many lives, how much money and energy has been spent fighting this war with no result. At the beginning, the 38$^{th}$ parallel marked the split between the North and South, and that won't change when this is over. What we can do is make a difference."

"I also like the clarity," Sophia said. "But there are limits to what men can achieve. You boys may learn a lesson or two from the fairer sex." She batted her eyes for effect. She didn't need to touch Max for him to feel the heat from her body.

"Let's see before we congratulate ourselves how great this is," Max said. He was beginning to sweat with an unfamiliar anxiety. He had never killed a man and didn't know if he was capable. He didn't sign up to be an assassin. He wanted to use his brain, break codes, and assist from the shadows.

Corporal Parker entered and placed a file in front of each of the members. None had moved since Smith stalked out. Each watched as she silently made her way around the room and then left.

Max opened his and saw a sheath of onion-thin papers clipped with a photo on top. Its black and white grains made the target hard to see, but he easily recognized him. When Bull and Sophia opened theirs, they held the same photo.

"Looks like we're a team," Sophia said. Her body nudged close to Max's but didn't touch.

"Unless they want us to get to the target independently. Maybe the entire class has the same target and this is a test. Whoever succeeds first wins a prize."

"Like what? More lies? I liked it when I thought things were clear."

"Like when you were five years old?" Max couldn't help himself.

"Calm down," Sophia said. "We have an objective. Do we need to sit here like lemmings or can we leave?" She looked around and only saw blank faces as each member read through their file and began looking at each other, also wondering what to do.

"Let's leave and see what happens," Max said.

They stood to leave but no one else moved. Parker stopped them as they walked through the connecting office.

"One second please. Yes, you three. Hang on. No, sir, a group of three just came out. Yes, sir, I'll send them in right away. Okay, please go in." She motioned to a closed door, which was not the way out.

They walked through the door and closed it. Smith sat behind a large desk. Sophia stared at the desk. It didn't have one piece of paper on it. Not even a phone. It was completely bare.

"So, you are it."

"Sir?"

"It is a technique to weed out the doers from the talkers. You're it."

"So this isn't our target?"

"It is, but not in the way you think. We can't take him out directly. That would cause a third world war and make this Korean police action a military footnote in comparison. We need to infiltrate his inner circle and begin a campaign that will be effective in the long term."

"Why not attack their money instead of people?" Max suggested.

"We're working on it. China doesn't trade its currency internationally so that is difficult. They are barely above subsistence-farming and not really a threat yet. But their numbers are terrifying—both militarily and economically. If they get their shit together, America is going to be in trouble."

"So what do you want us to do?"

"Figure out a solution and get back to me. You have one week to come up with some suggestions. If they make sense, I'll run it up the line and we'll take it from there."

Bull was silent, taking it all in. Max had nothing further to say. Sophia nodded and saluted. "Yes, sir."

∞

"How are we going to be effective against something like China? They're too big. Anything we do will be irrelevant—apart from assassinating Chairman Mao. And that, I agree, would start World War III."

"He's only been around for four years. How bad could it be?"

"He also just brought China into the Korean War last year. He has the ability to mobilize hundreds of thousands of men at arms. And the colonel said he wasn't the target, so that gets us off the hook."

Bull was staring out the window as the other two brainstormed. "If we are all about fighting the next war, why don't we look to where they are going to expand and stop them or frustrate them? That must be as good as a victory."

"Don't you think our military strategists will have thought about that already? This is like giving children advanced mathematical formulae and then wondering why they can't solve it." Sophia slunk back in her chair. "What can we do that the suits in Langley can't? They have more resources, and more people at their disposal. We're just a handful of spies."

"Novice spies at that," added Max.

"But anonymous spies," said Bull. "Remember what Smith said. That is our greatest advantage."

"Okay, then how do we do something relevant?"

"We don't fight a tank with a switchblade, that's for sure. The more I think about it, the less I see our ability to make a difference here at all. First, we are not Asian. We should recommend an aggressive campaign to recruit Americans who look like locals. I've seen our Chinatown back home. There are lots of 'em."

"Do you think they'd fight for the United States?"

"That's not for us to determine. I'm just looking at our strengths and weaknesses. Not fitting in makes it difficult for a spy to operate."

"Our country needs us here, not the south of France." Sophia smiled.

"I think Mao needs this war to legitimize his new government and gain favor with Russia."

"That's a lot of blood for good will."

"Isn't that what this is all about? Good will, saving face? America needs to fight or it loses credibility on the world stage. China needs to fight to establish its credibility. Russia needs to supply arms and keep up its façade as a great power."

"It is a great power, nukes and all."

"You know what I mean. They are kicking the shit out of us and we're kicking the shit out of them. Unless we do targeted assassinations—like with Stalin—we can't have any effect on the war."

"Maybe that's the solution," Sophia said. "Forget China and Korea and go right to the source. Russia supplies the arms. Let's do something that affects them. That will in turn affect China, which will help America."

"What are you thinking?"

"If Stalin was killed by one of ours, it means that the people closest to him are complicit with us."

"We don't have any information on this."

"We don't need to. Only a handful of people would dare do this. Stalin must have been something like a god in his country. Would you kill President Eisenhower or Roosevelt?"

"Or Churchill?" said Bull.

"Exactly. You only do it if you have something massive to gain."

"Like power," smiled Max.

"Exactly," said Sophia. "Using that logic, we know who killed Stalin for us."

"For himself and us," said Bull.

"Khrushchev."

"Absolutely, and perhaps an assistant. He may not have wanted to get his hands dirty."

"How do you anticipate infiltrating his inner circle? Each one is more suspicious than the other, with people spying on each other to the point where society has become dysfunctional."

"If you are to believe the reports, yes. But there is always a way. And with men, the way is fairly simple." Sophia twirled her hair dramatically.

Max ignored the idea of Sophia with another man. "I think we need to contact them when they visit a foreign country. That way, we will have the upper hand amidst the confusion."

"Like a trip to Geneva or one of the eastern satellite states?" Bull said.

"Exactly. Or perhaps on an unofficial holiday outside of Russia's borders. If you are one of the most powerful men in the world, what is the one thing you can't bear?"

"To be told no by some underling," said Sophia. "Good. I like this. We use G29's existing contacts to get us the travel schedule of Comrade Khrushchev and we happen to be there when he arrives."

"What do we do then?"

"Hope he killed Stalin and has a plan. Otherwise we're all dead."

"Or worse, captured, tortured, and then live out a broken, humiliated existence in a Gulag until we die of exhaustion."

"Charming," Sophia said. "Bull, you really are full of shit."

"Don't forget charm and enthusiasm," he said. "It keeps things in perspective."

"Let's not rely on this. We need to come up with viable plans or slide back down the greasy pole into the ranks of do-what-you-are-told." Max knew this was their shot.

"You mean, become ordinary CIA spies instead of G29 superspies?"

"Yeah, something like that. A few weeks ago, I was happy being an analyst. One magical night, a couple of briefings later, and now I wouldn't return there for anything." Max felt a fire inside him. It was excitement for something larger than himself. He liked it.

∞

"Are you sure we can trust this guy?"

"He's the mole and Khrushchev is meant to be here any day now."

"I'm not sure how much longer our cover will hold."

"I wouldn't worry. It will work or it won't. Too late for doubt."

"I wish I shared your certainty, Max." Bull picked up one of the large rocks on the beach and threw it into the water. "Why can't they have sand like other beaches? This is crazy."

"I think it has a natural ruggedness. Look at the water. It is the perfect holiday destination. I can see why he would come here." Sophia kicked the stones and looked into the horizon of never ending gray rock with blue-gray water lapping the shore. "It feels like the unmovable earth meeting the irresistible sea. Both seem so impossibly strong, yet they co-exist."

Max wanted to reach out to her at that moment and hold her close. He settled for her fingers brushing against his as he drew near to her. The autumn air was crisp. "Winter is in the air," he said. "I guess Pitsunda is south when you come from Moscow."

"He's originally from the Ukraine, so it must be like us going to Florida," Bull said.

"We can give this another few days and then we'll need to hop back to Turkey and chalk this up to poor intel." Max joined Sophia in kicking stones. He stopped after his toes became sore.

"I wish we could have a backup team," Sophia said. "I feel naked out here."

"Maybe it was a mistake to come with so many of us."

"One is a spy, even two. Three is too many for spies, which makes it perfect as a cover. It's too stupid a move. Nobody will doubt we're educators from Canada trying to help the Georgians with our mining expertise. The worst they will do is deport us."

"As we just happen to be hanging around the dacha of the Soviet premier."

"Yeah. What do we say when their security detail comes over to see us?"

"Act surprised and have the guts to ask to meet him. Sometimes the boldest and most audacious moves are the best."

"I'll leave you to do the talking," Bull said. "I'll be busy changing my diapers."

Max knew Bull to be ice cold under pressure. He had seen him tackle Sophia and himself to the ground when they ran across unexpected hostiles on route to Seoul. In a smooth movement he will never forget, Bull recovered his own sidearm and returned fire. His voice never raised above conversation level. The rest of the contingent they were travelling with did the rest, opening fire with automatic weapons until whomever was firing at them was dead. It was the first time Max had been fired upon. He was glad Bull was there for him.

"I think your moment is coming. There's activity in his dacha. See the vehicles?" They scanned the building at the edge of their line of sight. Four cars had arrived. "Are those Packards?"

"No, but they look like them. Big and decent-looking. I think they're called Chaikas or something." Bull observed without appearing like he was looking.

"I assume the security will take the dachas on either side to leave him some privacy."

"Wait. Take a look at that." Max nodded in the direction of a single Lada that stopped next to the four black Chaikas. "Enter the mistress."

"I think we know how we're going to get to him," Sophia said.

They packed up their picnic and began walking back to their guest room. The area they needed to observe was heavily wooded but the beach was free for people to walk on. It stretched endlessly in both directions. Khrushchev's dacha was at the southernmost tip of the landmass that jutted into the Black Sea, giving its occupant an unrivalled vista over the water. Looking out, only his back would see the trees and stone.

"I'd like to go back alone," Sophia said. They were sharing a room, Bull acting as the brother and Sophia as Max's fiancé.

"I don't like it but I think it is the only way we'll make contact." Max never liked the plan as it had evolved.

"I'll put on something attractive and see if I can happen across the mistress. Hopefully I can get talking."

"How's your Russian?"

"Better than your Korean. I'll get by. I don't need to be fluent. I only need to be willing and smile a lot. The shorter my dress, the less my language requirements." She said it with a smile but knew it could go terribly wrong very quickly. She was rummaging through her luggage to find the right outfit.

Max put his arm on hers. He could feel her trembling. "Sophia. You don't have to do this." His eyes said the rest.

"Don't be foolish. It's what we've trained for. It's what I'll do." She gathered her things and went to the shared toilet down the hall to change.

"It feels a bit rushed," Bull said when she was gone.

"I agree."

"She seems very eager."

"I'm concerned as well."

"Shall we pull the plug?"

"Not our call. She's the only one who can do this. No one will let two men get close to the target."

"We're not killing him. We just want to talk."

"They don't know that."

"I'm sure it'll change as security tightens. I have a feeling every time we do something like this, we make it harder on ourselves and people in our line of work. Some guy who gets killed in an innovative manner means security forces have to take that into consideration. Today, we use women to get close to powerful men. Tomorrow, even that may not work."

"True, but people are people. The more powerful you are, the less you want to be restricted."

"And those restrictions may be the type of danger that turns you on. Agreed. So maybe sex is the one thing that will stay constant. But we're talking about Sophia."

"I know. Don't remind me," Max said.

"I know you like her, my friend." Bull put his hand on Max's shoulder.

"Too much. Maybe it was a mistake for us to be a team. It's clouding my judgement."

"Maybe. Maybe not. Let's see how this goes."

Sophia opened the door and was shy at first.

"Wow. Can I have a squeeze?" Max hugged her. He didn't want to mess with her makeup but wanted her lips on his as much as any time before.

"You look great, Soph," Bull said. "Are you sure that skirt's legal?"

"I told you I needed some help with my Russian."

"I think you've found the perfect translator."

"Okay, I'm off. Don't wait up for me. If all goes well, I'll see you tomorrow."

"I'll walk you to the corner," Max said. He saw Bull nod.

"I'd like that. See you, Bull." She gave him a peck on the cheek.

"See you, gorgeous."

The door closed and they walked in silence down the narrow hall. Its carpet was clean but still smelled of smoke. The rest of the house smelled of whatever was being cooked at the time, usually cabbage or a fatty sausage. Its owner was well fed and had lost her curves many years ago. She wore a floral dress that hung straight from her shoulders, with two bulges for her breasts and a belly that pushed out just a little further. They never caught her name and she was always smiling when they met her. When she wasn't aware that they were looking, her face became set in a mask formed over many decades of trying to stay alive.

The fresh air was welcome and they both breathed in deeply, partly because they didn't know what to say. Sophia put her hand in Max's and they walked in silence until they reached the edge of the stony beach.

"I love you, Sophia." Max wanted to get this out of him before the moment passed. He had told her before, but never meant it more.

"I love you too," she said and kissed him gently. "Careful with my lipstick. I can't be changing anything."

"Careful with yourself. I need you back in one piece."

"Don't worry. I'm only going to talk. We need to see if he is the asset that we've been looking for. If we're right, it may even end this Cold War."

Max held her arms lightly, looking at her, memorizing her face.

"I'm coming back. Don't look at me like that. It makes me nervous." Sophia touched his face and pulled away. "It's worth the risk."

Max silently watched as she backed away, turned, and started walking. As she was about to walk past his line of sight, she turned to look at him. He waved and she lifted her hand a little. *Now the worst part begins,* he thought.

∞

"Another drink?" Bull was keeping positive and passing the vodka.

"Sure. I shouldn't really."

"If not now, when?"

"I know we're supposed to be hard bastards and we've seen a thing or two since we arrived in Korea, but this has a bad smell to it, doesn't it?"

"No more than dropping the nukes on Nagasaki and Hiroshima. It was terrible, but it ended the war and saved millions of other lives."

"You're equating Sophia getting man-handled, or worse, by Khrushchev and his thugs to the nuking of Japan?"

"Yes." Bull said it straight faced but it didn't last long. His toothy grin gave him away.

"It's still tough."

"Would you go if it was a female president and you'd have to give your body for your country?"

"Depends on what she looked like," Max said.

"Like Khrushchev."

"Nasty image. I'll have another shot."

Bull glanced at the clock. "I don't want to be a spoilsport, but I think we've had enough."

"What's the time?"

"Getting there. Just past midnight. Maybe we should get some shuteye before it gets light. She's not coming home tonight."

Max turned around and verified the time. "Okay, lights out. I'm going for a stroll at dawn."

"Deal."

The vodka did its job to get the first few hours of sleep done, but the anxiety forced Max's eyes open before it was light outside. He got dressed and tried to sneak past Bull to get out of their room.

"Where do you think you're going alone?" Bull was on the sofa but his voice was sober and wide awake.

"I need some fresh air."

"Sorry about that. The cabbage does that to me."

Max had to laugh. "Not that, but now that you mention it, try to get control over it."

Bull shrugged. "My body is a temple. It reacts to what I put in it in a natural fashion."

"Then I'm putting you on rations."

"Fine by me. Just hang on, we'll go out together."

Outside, the light was black with a hint of blue. There were no road lights and they had to navigate by the moon, which was two-thirds full. It provided enough light.

"Glad there are no clouds."

"We need to be thankful at all times, my friend."

Their feet touched the rocks as their eyes began to play tricks on them. "Is it getting lighter out here or are we getting used to it?"

"I think the sun must be coming up."

"I remember a bench around here. Let's wait a second. I don't want to twist my damn ankle."

*Saving the love of your life?* Bull refrained from saying it out load. "Sounds good. A few steps, yep. I can see an outline. It's a little wet, not too bad. Okay, that's good."

The morning air sobered up whatever was resisting their adrenaline and nerves. The sun began its ascent as the moon almost disappeared on the horizon. The blue black of the moment had passed and their eyes began to make out vague shapes and patterns. The horizon loomed black and seemed to shimmer in shadow until enough light defined its woods. Max stood, Bull followed, and they began their walk on the stones.

Thirty minutes brought them to the portion of the beach nearest Khrushchev's dacha. The lights were still on and they could make out the shapes of the black cars that looked like American Packards.

"Looks like the party is still going. The old fart must have more in his tank than I gave him credit for."

"Wait."

"What?"

Max squinted his eyes, willing them to focus the distance. "Why aren't there any guards stationed?"

"Good question." They walked the perimeter of the beach, scanning the dacha from all available angles. "I don't see anyone."

"I'm going in."

"That's crazy."

"I know, but something doesn't smell right."

"I told you, it was the cabbage." When Max didn't reply, Bull followed behind.

They approached the dacha from the east, trying to gain some advantage from the sun's morning show. Three cars were parked nose to tail with the front one pointed at the gate, ready to exit at a moment's notice.

"One car has left since yesterday."

"And the Lada is also gone."

"Big Cheese and his mistress?"

"Probably. Which makes me wonder what the rest of the guys are doing in there."

They walked past the rows of vegetables, perfectly hidden amidst the tall rows of corn. Max had taken the lead and took the shortest route from the edge of the woods to the house. Still, no guards could be seen.

They could hear the oom-pah ostinato of the traditional Russian folk music being played by a phonograph. Max dared to come next to the outer walls and peek into the glass windows. The sun was pouring into the eastern and southern windows. The blinding yellow and orange light filled the rooms. Inside, he could see bottles, food, and bodies. Six men lay collapsed on the floor with barely more than their underwear on. Under one, a familiar leg stuck out. It was bloodied.

Max turned to see Bull looking in on the next window. His hand went to his sidearm and they each nodded as they turned their safeties off. Max raised three fingers and pointed at Bull, and then raised the same three fingers and pointed at himself. Bull nodded.

They made their way around the corner of the dacha, looking for the guards they knew were inside. Brazened by their luck so far and the scene inside, they turned the handle on the front door. It was unlocked and opened without a sound. They left it open and went inside, intent on cleaning up their mess.

As they put a bullet in each guard's head, they counted. One. Two. Three. Then they went back to number one and put another bullet in his chest, just in case. The same with two and three. Max pulled the guard off Sophia while Bull rushed through the rest of the dacha to ensure no further surprises were in store for them.

"You came for me?"

Max's eyes flowed tears as he found some clothes to cover her up. Blood-stained, her legs and her face were swollen. Her mouth had dried blood smeared around it and there were two trails of red from her nose to her mouth. Max didn't see any of it other than her eyes. It was the first time he had ever seen Sophia afraid, and it made him cry.

∞

Unlike their mission, their exit strategy was flawless. The importance of planning multiple options was drilled into them in their training. They all silently thanked the sonsofbitches who made their lives hell during training. It was the only thing that helped them stay alive. They had a small boat with an outboard engine in waiting. They followed the shoreline in the early morning hours until they reached Hopa in Turkey in the afternoon. Time seemed to crawl by. They were torn between being seen and hauled in by some coastal authority and the fear of being out too far and drowning in the unforgiving Black Sea. They all relaxed when they reached their safe house.

"I'm sorry," said Sophia, over and over.

"Drink this and sleep. We'll deal with this later. All that matters is that you rest." Max covered her and kissed her gently. They had bathed the blood away but the bruising would take some time.

He left her upstairs to sleep and went downstairs. It took everything he had to keep from smashing up the place. "Those were the first men I ever killed," Max said. "And I feel nothing for them but rage. I could kill another hundred right now."

"Try this raki instead. It's just like ouzo."

"I never liked ouzo." He took a drink of the clear liquid and grimaced. "Is this the only shit we have to drink?"

"Never look a gift horse, my friend." He put some water with his, making it go milky white. He sipped it contentedly.

"We need to report back," Max said after a few moments. "This is a royal mess."

"Which part, the bad intel or the massacre we committed?"

"Both. I am beginning to wonder if the big man was ever there."

"You're thinking we were set up?"

"Yeah."

"That our mole may be playing both sides of the fence?"

"Yeah."

"And this may be intel our CO would want to hear?"

"Fuck yeah." Max took another swig.

"Agreed, but let's get drunk first. Sophia won't be needing our immediate attention; she needs to sleep. We can get in touch tomorrow. In some ways, I kind of liked it. Not the Sophia thing, the other stuff. I may be more suited for this than I thought."

*Me too*, thought Max.

# CHAPTER SEVEN

# *Kennedy*

"Are you ready for the big event?" Bull elbowed Max but could see he had his mind on other things.

"Sophia can't get pregnant."

"Don't you think you should get your mind around what our next mission is?"

"I think it was because of that day ten years ago."

"Max, sometimes these things happen. Lots of couples can't have babies."

"I'm not lots of couples. I think it's changing me."

"Look, I know it's important to you but don't you think what we're about to do is too?"

"We do what we do. We'll do what we're told. Don't worry about me. I'll pull my weight."

"This isn't just some schmo, you know."

"A man is a man, and a bullet is the great equalizer. If he's a god, then he has nothing to worry about."

"It's going to shake things up quite a bit. We'll need to stay low for a long time."

"It will either be a success or it'll fail, in which case we're both dead. The key is our exit strategy. We can both fire straight. That isn't my concern. How we get away or pin this on someone else is what we need to think about."

"Do we know anyone else who will be there?" Bull was glad to have dragged Max from his obsession about babies. Ten years of missions going according to plan had inured themselves to the requests from control.

"The only way we stay safe is not to question our orders. I haven't heard about anyone else being there. But if it were up to me, I'd have half a dozen rifles pointing at the target just in case."

"This has never been done before."

"Not here, not by us. But history is littered with assassinations."

"Do you think about what we're about to do?"

"Yeah. They call it the big event. It'll be big alright. The public doesn't know what we know and we can't let him stay in power. It's too dangerous."

"That's the only thing letting me pull the trigger," Bull said. "As an American, it's a tough call."

"You know," Max said, sitting back against the metal structure, "G29 should figure a way to create a more credible enemy. The Soviets are a good bad guy, but their army and forces are too real. If we push things too far, we'll end up at war. We need a bad guy who is shadowy, unknown, and potentially powerful. This will allow the government to blame it for whatever it wants."

"Like today's events."

"Exactly. After today, we need to put together a brief outlining a strategy for a more effective bogey-man. It needs to be foreign so pain-in-the-ass civilians don't get too involved. It needs to be in a dangerous location so it is difficult to get to—and we can neutral-ize anyone who decides to become brave."

"Vietnam and Korea? China?"

"Good bad guys. Vietnam, maybe, but that brings in Russia again. The problem is always Russia."

"They probably think the problem is us."

Max laughed. "I know, and I bet there are two schmos like us on the other side talking the same way about us."

"Life." Bull liked this about Max. They were on the edge of an historic day and talking shit.

"Have you taken a look recently?"

"Elm Street is clear. Secret Service agents are eve-rywhere."

"And even where they're not, they claim to be."

"I bet they've disguised some bums as backup if things go wrong."

"Things can't go wrong. This is a one-time deal," Max said. "We'll never get this chance again."

"Do you think about Khrushchev much? How we could have changed history?"

"I think about other things from that day," Max said. Bull could see his eyes cloud over and regretted bringing it up. "But today isn't the fault of Khrushchev, for once. From what I understand, he's been trying to form some type of peace with us."

"Is that a good thing?"

"If it's real. Hard to tell with those Commies. They're all liars."

"It's hard to find honest people with morals anymore," Bull said.

"War brings out the best and worst in people," Max said, rifle now laying on his lap. He sat with his legs out, back against the metal framing of a large sign for Hertz Rent a Car. There was a second set of heavy metal framing holding up a sign advertising Chevrolet. The signs were twenty feet above their heads as they sat on the roof, overlooking the expected route of their target. "To win, war needs moral men who can remain moral while still being able to kill on command."

"Clarity is strength." Bull recited their lessons.

"And enlightenment confuses a fighting force," Max finished.

"Perhaps we aren't supposed to question?"

"I don't think so. We can question everything. That is what makes us free and American. But an order is an order and must be followed. We can question when we're off duty."

"I believe that we make a difference. Otherwise, I couldn't do what I'm about to do."

"Agreed. Do you have the time?"

"Just before noon. We'll hear the sirens before we need to get into position."

"Make sure your arms or legs don't go to sleep. We each need to put two rounds into him to be sure."

"I'll do my part," Bull said.

"Do we go for head or heart shot?"

"I would start with a high percentage shot. We'll be shooting as he is driving away, so aim for the vital organs. We'll go for the head after we plant at least one in him."

"Protocol will give us a small window of opportunity."

"Don't overthink this. He's just a man. Try not to hit his wife or the Secret Service agents. They're not targets."

Max was clearing his mind, looking into the distance. "Do you think the same applies here as in Russia?"

"What do you mean?"

"We are almost certain Khrushchev killed Stalin. He had help, granted, but he was the one to give the order. On that logic, who would you say gave this order?"

Bull didn't want to think like this. It was unpatriotic. "You know what I think."

"I know. Who has the most to gain?"

"Only one man."

"I know." Max checked his rifle and scanned the scene below, barely poking his head above the edge of the short wall that ran around the perimeter of the roof. He could see the crowds gathered. "There isn't much of a police presence here at all."

"I think that has to do with the man who has the most to gain from today."

"It is his state."

"I'm glad I'm not in politics. Too much gray for me. I like the clarity of our work. We don't have to determine who or what is bad. We allow others to figure it out and act as their sword."

"We are the dog's body," laughed Max. He enjoyed the banter. It relaxed him.

"Hang on, I can hear something. The crowd is waking up as well. I think it's show time." Bull moved forward and they got into position. Each had two extra shells placed next to them. There would be no time for thinking or looking when the shooting started.

"Remember the exit strategy," Max said as he looked through his scope and found where he wanted to take his shot. They had examined this closely earlier so there was nothing to do but wait for the target to move into their sights.

There were three police motorcycles escorting the president's Lincoln Continental convertible with a handful more along the side. There, as expected, the president of the United States sat waving next to his wife. There were other people in the car, but there was only one target. Bull and Max had him in their sights and waited for the precise location where they agreed to fire.

Max had already slowed his breathing, waiting to fire between breaths. He waited until his lungs had exhaled, not forcibly, just naturally. His finger touched the trigger.

The first shot didn't come from either Bull or Max. They could see the occupants of the car look to their left, trying to identify the source. Anyone who had gone hunting knew the sound of a high-powered rifle.

The second shot was from Max. From their position, they couldn't see much of a reaction. The third came from Bull. Max didn't fire a second time as he saw the president's head explode in a red burst. He was already cleaning his rifle of any prints and placing it in the prearranged location on the Hertz metal framing. Someone would remove it later. Bull did the same.

They heard some more shots from below them as they implemented their exit strategy. "This place'll be crawling with cops before you know it. Do you have your ID? Good. Let me see it? Okay. Wait a bit. Now."

Max hurried into the sixth floor of the Texas School Book Depository and began looking for whoever was taking the other shots. Not seeing anything, he motioned Bull to follow him. Both were dressed as local police officers.

"Where the hell are they?" Bull asked.

"I don't know. Makes you wonder."

"Just keep walking. If we meet up with anyone, we'll join the hunt for the assassins. Otherwise, let's get the hell out of here."

Max nodded as they began their descent down the stairs. They came across no one and exited onto the rear entrance without incident.

"That was too easy," Max was breathing hard. "It's frightening."

Lyndon B. Johnson was sworn in later that day as the thirty-sixth president of the United States. Lee Harvey Oswald, an employee at the same Dallas School Book Depository, was motioned over by an officer, J.D. Tippit, on Tenth and Patton. Oswald responded by shooting Officer Tippet three times with a revolver before walking over to him and shooting him in the head. Oswald was arrested thirty-one minutes later in a movie theatre for shooting Officer Tippet. Later, he was charged for assassinating President Kennedy. He denied shooting Kennedy, claiming he was a patsy. Two days later, escorted by police and surrounded by cameras, Oswald was fatally shot by Jack Ruby. Ruby was convicted of Oswald's murder and then had his conviction overturned. While waiting for his retrial, Ruby died in prison of a pulmonary embolism.

No mention of Max Harding or Timothy Bull was ever made.

# CHAPTER EIGHT

# The Hildebrandt Dossier

"Is Bull okay with it?"

"He'll have to be. Besides, he's a big boy."

"But you've been working as a team for over twenty years."

"So have we." Max gave Sophia a kiss and used his arm to bring her closer to him. They sat on a bench on the Moanalua Ridge overlooking Honolulu.

"Maybe they're wrong."

"Whatever happens, I'm happy if it's just the two of us."

Sophia looked at her hands. "I've been able to do anything I have set my mind to my entire life. We've travelled the world, made an impact through our work, and survived things that we probably shouldn't have."

"Like Oleg?"

"And the rest."

"We'll be fine."

"I feel like a failure. It's the one thing every trailer trash girl with a glint in her eye can achieve. Any cow can get pregnant and give birth, but not me. Why can't I get pregnant?"

I *don't mind the trying*, Max thought. Then he was pleased he didn't verbalize it when he saw her face. "There are plenty of women who can't get pregnant. We'll be fine. We can adopt if you want."

"I thought Tripler would be able to sort us out. At least we know your sperm isn't the problem." The tears were on the cusp of falling and she willed them back.

"At least the hospital is pink. That's a start." Tripler Army Medical Center was painted a coral pink. Its massive structure sat overlooking Honolulu.

Sophia glared at him.

"And they said there was nothing wrong with your eggs," he added quickly.

"Maybe there's something wrong with us?"

A *part from killing and torturing people for a living, knowing that we will be disavowed by the CIA and government if we get caught? No stress at all*, Max thought. "Maybe we need a break? Why don't we clock off for a few weeks and hang out here. It's beautiful. We can walk on the beaches, spend romantic evenings together, and try to forget babies or the rest of the world."

Sophia became soft and leaned against Max. "I'd like that." She let her head roll against his shoulder until it found the best resting place. "Are you sure about the other thing?"

"Yeah. I've had enough. It's time that we got out, took a job that allowed us to raise a family—God willing—and live happily ever after."

"Do you think people like us are allowed to live happily ever after?"

"I hope so. You never know, we can always go back if we can't tolerate small town American life."

"Do you regret our lives? Our decisions?"

"Do you mean would I rather be a professor in Harvard exchanging A's for sexual favors?" Sophia punched him hard. "Ow! I'm kidding! No, I don't regret a thing because it led me to you."

She kissed him on the side of his chest where she rabbit punched him. "Better answer."

"You are the only thing that makes sense in this world," Max said. *I don't think I could go on without you.*

"In light of our new romantic intentions, perhaps we should walk back to the hotel. We can watch the sun set in paradise." She kissed him and the anxiety began to melt away.

When they returned to their hotel, there was a telegram from their commanding officer under the door. "I'll get some wine," she said. "You check what that's all about." Their hotel suite had a kitchenette and a lounge, with their bed in a separate room.

Max grabbed the telegram off the floor and kicked off his shoes. His feet were already feeling the walk. He sat down in the armchair nearest the television.

"Anything good?"

When Max didn't answer, Sophia popped her head out of the fridge, where she kept her white wine. She moved next to him and crouched down.

"Don't cry, sweetheart. What is it?" She got up and put herself on his lap, holding him. He hung on to her before answering.

"My dad. He's gone."

She took a moment before registering the meaning of his words. They never talked about his father. "I'm sorry, Max."

"He was such an asshole, you know?" He looked up to her, eyes red. "But he was my dad."

"I know. It's complicated." She smoothed his hair and kissed him.

"I just wish there was more time. I wanted to talk to him, understand him and why he did what he did."

"How is his family? Any children? Wife?"

"I haven't kept in touch. Since my mom died, he became weird. It was as though he didn't want me around him. Like I was bad luck or something."

Sophia paused. "Are you going to the funeral? Do you want me to come?"

"I wouldn't go without you." He turned and kissed her until his tears ran down her cheeks. It made her almost as happy as when he proposed to her.

"Just hang on a bit. Let me get us a bottle and some glasses and we can drink them in bed." She looked back at him over her shoulder and she could feel the excitement growing in her, warm and nervous, and an unspecific sense of longing that never went away whenever they were together.

Max got up, feeling flat from the news, and strangely turned on by Sophia's actions. He began to take off his shirt and walked into the bedroom.

∞

"I don't know what it is, but I'm exhausted. The flight wasn't bad. I think I slept through most of it."

"Booze and sleeping pills will do that."

"Maybe it's my dad. I can't seem to shake this feeling that I never gave him enough credit. As though there was something more to him."

"You always told me you were raised by your nannies and never saw him growing up."

"Yeah. If I didn't have a picture of him, I wouldn't remember what he looked like. I have almost no memories of him growing up and none as an adult."

"We don't need to go."

"I need to. We just flew half way around the world to see him. And the bastard's dead. Why couldn't I have done the same when he was alive?"

"We don't need to stay at the Savoy, you know. It's far too expensive and your family is in Hampstead."

"I stole you from what I had hoped would be a romantic month away from our mad existence. At least I can pamper you with a good hotel."

"This isn't just a good hotel, Max. This is the best."

Max shuffled his feet and shrugged. "I want to learn from my dad. I don't want to wait until it's too late to spoil you and tell you that I love you."

Sophia kissed him on the cheek. Her arm was already around his and she hugged it appreciatively. Max was good to her at the best of times but, since his father's passing, he was going out of his way to make her feel special and wanted. It was a selfish thought, but she liked this new Max.

"The solicitors acting for Dad aren't far from here. That's another reason I chose this place."

"I thought you were joking about the name. Talk about scary."

"No more than a chiropractor called Dr. Bones."

"A firm called Slaughter and May seems a little too much, don't you think?"

"It is a bit intimidating for the other side, I would think. It is the oldest and most prestigious firm in London, probably the world."

Sophia raised her eyebrows. Max had a past she didn't know about, and his father was it. *He must have been loaded,* she thought.

"When's the funeral?"

"Tomorrow. The reading of the will is after that. I was told to stick around. I hope you're okay with that."

"Uh huh. You think he left you anything?"

"I don't know. I'm not sure I want anything."

"Whatever happens, I'm here."

The next day, the sun shone, defying the rain they had endured the rest of the week. Max stood with Sophia after giving condolences to his father's new wife. The service was short, the grave site shorter, and there was no wake.

"You think they would have introduced you as his son. Even his wife treated you like a stranger. And why did he go by a different name?"

Max pursed his lips. None of it made sense. "I don't know, but I didn't want to cause a scene. I had never met his wife and, obviously, she was never told of me."

"Then how did you get the telegram?"

"That's what's been bothering me."

"Maybe the solicitor will have some answers."

"They couldn't give me any more questions than I already have."

She held his arm as they walked along the Embankment, Big Ben silhouetted by the bright sun. The Thames gurgled past contentedly, as did everyone else. "From the papers, you would think this country was going to pieces, but it looks pretty good from where I'm standing."

"I could be in a warzone with Satan and feel pretty good as long as you're on my arm," Max said. Even he groaned inwardly as he said it.

"Max Harding, are you trying to butter me up for something? That's the corniest nonsense I've ever heard." She put her hands on her hips, trying to act the part. "But I forgive you because you are so adorable and you're trying to be romantic. Full marks." She gave him a kiss on the cheek.

The next day they went to 18 Austin Friars. "This is just how I imagined it," Sophia said. "The heavy wooden doors, the stone and brick. All dark from soot and age. I love it." She squeezed Max's hand. He hadn't spoken a word since they got up and she made up for it by not stopping.

"I wonder if he'll be wearing a monocle or something outrageous. Perhaps a walking cane?"

Max looked at her and grimaced. She stopped talking.

They were shown into a large room with a boardroom table and armchairs for twenty-four people. Stone ashtrays set in polished brass were conveniently located within an arm's reach of each chair. There was no view to speak of and the lighting was dulled by glass with years of smoke-stains. The room smelled of wood, books, and smoke.

At the center of the table, with his back to the windows, sat an elderly man with scrolls, leather bags, and four large books. Next to him was a middle-aged woman who must have been his secretary, as she waited on his every word. When Max and Sophia entered, the man stood.

"Max Harding, I presume? I am Sam Gren." He extended his hand and Max had to walk around the table to shake it. He didn't move. Sophia nodded and took a seat.

"When are the rest expected? Am I too early?"

"No, no. There are no others."

Max's head turned, trying to understand what he just heard.

"I'm sorry. I thought this was the reading of his will."

"It is. I think you should sit down, Mr. Harding." The man's face was etched with concern softened by a life lived with books.

Max made his way next to Sophia. As he walked around the table, the man began unfurling the scrolls and opening the books, which turned out to be ledgers. When Max was seated, he began.

"I'm sorry to hear of your father's passing, Mr. Harding. He brought a lot of business to our firm on the understanding of our reputation for discretion. We have had many powerful men as clients in the past. It's no secret that we have acted for the Rock and Roth families in the past, as well as most of the wealthiest families of Europe. Your fortune was slightly different for a number of reasons."

Max's ears began to ring. *My fortune? Did I hear that right?*

"First, I am instructed to give you this." He handed a scroll with a mark of a seal in the wax next to a signature Max didn't recognize. "I am to provide a brief background and then let you familiarize yourself with the documents and the contents within."

Max's face was a mix of disbelief and shock. He looked briefly at the scroll and put it aside, preferring to hear it from Gren directly.

"Your father was not a wealthy man, you must understand, but he was wise and wanted to protect the most precious thing he had in the world. You." Gren paused for effect but received only a cynical look from Max. "You may have wondered at the difference in names between yourself and your father's wife. It is because your name was given as a shield, to protect you from enemies."

"Enemies? Are you sure you have the right person?" Max couldn't keep quiet any longer. This whole escapade was becoming farcical. It was also destabilizing his memory of himself and his father.

"There is a reason your father left you. Your entire family was killed and they didn't know about you."

"My family died in an accident. They weren't killed." Max was sweating. He sat forward in his seat.

"I will leave you all the documents. You can determine that for yourself. The main concern for your father was that you weren't killed. He was never able to find out who was behind his wife's, your mother's, murder. Significant sums were spent trying to track down the agents behind this, to no avail."

"I'm sorry, Mr. Gren, but none of this makes sense."

"I'm sure this is a lot to take in, and you'll need time. This firm is at your disposal if and when you need us."

"Thank you, but I'm not sure if I can afford this." Max looked around and shrugged.

Mr. Gren laughed genuinely and caught his secretary off guard. She looked mortified at his behavior. "Mr. Harding, my good man. You are richer than the Queen of England."

∞

With Gren and his secretary gone, Max looked at the paperwork. His training let him disassemble the data and make connections. He took notes on the pad of paper they gave him. He ensured Sophia had a pad and she was given half of the ledgers to examine.

"This is going to take us all week," she said. "We've barely scratched the surface and it has already been a couple of hours."

"I'm not too concerned about the money. It's great that we have it, but I want to know what happened to Mom. If what Gren said was true, my dad wasn't the bastard I always thought. He may have saved my life."

"And who killed them? That's a long time ago."

"We've got time. We'll need a leave of absence from work, but we'll find the bastards who did this. First, I need to find out how." He was speed-reading with his fingers along the pages of documents. When his finger stopped, the rest of his body froze. After a moment, Sophia noticed.

"You find something?"

"I think so. It looks like they died in a concentration camp."

"What? Are you Jewish?"

"I don't think so, but more than Jews died in those places."

"But they had money. Shitloads, from the looks of it. They could have bought their way out."

"Which makes this more mysterious. When does money not buy you everything?"

"Love?"

"Hate. And political expedience. We need to follow the power and who benefits from my family's extermination."

"Why didn't they go after your father?"

"No money, no influence, no reason. It looks like all of the money came from someone called Meyer Hildebrandt."

"It looks like he was your grandfather, or maybe your great-grandfather."

"I don't know. It looks like he siphoned out a lot of money before he died and placed it in Switzerland, England, and America. He wasn't wiped out during the inflation after World War I or the reparations after World War II. His money sat quietly, growing. And there is only one heir. It wasn't my father. It's me."

"Mr. Gren or someone must have been tracking your whereabouts. Otherwise, how could he have found us in Hawaii? I didn't tell anyone."

"Okay, great. We're rich. My mother and her entire family were killed in a concentration camp after they were accused of being Jewish, from the looks of these records. But they don't say who brought the charges or how they were enforced." Max was intense as he scanned the documents, excited because it filled in so many holes in his past but not wanting to believe the reasons were so macabre.

"Maybe we can use the resources at work to find out? Perhaps pull some strings?"

"I like that, but we need to keep quiet on the money. We can't change the way we live. I'll talk to Gren about keeping this hidden. Hopefully, our children can use it. I'm content enough without the hassle of fending off all those leeches who want to part us from our money."

Sophia pouted. "Are you sure? Even just a bit, you know, for the little luxuries?"

"Absolutely. Hotels have all been officially upgraded to five star. We can sit in the front of the plane and we don't have to eat pizza if we don't want to." He was smiling, despite himself. The amount of money was staggering.

"Maybe we can retire from the agency?"

"That may not be so easy. You know the rules."

"'Til death do us part." She crossed herself in mock seriousness.

"Exactly. That's why we can't let those bastards know about the money. We can show some to justify our increase in quality of life, and I can explain that with the death of my father."

"You know, I just noticed you've become even more handsome since I found out you're a multimillionaire." Sophia got out of her chair and sat on Max's lap, facing him. "I don't know if I can let you out of my sight." She kissed him slowly, running her hands through his hair.

"I think you're right," he said. "But first, make sure the door's locked."

# CHAPTER NINE

# Illuminati

"I'll do it." Bull was leaning back, finding the point of balance where the chair was on two legs and his legs dangled. He touched the table lightly, calibrating himself.

"Not if you fall and break your damn neck." Max took a sip from his beer.

Bull ignored him and finished off his beer before placing the bottle lightly on the table. "Soph, could you pass me another? Thanks."

"You plan to drink and pass off your shit-eating grin as a conversation?"

"It's worked for me so far, my friend." He was rocking his chair, no longer trying to balance.

"Yes, it has, though I'm not sure why." Max leaned over and clinked his bottle against Bull's new one. "Sophia, why do we tolerate this guy?"

She smiled and kissed Bull on the cheek. "He's a bit like an ugly stray dog that grows on you."

"Ruff ruff." Bull played along and grabbed her hand before she sat down. He kissed it gallantly and bowed.

"See, he does stuff like that," she said. "How can you say no to him?"

"Everyone else does," Max said. "Seems to work for them."

"Okay, I get it. I need to find some more friends," Bull said.

Max got up and went to the other room for a moment. He returned with a manila folder that had a red rubber band around it. He put it in Bull's lap. He put all six legs on the floor.

"What's that?"

"Our next assignment."

Tim opened it up and began scanning. The first two pages contained a summary of the file's contents. "This doesn't look official. Is this off the books?"

"Sort of. I need to find out who killed my family."

"What? Is that why you took so much time in London? I thought your father died an old man. I didn't hear about any suspicious circumstances."

"Not my dad. My whole family. The memory of my existence was eliminated. I need to know everything."

"This dossier contains a lot."

"It is a history of them as people, their accomplishments. Not who they were."

"That may not be possible," Bull said softly.

"True," Max said. "But we can find out who did it to them."

"War crime?"

"I think it's more than that. Whoever did this was able to short circuit all the normal corrupt channels that keep wealthy and powerful people out of places like that. If it was some petty politician, the money from my family would have set him up as a dictator of a small country on the edge of the world. Whoever did this wasn't interested in money. They wanted this family eliminated from history."

"Maybe you're getting a little paranoid?"

Max tensed up. If it was anyone else, he would have punched him. "You've seen what we do. We've all seen it. There is an alternative reality. Most people live in a willful daze, not seeing the petty crime on their block. Not only don't they see it, but they're fed lies from agencies like ours."

"Calm down, Max. You don't want to be verbalizing all of this. This isn't a secure location."

"Understood. But this smacks of something our friends would do." He never referred to their organization by name. The G29 remained anonymous because of the discipline of its members.

Bull leafed through some more pages before returning the folder to the table. "It doesn't look good. If this is as you say it is, then we are dealing with a group who operates at the highest levels and who has the protection only armies and spies can provide."

"I don't think we're dealing with a country. I think it's a small handful of people. I've read all the notes from my father. His investigation led him in circles. There was one entry that was dismissed with a note from him."

"How do you know?"

"I learned what his handwriting looked like. It is very slanted and he used too much ink in his fountain pen. There were blotches everywhere. He would make notes in the margins of the papers. I learned that those papers were never copied and remained at the solicitor's offices at all times. They were kept in a secure box within the firm's large walk-in safe."

"Sounds interesting." Bull was leaning forward, all nonsense gone. Sophia sat quietly on the sofa, watching them. "What did the entry say?"

"Illuminati." Max said it and waited. He received no response from Bull. "Doesn't mean anything to you?"

"Nothing."

"It was a secret society set up in the eighteenth century. It was broken up and publically disbanded. That's why my father would have dismissed it. He didn't want to be chasing ghosts."

"You seem to think there is something to it?"

"I do. Forget about the label of the group. It may go by some other name. But it could explain the lack of records and our inability to learn anything. It also explains how they could walk away from so much money."

Bull was silent. He resumed rocking his chair. "Unless they didn't know about the money."

Max leaned back. His eyes counted the lights on the ceiling and then closed. His legs began to bounce. He sat up, nodding. "Maybe that's what we're missing. I assumed that whoever did this wasn't interested in money, but that goes against everything we know about human nature."

"Amen, friend. Money is everything."

"And power. When does money become power and power beget money? Or is power always beholden to money?"

"And money is beholden to power. Nazi Germany was a time when the rules ceased to apply," Bull said. "Perhaps the power that protected money turned its back long enough for those with money to be eliminated along with everyone else."

Max nodded. "By the time cooler heads took charge, it was too late."

"Maybe it was even simpler than that," Sophia said. "Maybe Meyer Hildebrandt hid the money so that it couldn't be found and wasn't known about. He sounds like he was a connected man and knew how to pull the strings behind the scenes."

"Those are a lot of maybes."

"So how do we proceed?"

"We need a team to help us. This is the proverbial needle in the haystack."

"The team can't be too big or they will know about it."

"They're not God."

"They might as well be. Think about the stuff we hear. There are always snitches trying to ingratiate themselves to their bosses."

"Okay, let's keep this small. Just ourselves and a couple others."

"G29?"

"Exclusively."

"What do we do when we find them?"

"Return the favor."

∞

"You want me to do what, to find whom, and how?" Colonel Smith's face said everything Max needed to know. He wasn't going to get any cooperation.

"Sir, I believe that there is an organization that is a threat to America's national security. They operate as a pseudo sovereign entity inside and outside of our borders. At the very least, we should determine who these people are and what their agenda is."

"And you believe this why?"

Max was silent. "I have received some intel that suggests they exist and have operated for at least a century. That would lead me to believe…"

"You don't need to waste any more of your time on chasing chimera. You will cease all talk of this nonsense and return to your missions. Can you do that, soldier?"

Max didn't want to quibble with his rank. He had been promoted to lieutenant colonel and Smith was now a full colonel. He assumed Smith was rankled for not being promoted to general. A glass ceiling made it difficult to make that leap and Smith didn't have what it took. Max wanted to use his investigation as a path to Smith's promotion. *Alignment of interests*, he thought, *was better than any other persuasive argument.* "Yes, sir." If he were going to do this, it would have to be under the radar.

He nodded to Tim Bull as he left the office. It was up to Bull to put the next phase of Max's plan into place.

"Sir, we are in need of more quality staff in G29. I suggest recruiting from within the ranks of the company, or possibly civilians."

Smith was always looking to expand his empire so he took Bull's comment to heart. "Agreed, Major. I've reviewed your report. Happy to authorize civilian recruitment. Start them slowly in the company but have them fast tracked into G29 if they are the right stuff."

"Sir. Thank you, sir. Priority?"

"We keep our eyes open and have a list of potential candidates. Check them out and see if any are suitable."

"Yes, sir." Bull saluted and left. The colonel and his secretary didn't catch the small smile at the corners of his mouth.

∞

Max arrived home to find Sophia already there. On the table was a salad ready to be served in its bowl, all cutlery and plates in place, and two candles recently lit. *She must have seen me coming or heard the car door slam,* he thought. A bottle of red wine was already open; it looked like the one they bought for special occasions. It had a particular label that looked like a title deed. Something Rothschild. He could smell the root vegetables and meat cooking, and garlic filled the air.

"It's been breathing for over an hour," she said. Her cheeks were rosy and her face was lit with her smile.

"Stew or roast?"

"Beef on the bone, reduced sauce I pulled from the freezer, and all your favorites. Potato, sweet potato, parsnips, onions, and garlic."

"Special occasion?"

She twirled, forcing him to notice the summer dress she was wearing. It was light and airy, the type designed for someone twenty years younger. It hung lightly on her body, hugging her enough around the shoulders to keep it from falling down. The rest flowed and allowed him to catch glimpses of her skin. "What makes you think that?" She smiled and twirled once more before kissing him on the lips.

He looked down and saw that she wasn't wearing socks or shoes. "Are you okay?"

She laughed and hugged him. "Let's eat." She took his briefcase and jacket and made him sit at the table.

"I should change first," Max said. He really didn't want drops of gravy on his uniform.

"Just relax. Sit there and I'll put a plate together for us."

Max watched her twirl between the table and the kitchen island. She opened the oven and released the rush of warm flavor into the room. His mouth began to salivate. He watched her cut the meat, then scoop out the vegetables from the roaster and, finally, apply the gravy over everything. She finished her plate and brought both back to the table. She glowed with excitement.

"This looks magnificent, sweetheart. Thank you. Almost as good as you. You look ravishing today." She rolled her left shoulder upwards as she tilted her head like a shy schoolgirl on her first date. It always had the same effect on him. He reached for the wine. "This must be a special day." He motioned to pour her glass first but she put her hand over it.

"That's the special news," she said with a smile.

"You gave up drinking?"

"Yes."

"Why?" Max was slow to catch on. Then his eyes opened wider and tears began to form. "Really?"

"Yes. I've been waiting all day to tell you." Her eyes were blurry as the tears began to run freely.

Max put down the bottle and got up. Sophia did the same. He began to laugh and they held each other and cried. "This is the best day of my life."

"Until our daughter arrives."

"Are you sure?"

"Today. I found out today." She could barely get the words out. I guess there was nothing wrong with me after all.

"I love you, Mrs. Harding."

"I love you, Max."

They held each other in the kitchen until the food was cold. Neither noticed.

The next morning, Max got up early to fix Sophia breakfast in bed. The coffee was black and he had warmed milk in a cup next to it. "You need your strength. You're eating for two," he said in response to her raised eyebrows. She always had black coffee, like him.

"Lovely, Max, but are you going to clean the crumbs from the bed?"

"I'll clean whatever I need to. Your job is to stay healthy and carry our baby."

"I can get used to this." She smiled.

"I can't wait until our daughter is climbing into bed with us, crying because she has nightmares, and desperately in need of our hugs."

"And the boyfriends?"

"She'll be celibate until she's thirty. If any boy comes sniffing around, I'll have a firm word with him." Max's head was swimming with images of being a jealous and over-protective father, chasing off would-be suitors from his princess.

"And if there are others?"

"The more the merrier."

"I don't want to jinx this, Max. Let's take it one step at a time." A cold shudder passed through her body and she turned to hold him.

"Everything will be okay, don't worry." He smoothed her hair as she lay against his chest. "Careful. Here, have some coffee. You'll feel better."

She had her first cup and her body responded with tingles of alertness. She took a deep breath and shook off sleep. "You make the best coffee."

"I make the best babies." He kissed her with his permanent grin, unable to do more. "I don't know when I'll come down. I don't want to. Every moment, we are closer to meeting her. Every moment, I am closer to you." He got out of bed and did a little dance. Sophia laughed.

"Are you sure you're happy or did you slip something into your coffee?"

"Something's changed in me, Soph. I feel different inside. It's as though nothing is bad in the world and everything is sunshine and light."

She put her coffee down. "That's a bit of a dangerous outlook in our line of business, don't you think?"

"Absolutely. I don't want to hurt people any more. I don't even want to know who killed my family. I just want to hold you and kiss you and make love to you. I want to raise our little girl without looking over our shoulder. I don't want her to become a bargaining chip for the bad bastards in the world."

"Are you saying what I think you are?"

"Yep. I want out. I want us out. I woke up this morning a different man. I'm re-wired. I'm a father. I can't and won't live that life anymore."

"This is dangerous talk. I love it, but it's dangerous. Let's talk to Smith."

"Smith's a stuck up asshole. He won't understand."

"But he's the one who needs to sign off on this."

"I've got a card or two to play," Max said. "We've done some jobs that history will not be kind to."

"Talk like that will get us both killed."

"I would never say it. They know it. They also know I'm too valuable alive. We have twenty years in this business and we're able to make contacts in Russia and China before the iron curtain came down. Now, it's all about Checkpoint Charlie in Berlin and a few entry points where we can interact with their spies. We are on a first name basis with spies who will become their leaders in due course. No, I'm confident we can transition ourselves into a less dangerous life."

Sophia was silent as she finished her coffee and toast. She poked at the eggs but they didn't smell right to her. She left them for Max; he always finished her plate.

"I know what you're thinking. We can only try. I'll tell them that my heart's not into it anymore. That is more dangerous for the agency than anything. I can still consult. We can still be passive participants. We have enough money not to work, and they'll understand that. I'll explain we have enough for a house and a hundred thousand dollars in the bank. We'll worry about things when that runs out."

"They can't know about the other money," she said.

"I know. I can't put my finger on it either, but let's keep that between ourselves." His bouncing dance had ended and he was back in bed. He started on the unwanted scrambled eggs and toast.

# CHAPTER TEN

# San Francisco, 1968

"They said the hippie was dead."

"Who did?"

"Some fascist, probably. They held a funeral and everything last year."

"Were you there?"

"Never left. Best summer of my life."

"Cool."

"Anything on you?"

"Just a little. You?"

"The normal stuff. Nothing exciting. My weed is weak and I'm outta tabs."

"I got some 'shrooms."

Junior's face lit up. "That'll do me. By the way, what's your name?"

"James. Yours?"

"Everyone calls me Junior."

"Cool. There's a party on Haight Street. Wanna go?"

"There's been a party on Haight and Ashbury since last year. Groovy stuff. Yeah, I just need to grab something to eat. I keep forgetting."

James laughed. "Me too. I saw a place selling beansprout sandwiches just up there."

"Hey, I'm cool with all of that and I'll have one when we're with the chicks, but I'm a carnivore, know what I mean? I need meat."

"I think we're going to get along. There must be something up the way."

"Excellent, my friend. Lead the way."

A family run shop less than a block away had been enjoying the sudden popularity of the area. They had painted flowers on the windows and the woodwork was in a sunshine yellow with sunflowers. Inside, it was a normal greasy spoon with a grill, grease, and lots of meat. There were four burgers sizzling as they entered.

"This is exactly what I've been looking for," Junior said. He knew the place but he also wanted his new friend to feel special.

"I saw it coming down and ear-marked it for when I needed to eat. Look at that one, it's huge! I think I'll have what that guy just ordered."

"Make it two. I'll grab a table. Here's some cash. I'll have a coffee as well. Thanks."

They ordered, ate, and sat back contented. James was wearing a tie-dyed shirt and jeans. He looked to be in his early twenties and had intelligent eyes. His movements were smooth and certain, like an athlete's.

"What kind of party is it going to be?" Junior asked.

"Not sure. I was told by some friends to be there."

"Okay. When does it start?"

"I don't know. I was thinking of scoping it out now and then see how it goes."

"I'm in. Burger was perfect. I can feel it digesting inside of me."

They walked to the junction made famous by the summer of love the previous year where a hundred thousand people joined in the party. It was a social phenomenon with little to no violence. The police and media couldn't explain it and the young hippies did what they wanted to do—sex, drugs, and rock and roll.

They could hear the music before they saw the house. The building was like all the rest in the terrace, with stairs leading up off the slanted road onto a level Victorian-styled house. There was no garden or yard to speak of; only the road, steps, and house. Inside, the doors were all open, the windows shut, and people were standing or lying on the floor in every room. When James saw her for the first time, his body jolted. Junior noticed him stop moving and followed his eyes.

"Introduce yourself."

"I will." He wasn't shy.

"I'll make myself scarce but I'll be somewhere in the house. Good luck, my friend." He put his hand on

James' shoulder in solidarity. James was already moving towards her.

"Hi, I'm James."

The girl turned to look at him, her eyes connecting with him for the first time. James could have sworn that he saw her body jolt as well.

"I'm Denise."

They both stood looking at each other, saying nothing, not noticing the rest of the party.

"Can I get you another drink?" James snapped out of his reverie first.

"Sure. Coke if there is one."

"I'll be right back."

"I'll join you."

When they got to the kitchen, there was no one there. James located the fridge and opened it. When he closed it, she was next to him. When he opened his mouth to speak, she kissed him. It was all he could do to keep hold of the two Cokes.

She broke from the kiss, he handed her a can, and she took a long drink. "I've been waiting my whole life for you," she said.

"I think I may have been as well." He put down his drink and took her hand. She knew the house better and led him to the top floor where there was an empty room.

"I want your body," she said. "And maybe your soul as well." She let her dress fall. She wasn't wearing anything underneath.

James' mouth was dry and he began to wish he brought his coke with him. He knew better than to say anything and felt her fingers pulling off his shirt and undoing his jeans. He raised his eyes to the ceiling and mouthed 'thank you Jesus' before turning all of his attention to her.

∞

"You hit it off pretty quickly," Junior said when they emerged. "Score anything to smoke yet?"

"I think there's something over there." He pointed to four long-haired guys without shirts dividing up a pile of marijuana.

"I'll get it in a bit. So? Is this normal for you?"

"Never. I've never experienced anything like it. It was as though God wanted Denise and me to be together. I hope you get to experience something like that, man, 'cause it is blowing my mind."

"And you're clean? Not on anything?"

"That's the thing. We're both stone cold sober. I can't wait to do it on LSD. She's also looking forward to it."

"You're an animal."

"Just lucky, I guess." He smiled and it wouldn't leave his face. It wasn't cool to be smiling all the time, but he tried to be true to his feelings.

"What do you normally do? I am guessing this hippie thing is a hobby, not a career choice."

"I've got a degree in statistics from Nebraska State U and a dab of English lit. Nothing to speak of. Nothing that'll get me a job."

"Are you looking for a job?"

"I wasn't until I met Denise. It's crazy but I think she's the one. I don't want to mess it up."

"Cool it, my friend. She's hot and sexy but you've just met her. I don't want to state the obvious, but she did you without even knowing your name."

"She knew my name."

"You know what I mean. She's a party girl. I love party girls. Hell, I wish I had asked her if she needed a drink."

"Watch it, man."

"We're cool, friend. I'm just looking out for you. These girls can mess you up more than any drugs."

"Amen to that." James drifted into his own thoughts and Junior stopped pressing the issue. Denise returned shortly after.

"Hey you." She slid her arms around his waist and kissed him long and slow. Junior pushed off from where he was leaning as if to leave. "No, don't go. I was just saying hello. Hi, I'm Denise." She put her hand out.

"Junior."

"That's an odd name. Don't you have a regular name?"

"Tim."

"That's a good biblical name." She smiled and eyed James. Her other arm was still around him.

"My father wasn't a religious man but he gave me his name. I guess my grandparents were religious."

"And your old man doesn't mind you being here? You can't be much more than eighteen."

"Eighteen last month. Been here a year. When that shrink guy from Harvard said 'turn on, tune in, drop out' I did just that. My dad thought I was crazy but he said it was better than me getting killed in Vietnam."

"Your dad sounds cool."

"He's a vet. Fought in Korea. Now he does consulting work for some big company. I'm hoping to join the firm when I get older."

Denise eyed him. "Are you a cop?"

Junior's hands became sweaty. He hadn't anticipated such a direct question. "No. Why?"

"Because you don't fit. You're a young, blue-eyed boy with parents who let you do what you want with their blessing? That sounds like a bullshit story to me."

"It isn't, but I see what you mean. Would a pig do drugs?"

"No."

"Then give me what you've got. Let me prove it to you."

"Careful, Junior. I don't want you over doing it."

"I'll be okay." He took a pill from her and popped it under his tongue. He took a swig of James' Coke and then waited for it to kick in.

"That was an aspirin," Denise laughed. "I believe you. I was just busting your balls." She put her hand into James' back pocket and squeezed his bum. "Speaking of which, I need to have a word with your friend." She smiled over her shoulder and disappeared with James upstairs.

Four years later, Tim's father approached them to join the CIA. Denise and James said yes. By then, Junior was already an old-hand.

# CHAPTER ELEVEN

# Isabella

"How could you have kept a secret like that for all these years?" Max was furious at Tim. "You're my best friend. We've saved each other's asses more than I can remember. How could you not tell me you had a son?"

"For the same reason you're thinking of quitting. It's too dangerous. I love you like a brother but you need to understand. Our life is not conducive to family. Everything we touch dies. You remember the two brothers we had to take out? Five years apart, but our instructions were clear. It didn't matter their station in life. They were targets and we were the tools. If they can kill presidents, what would they do to kids of nobodies?"

Max was silent. He took a slow sip from his scotch. He needed something strong. The news made him question everything he knew or trusted. Tim Bull had a son, also named Tim. He also worked for the CIA but not for G29—yet.

"And you never thought it was important for me to know about your recruitment efforts? I still outrank you, you know."

"That doesn't mean the same thing in our division, and you know that. We are about results. The end justifies the means; it should be tattooed on our arms."

"It probably would be if they could be certain we'd never be captured."

"They'll kill us themselves if we get captured. Bomb the whole fucking place to keep us quiet." Bull was in a good mood and his friend's attitude wasn't going to get in the way.

"Do you think we can have these cigars now?" Max had two in his pocket and had given another two to Bull.

"It'd be a waste if we didn't. She'll be in there for a while. You never know when those little guys come out. It was the same with me."

"What happened to the mother?"

"I wasn't the marrying type. She gave the child my name and raised him. I sent money but was otherwise invisible until he was in his teens. It was impossible for me to be there when I was stationed in Korea and doing missions all over God's green Earth."

"I'm sorry to hear that. This whole thing's too bizarre for words. I still can't believe you didn't tell me."

Bull ignored him. "Do you think they'll allow us to smoke in the hospital or do we need to go outside?"

"What the hell, Bull? We'll smoke in here like Americans. Since when do we need to be embarrassed to smoke a quality cigar? These are Cubans. Best in the world. Not like some of the shit the doctors are smoking. Most of them just smoke cigarettes anyway."

"Just asking. My grandfather smoked cigarettes in the house but my grandmother forced him to smoke outside when it came to cigars."

"I'm smoking mine here. If they want me to leave, they'll need to ask me.

"To the new father." Bull lifted his cigar and they touched them together before lighting up.

"To me," Max said. "The most undeserving sonofabitch father there is. That's why I'm going to be the best there ever was."

"You'll be great. Now pass your flask before you finish it all off."

"You know," Max said as he lit his cigar, "there's nothing like a good cigar." He rolled it as he lit it, the red ember glowing on the end beneath the flame. The puffs were practiced and efficient. Within a minute, both cigars were lit and the room became hazy.

"I can't believe they don't have a window in here," Bull said. "How are we supposed to enjoy our cigars?"

"Stop complaining."

"Who's complaining? I'm just saying..."

The door opened to their waiting room. The doctor filled the frame.

"Mr. Harding?"

"Yes?" Max jumped to his feet. He put his cigar in the tray, his hand ready to shake the doctor's.

"I need to have a word with you."

"You can speak in front of Tim. We're all family."

"It's serious. It's about your wife."

"What's wrong?" Max's face lost its smile and became creased with worry. It mirrored the doctor's face.

"There have been some complications."

The rest of the conversation passed over him like a fog, forcing him to piece it all together at a later date.

"Is she going to live?"

The doctor's face said it all. "She lost a lot of blood. We're doing all we can."

"And the baby?"

"It was touch and go, but she's alive. She's being treated in our specialist unit. She's in good hands."

"When can I see my wife?"

"She's under sedation right now. We need to go to surgery but I didn't want to proceed until I talked to you. You need to make a decision."

"What are our options?"

"You will recall I warned you both about bleeding. Redheads are known for hemorrhaging during and after childbirth. Your wife's was particularly heavy. We could try to do nothing and take the chance that every-thing will heal naturally, or we open her up, locate the tear, and make sure through surgery."

"That doesn't sound too bad," Max said. He felt re-lief spreading through his body. "If there is an option to do nothing, I think that must be the best. Her body is strong and she's a fighter. She'll be okay."

"I need you to be aware of the issues. If she has a further complication, she won't be strong enough to have the surgery in time."

"Isn't that what intensive care is all about? You can operate on her right where she is, can't you?"

"It isn't as simple as that."

"Is your preference to operate?"

"I can't be making this decision."

"Can't we wake her up and let her decide?

"It's risky."

"Why?"

"She's ready for the theatre. Every time we anaes-thetize we run the risk of death, so it is not something we do lightly. With her condition, bringing her out will take time and she will need to recover."

"But you said the natural way was an option."

"Yes, but…"

"I think if it is possible, we should let Sophia decide this. We're in a hospital. What can go wrong? If need be, she can be operated on."

"It is a tough decision. As long as you know that there are risks, I will do my best. Medical science can only do so much. The rest is in the hands of God."

Max didn't like talk of God from a surgeon, especially when it came to his wife. "I want Sophia to make this decision."

"Okay. We'll put her in the recovery room. We'll be able to talk to her in a couple of hours."

"Doctor?"

"Yes."

"Can I see my daughter?"

The doctor smiled. "Of course. Follow me. I'll take you to the nurses' station and they'll be able to take you to your little girl." He was already walking away from the smoke-filled room. Max followed. Bull sat dumbstruck, watching Max, cigar in hand. As the door closed, he dropped it in the ashtray and ran after him. He just about ran over a woman as he did so. She was already crying and didn't take any notice of him.

"It'll be okay, Max. These little buggers are stronger than you think."

"I hope so," he said. From his voice, Bull could hear he was barely holding it together. Bull remained quiet and walked next to his friend, following the doctor. The polished floors reflected the harsh lights and their steps squeaked in the silence.

The doctor introduced them to Nurse Wiggin and then went to deal with Sophia. Wiggin led them to the neonatal care unit. They had to wash they hands and put on gowns to enter the room.

"I'll stay here," Bull said.

"No you don't. You're coming in here with me. You're the only family I have."

Bull didn't respond. His eyes had become watery and his throat tight. He had never felt more loved than he did at that moment. He followed the nurse's example and washed his hands and then put on a paper gown. They had to wear masks and a cap over their hair. They entered the room with the reverence reserved for a cathedral.

"Is that her?" Max asked the nurse.

"She's in that incubator, yes." She indicated to the one in the corner of the room.

The room had six stations, each with instruments surrounding a translucent glass box. Each box had holes for hands to access the precious contents inside. The babies had tubes inserted into their noses and, sometimes, their hands. The room was warm and moist.

"May I put my hands inside? Can I touch her?" Max looked for approval from the nurse.

"Absolutely."

He turned the piece of plastic covering the hole and put his hand inside. She was sleeping on her front, her back legs tucked in tight with her diaper sticking out. Her arms were also held tight against her body. He touched her little arm. He couldn't see much more through his tears.

"She's beautiful."

"Do you have a name yet?"

"I'm waiting for Sophia before we make a final decision."

"Wise man." Bull put his hand inside and let his fingers run along her back. She was sleeping but her body responded with a little movement. It made him feel connected and relevant to this little bit of life. It made him think about his own son and what a poor father he was.

"Can I hold her?" Max asked.

"Not yet. We are monitoring her. Does your wife intend to breastfeed?"

"I don't know. I think so."

"We'll need to get her onto the breast milk soon. We are drip-feeding nutrients but mother's milk is best. We'll send down a pump to collect some milk until she is able to come up here."

"Thank you, Nurse. Do you mind if we stay here a moment before we return to the waiting room?"

"Fifteen minutes, then I'll shoo you both out."

Max and Bull made the most of their time, opening the other hole in the incubator so they could both touch her at the same time. Their hulking frames crouched delicately over the glass box, cooing and making baby sounds. They left reluctantly when their fifteen minutes were up.

Back in the waiting room, their cigars had been removed. "Probably the nurses," Bull said. "They don't get to see such quality cigars all the time. Probably took it home to have later."

"Or they just threw them in the garbage."

"No one throws cigars away. I bet you they're smoking them in some back alley as we speak."

"Bull, you're full of it. There's more where that came from. Here, enjoy." He handed him a fresh Cohiba and took one for himself.

As he raised the cut end to his lips, the doctor opened the door again. This time, his face was set, motionless. Max dropped his hand to his side, eyes locked on the doctor. As the doctor stepped inside and closed the door, Max's blood ran cold as his fingers became numb. Bull had also become quiet.

"I'm sorry, Mr. Harding. We did everything we could."

Max's mouth opened silently. He wanted to say something but the words became irrelevant. He knew the moment the door opened what the news would be.

"Your wife suffered a severe stroke in the recovery room. We think it was from a clot formed during childbirth. We won't know for sure until the post mortem. I'm very sorry." He walked next to Max and put his hand on his shoulder. He stayed for a moment, head bowed, and then left the room.

In the hall, a woman sat weeping. It was the same one Bull nearly ran over earlier. Neither man noticed her looking at them as the door closed.

∞

"I can't keep her." Max couldn't look at Bull.

Bull said nothing. He reached over and filled Max's glass before topping off his own.

"I know what I said earlier, but that was with Sophia. I can't do this alone."

"You don't need to decide now."

"I need to give her a name. How about Isabella?"

"Sounds beautiful."

"It was Sophia's choice."

"She'll grow up and, if she's lucky, will look just like her mother."

"That's what I'm afraid of."

"What are the options?"

"Foster care. Adoption. Maybe you'll take care of her." Max rattled off some options, deadpan.

"I couldn't take care of my own son. His mother did that."

"I know. Children need mothers and I can't think of finding another woman to replace Sophia."

"Talk to a counsellor, talk to the nurses. Maybe one of them will be able to give you some insight."

"Thanks, Tim, but I don't see how that's going to be possible. The baby's too weak to be taken anywhere. The hospital will deal with her for at another week or so. I've got that long to deal with Sophia and get my own shit together." He paused and Bull didn't push him. "I can't even leave this place to go back to the hospital," he said eventually. "They tell me they're going to do a post mortem. I don't want them defiling her body, Tim. I just want to sit here."

"We'll sit here until you're ready." The music in the bar was low and there were no customers yet. The place smelled of stale smoke and beer. Its carpet was a black and red pattern and they sat on red leather benches with dark brown wood tables. In front of them were four empty beer bottles and half a bottle of scotch whiskey. The bartender let them keep the bottle next to them when he heard what had happened.

"If I had a mother, she'd know what to do. Hell, I could leave Isabella with her."

"If you need some time, I can help," Bull said.

Max's face was becoming red. His bloodshot eyes burned. His neck thickened as the adrenaline pumped his blood faster. "I'm gonna kill those motherfuckers."

"Whoa, calm down, Max. Remember where we are."

"I'm gonna kill every one of those cock sucking, motherfucking sons of whores." Max was standing and the veins in his neck were standing out. He had slammed the table with his fist as he stood and one of the glasses cracked.

"Sit down, Max. Calm down." Bull was standing as well. The bartender stopped wiping the bar to see what the commotion was about.

"Calm down, like my mother and grandmother as they were shipped to a concentration camp? Like my uncle? Like my father?" Emotions blurred in Max's head. He felt the pain of being alone as a child as though it was yesterday. Now he knew more of the story. He could understand accidents; he could accept them. His wife's death was an accident. But the murder of his family was something he wasn't going to accept. If he couldn't do anything about his wife's death, at least he could avenge something.

Bull was silent again. There was never anything to say when confronted with Max's true history.

The red mist receded from his eyes and he saw Bull, the bartender, and the empty room. He sat down. "Sorry. It all hit me at once. Isabella is the last of my bloodline. If I don't do something, she'll end up in the cemetery next to Sophia. They're going to kill me, then her."

"You don't know that. Why are you still alive? If they're that powerful, they would have found you."

"We don't know. They didn't find me because they weren't looking." Max sat fuming a moment longer before continuing. "Maybe they were behind Sophia's death. What if they're already following me, Tim? What if it wasn't a blood clot that killed Sophia?"

"Don't go paranoid on me. You just had a big shock. Let's see how the next few days look before you make any plans."

"I know what I am going to do. If you want to help me, you'll take care of Isabella until I'm back. I'm leaving after the funeral."

"Where? To do what?"

"To do what I should have done when I found out. Find them and kill them all."

# *Hoover and Hoffa*

"Real violence is different than a blade cutting leather or skin. It is the imposition of one person's will over another. The fear is palpable as the victim's eyes see what is about to happen and can do nothing other than submit, hoping for mercy. When the first blow strikes, it is the fat, as much as the fear, that trembles. To see a body absorb a fist is more frightening than watching it being blown apart from an explosion. The latter is abstract and equated with death. The body blow, flesh against flesh, animal against animal, is primal and strikes one of two reactions in the viewer: fear or excitement. People are sympathetic creatures, so we tend to register disgust, but that is on the spectrum of fear. For the predators amongst us, we register the desire to fight, which is within the spectrum of excitement.

"The asylum seeker illegally squatting knows that he has no chance against the police who come knocking at his door. The police stand an inch away and berate him, knowing that even a predator will succumb to the power of the state. The insane will be unpredictable but will meet with the expected violent reply from the police. Within the flesh of the poor bastard, he is torn between his natural fear and excitement and the reality facing him in the guise of a uniformed man of the state." Max could hear Colonel Smith's voice drone even though the lesson was a decade old. *He's an asshole, but he's good when it comes to the visceral elements of life,* Max thought. *Think, dammit, think. First who, then why.*

Max rifled through his father's papers. He had taken the first plane to London after Sophia's funeral. Bull wasn't happy but did his best to smile and wish him luck.

*They weren't government but they could influence it. Control? Not likely. Where could they influence? Army? Unlikely. Justice system? Yes. Penal system? Definitely. How could they have kept them there?*

Max retraced each step. The justice system conformed to Nazi political goals. Where a person of interest was detained, it was for their protection. This protected custody was carried out in concentration camps. Concentration camps were under the strict authority of the Schutzstaffel, the elite guard of the Nazi state.

*Whoever did this had sufficient clout in the SS, and the only man other than Hitler who could overrule everyone was Heinrich Himmler. Shit. He's already dead. Was he controlled by someone else or was there an underling who was acting on his own?*

*Why? Money? Revenge? Sex? Unlikely. Love? Weird, but unlikely.* Max couldn't find any traction to his brainstorming. He looked down at the name that kept resurfacing in his father's papers. "It can't be. That's impossible," he said aloud.

∞

*Summer, 1929*

*The Stork Nightclub, Manhattan*

"Behave yourself or Saint Peter won't let you in." John was all smiles as he led his friend to one of New York's hottest new clubs.

"Why do they call him that?"

"Because he determines who gets into paradise."

"Is it that good?"

"Better. You can be yourself, be around others like you, and not be afraid of the little people."

"Are you afraid?" Otto Hildebrandt put his hand on John's arm and squeezed slightly.

John's eyes opened wider as he neared the door. The head waiter, nicknamed Saint Peter, was just plain Peter from 152 West 58th Street. Paradise was The Stork, a nightclub owned and operated by Sherman Billingsley, a bootlegger who wanted a place to play cards and enjoy a few drinks with his friends.

"Aren't you afraid you'll get caught?" Otto repeated.

"Here? No. They'd have to throw half the judges and businessmen in jail first." He turned to Otto and flashed a smile. John's black hair was slicked back in the style of the day and his suit hugged his frame. He was of average height and build.

"So prohibition is for everyone else?"

"Everyone who can't get past Saint Peter." They reached the door and were nodded in.

"That's Saint Peter?"

"No, that's just a guard. Peter is the head waiter. He determines who gets into the Cub Room."

Otto didn't say anything and followed his friend inside. His English was passable but his porcelain skin, fair hair, and impeccable tailoring set him apart as European aristocracy, or at least old money.

"John! Good to see you. I see you brought a friend. Hello, nice to meet you. I have a table for you in the Cub Room as you requested. Is there anything in particular you are looking for tonight?" Peter saw everything in the room while talking to John. It was his job to ensure the women were plentiful, well dressed, and friendly. He led the two men into the wood paneled room with no windows. He caught the attention of one of the women he assigned to the VIP Cub Room. "Claire, take care of these two. Mr. Hoover is a very special client." He shook John's hand and nodded at Otto before leaving them at their table.

"This is the most peculiar place I've ever been," Otto said. "It's lopsided. It's like an afterthought."

"I know. It shouldn't be anything special but it epitomizes New York more than anything I know. I wanted to bring you here." He put his hand on Otto's as he continued. "The rest of the club is full of mirrors and the usual cigarette girls, if you like that thing." He watched for Otto's response.

"The girls are beautiful. I could eat them up," he said. He saw John's face drop slightly. "But I'd rather be here with you any day." He smiled and watched John do the same.

"I'm glad you like it here." He relaxed and sat back into the curved leather bench. The table was covered in white linen featuring a green logo of a stork with a top hat and the club's name. The ashtray also was labelled.

"Why do they call it the Stork Club?"

"I don't know. I've tried to find out but even the owner can't remember."

"Or he's not telling."

"Does it matter? Look around you. It's the who's who of New York society."

"I only see one person," Otto said. He had fixed his eyes on John. "Let's get a few drinks into us. I'm parched." He let his hand fall onto John's leg and left it there. John didn't move it or say anything. Shielded by the tablecloth, he allowed his hand to feel the inside of John's thigh. He smiled when he found what he was waiting for.

"What'll you have?"

"Whatever's going."

"Champagne or whiskey?"

"Let's start with champagne."

"Claire!" He raised his hand when he spoke. The woman turned, her black jacket accentuating her shape. She was all legs with the shortest of skirts that glistened in layers. Her front was in white with a bra that made her breasts point up. It was similar to the hat-check girls' uniform, only more provocative.

"Yes, Mr. Hoover."

"We'd like a bottle of champagne and something to nibble on. Do you still do the fruit or can we get some meat?"

"I'll see what I can put together for you, sir. Can I get you something to smoke?"

"I'll have a cigar," Otto said.

"Me too."

"Coming right up, gentlemen." She turned and her skirt allowed them to see the curves where her legs ended.

"She's quite a specimen," Otto said, but his hand was somewhere else and John Edgar Hoover had no need to be jealous.

When the night was over, the two stumbled to a waiting taxi, hand in hand. John's body was on fire for Otto. He allowed himself to grab his bum and touch his legs briefly in the car. It was only when they reached

Otto's hotel room that he allowed himself to push himself against the younger man. He put his lips on his and felt his body relax. It was a tonic for the battle that raged within himself. He wanted the sex, needed it, but it was the simple touch that he longed for. He wanted to be held and caressed. He wanted to be loved.

Otto enjoyed his trips to New York. His family name ensured every door was open to him. Discretion was paid for in full with large tips to trusted middlemen. No questions were asked when men came back to his suite at the Ritz-Carlton. It was one of the reasons Hoover trusted him enough with his deepest secret.

"I'm not a homosexual, you know," John said afterwards.

"You would have fooled me." Otto was in his robe, having showered. His hair was wet and uncombed.

"I like men, I admit it, but there's something wrong about it."

"Perhaps we can get it right this time." Otto let his robe drop and got on top of John. "Relax and let me spoil you."

John put his head back and closed his eyes. He would deal with this later.

∞

"I want every homosexual, nigger, and communist flushed out of America. We cannot trust these types of people. They will infect our schools, neighborhoods, and way of life. I pledge to fight the criminals who sell the alcohol that is poisoning our great country. I pledge to clean up our streets from the filth that lie, steal, and cheat their way through life. I am talking about the mob, gentlemen. I am talking about the radicals flooding our shores with foreign ideas, like communism, spreading through our good universities and infecting our young minds. I am talking about inappropriate shows that could make people become homosexuals. I am talking about the discontent we have amongst our Negro population. Gentlemen, we have a problem. The Bureau of Investigation is here to draw the line. No more will the criminals get away with it. We have been given the power to cut through corrupt police who may be protecting them, to intercept and manage information of our good citizens. Gentlemen, in a word, we are the solution to the problem. Each and every one of you. Now, go and get 'em."

The assembled agents roared with approval at their director's speech. As they filed out of the auditorium, some came to shake his hand. Many carried on, trying not to draw the attention of their superior.

"Good speech, Director Hoover. I just wanted to tell you that you were the reason I joined the bureau. Your work against the radicals has been inspirational."

"Thank you. I appreciate your kind words."

J. Edgar Hoover watched the gait of the young recruit as he left. He sighed inwardly. He could still taste Otto all these years later. Why did he haunt him so? Their two month friendship scared him as no other. He began to contemplate a change, but the embarrassment would end his career. Otto had money and didn't care what people thought of him. *That's real power*, he thought. *I'll never have that, regardless of how many agents run around and call me 'sir'.*

"Have you been keeping up to speed with the new developments in Germany?" His aide was new. A young man, well-tailored and eager to assist.

"In what way?"

"Their security system. It is all handled by a specific department similar to ours."

"Oh, that. Yes, I'm in regular contact with its head, Herr Himmler. We agree on more things than I would have thought. I am looking into implementing elements of their regime here."

"I was hoping you'd say that. There's been talk of a shakeup at the bureau."

"I've heard, and I'm on top of it." He found his aide annoying at times. Too knowledgeable.

"You're a shoe-in for the directorship of the new FBI."

"It's the same organization, just new letters." He wanted to sound uninterested to the young aide, a trait he had mastered over the years. It added to his mystery and power.

"Just make sure there aren't any skeletons in your closet, hey sir?" The aide laughed to himself at the thought of his director being anything but a paragon of American virtue.

Hoover fell silent and found himself alone in the room before he realized what he needed to do. He went to his office and pulled out his official stationary.

*January 21, 1935*

*Dear Herr Himmler,*

*I thought you'd be interested to know that there is a prominent family living in your country pretending to be Aryan or, at least, a form of a German. They have come to my attention as they have hidden substantial sums of money I can only assume is rightfully owed to the German government. You will not be surprised when I found out they were secretly Jewish. Their perversion doesn't stop there. I have it on good authority that the grandson of the patriarch is a homosexual and the remaining family members are communists. I wouldn't be surprised if there weren't other sexual deviants amongst them. You would be doing my country as well as yours a great favor to deal with them as the subversives they are. You can count on me forwarding you any monies we are able to recover from these thieves in due course.*

*I offer this intelligence in the friendship that we have developed these last few years. If there is anything I can do to reciprocate, please feel free to ask. Details enclosed.*

*Yours very sincerely,*

*J. Edgar Hoover, Director,*

*United States Bureau of Investigation*

Hoover re-read the letter, sealed it, and had it sent by way of diplomatic post. *Sorry, Otto*, he thought.

∞

April 9, 1975

Max couldn't do anything about Hoover or Himmler. They were both dead. *That's it?* He thought. *The links were tentative at best, but still, why didn't anyone go after that psycho?* The answer was simple and succinct: power. No one wanted to pick at that scab.

"Well, I do," he said aloud. He had booked a flight back to Washington, DC. "I've got an appointment with a friend I didn't even know about." He laughed at himself as he instinctively looked around to see if anyone was listening. He was alone.

His taxi arrived outside of 4936 Thirtieth Place N.W. in Washington the next day. He stayed in the Watergate Hotel, as he wanted to be fully rested before he met Clyde Tolson. The street was affluent, with trees standing at attention along the road. They were all naked.

He approached the red brick Georgian house, amazed that there were no security guards or even fences. *I can't believe the most powerful person in America used to live here,* he thought. The house belonged on the street and was no grander than the others. It was quiet, the type of place wealthy grandparents lived in. He rang the doorbell. He could hear dogs barking and then the sound of movement as someone opened the heavy wooden door and then the screen door.

"Hello. Can I help you?" The man was frail. Max knew he was seventy-five years old.

"Yes. My name is Max Webber. I was a friend of Director Hoover."

The man looked suspicious. "I knew all of his friends and I don't remember you. How did you know him?"

"I didn't know him directly. He knew my family. Perhaps you may remember their name?" They were still standing in the doorway. Max hadn't planned anything. He wanted to talk first.

"And that is?"

"Hildebrandt."

Clyde Tolson closed his eyes and inhaled deeply. "Come in, please." He held the door and let Max go in first. "I'm afraid I can't offer you more than some juice. I'm here by myself today."

"No need. I don't want to take up too much of your time."

"No trouble. I've become largely irrelevant to most people. Any guests are welcome now."

Max smiled appreciatively and sat where motioned, on the edge of the sofa. "I am trying to track down who was responsible for the deaths of my family and I came across Hoover's name. It was only one reference within the file, but I have to think it is significant."

"I'm sorry, but I don't recall any of this."

"That's okay. Our family investigators were able to retrieve and remove a letter from Hoover to Heinrich Himmler setting out falsehoods about my family. It requested further action be taken against my family. I don't have any of their other correspondence. It looks pretty damning from where I stand."

"Are we talking about the Nazi SS leader?"

"The same."

"I know Johnny admired their techniques. There was a lot of talk of emulating them in the beginning when we were modernizing the bureau. But then, you know, the war happened and those ideas were shelved."

"You're not aware of this name?"

"I know it because they, your family, were amongst the wealthiest in Europe. I could never keep track of who's who. It changes so often, you know."

"I can appreciate that. Is there anyone else who may know something about this? Friends, enemies of Hoover?"

"He had plenty of both—more of the latter." Clyde laughed.

Max wasn't laughing. "Anything to point me in the direction that will give me some answers?"

Clyde became thoughtful. His back arched in pain and he adjusted his shoulders before looking directly at Max. "There is one person. He's powerful enough to know everyone but I can't say if he would know about this. It's so long ago."

Max sat forward, hopeful. "Go on."

"You'll know of him. Hoffa. He's big into organized labor, unions and all that. We always thought he was a communist but his ties to the mob dissuaded us."

"What's a gangster going to know?"

"Hoffa's no gangster," Clyde said. His years fell away. There was respect as well as fear in his voice. "He ran the Teamsters like Johnny ran the FBI. It was too bad for him that he wasn't the FBI because, eventually, Bobby Kennedy got him. They stuck him in jail for thirteen years. A crooked deal with Nixon got him out in '71. He's still got his fingers on the strings. If there is anyone able to tell you something, it will be him."

"Go on." Max saw Clyde hesitate.

"He was an enemy of Johnny. Hoffa had something on Johnny or else he would have been taken in by him and not Bobby. Johnny wanted to shut Hoffa up but he told me his hands were tied."

Max sat back, shocked. "Why would you tell me this?"

"I'm an old man. I have nothing else to live for. You seem a determined young man. Maybe you can give Hoffa the justice Johnny wasn't able to. Maybe it is one last gift from me to Johnny." Clyde blew his nose and then wiped his eyes.

Max was silent for a moment. "Thank you, sir. I really appreciate your help." He got up and then turned to Clyde. "You know, I think I will take you up on your offer. Do you have an orange?"

"Yes, in the kitchen. I'll get it."

"Sit down. I'll find it. Can I get you anything?"

"No, thanks. It's just over there on the right."

"If you're sure."

Clyde's head indicated that he preferred the young man to get it himself.

Max went to the kitchen and found what he wanted. He took five oranges from the bowl on the kitchen table and then put them in a large towel. He carried them to the lounge where Clyde was sitting.

"Did you find what you were looking for?"

"Yes." The harshness of Max's voice cut through the air and made Clyde look up.

He saw only a blur as the towel hit him from above. He raised his arms instinctively to block the blow. He was sitting and turned to cover his face, exposing his back to the full force. He suffered four hits before the beating stopped. His lips began to utter some sounds but nothing comprehensible came out.

"I can't believe that the former associate director of the FBI would live alone without security," Max said.

"I don't have enemies. I'm retired."

"You don't have enemies because you didn't do anything other than service your boyfriend, who just happened to be the director."

Clyde was silent.

"It's no secret and I don't care who you sleep with or how. What I do care is that you were part of something that killed my family."

"You're crazy. I had nothing to do with it."

"You were the second most powerful sonofabitch in the country."

"You give us too much credit. We're just civil servants like the rest."

Max hit him again with the oranges. Clyde was lying face down on the sofa, unable to fight back.

"You knew that your lover was being blackmailed by the only thing capable of hurting him. You did everything possible to ensure he wasn't hurt. I don't know how Hoffa found out but I have no intention of doing the dirty work that you weren't prepared to do."

"He's the one," Clyde cried. The dull thuds were taking their toll on his organs. "I don't know how that piece of shit found out, but it was the only thing that kept Johnny off his back."

"He still went to jail. He couldn't have been that good."

"That was Bobby Kennedy. He was an even bigger sonofabitch than Hoffa." Max put all of his strength into the blow. The white towel was stained as the oranges began to break.

"Then why is he still walking free?"

"Money and votes." He was struggling to breathe and put one hand on the ground to take the pressure off his lungs. He was now half off the sofa, face down.

"Nixon needed the Teamsters' support. He was desperate. That's when Hoffa set his terms."

Max slammed the wrapped oranges into Clyde's lower back three more times. He looked down at the pathetic figure of the man who kept the country's secrets locked in his head. The man who slept with the biggest homophobic, racist bigot in charge of America's secret police. The man who epitomized hypocrisy.

"I'm a nobody," he cried, his arms now outstretched towards Max. He could see the juice dripping on the Persian rug. He couldn't hear the dogs and wondered where they were. His body was sore with a pain he hadn't felt before. The organs near his lower back were sore from the inside. He was afraid to move.

"Wrong. You became a somebody as Hoover's right hand man. You were given choices but you decided to play ball instead of doing the right thing. Those were people's lives you crushed." Max hit him again, his anger growing as he pictured the grandmother he never knew in the concentration camp. The red mist covered his vision when he pictured his mother and the horrors she must have endured. No record of her existed, not in a ship's manifest or any of the concentration camps. She was simply erased.

A beast knows when the end has come. There is fear, anxiety, and then acceptance. The frantic shuddering of body mass makes it all the more terrifying for the animal. No quick stab to the heart or arteries, just muscle and bone, jostling to end the other's efforts. In this fight, Clyde gave up before it even began. He was always protected, coddled in the power of his lover. Now, alone and widowed of Hoover, he accepted his fate as the consequence of his life's actions. He lay beaten, conscious, but broken on the sofa. All resistance gone.

Max looked down at the pathetic figure of the man who was most likely faultless in the entire history of his family. He felt no remorse in killing an innocent man. *He's not innocent,* Max thought. *Maybe innocent of this crime, but there are countless others he is guilty of. And he's not dead, at least not yet.*

He could hear the dogs barking behind the closed kitchen door. He let them out. He opened the door to the garden and threw the broken oranges under the large elm tree. He returned to the kitchen and threw the towel into the garbage. He returned to the lounge to see Clyde in the same position. He checked that he was breathing. He then went around the house and wiped clean any surface he may have touched. The FBI had implemented a fingerprinting program and he definitely would be on file somewhere.

When everything was cleaned to his satisfaction, he called a taxi. He watched the dogs whimpering as they licked their master, willing him to respond. Clyde opened his eyes to look at Max sitting across from him. He said nothing, nor did Max. When they both heard the horn of the taxi, Max got up.

"I'm going to call an ambulance for you. You did not see me, nor will you repeat what has just happened. You are an old man. If I have done things correctly, your kidneys will fail. You'll die of some complication from that, possibly a heart attack in the next few days. Consider yourself lucky. If I need to come back, I will torture you and keep you alive until you weep and pray for death." He looked at Clyde and saw the resignation in his eyes. He called the ambulance and left the house.

Clyde Tolson was rushed to hospital with renal failure. He died of a heart attack a few days later, on April 14, 1975. He was buried within a few yards of his life's love, J. Edgar Hoover, in the Congressional Cemetery, Washington DC.

∞

"I feel nothing." Max was with Bull. His daughter Isabella was sleeping in the spare room. He had hired a full time nurse to care for her.

"It's bound to happen from time to time," Bull said. "It's not good to feel much anyway. Bad for decision making."

"I felt nothing for Clyde. I feel nothing for anybody or anything."

"Thanks for that," Bull said.

"You know what I mean. I'm numb. My entire life has been turned upside down. I'm not who I am. How is that even possible? My name is really Joseph Hildebrandt? Am I expected to change my whole existence?

Does this change who I am or does it make me something more?"

Bull said nothing.

"My family died in shame and anonymity in a concentration camp, labeled as Jews, homosexuals, and communists. They were probably tortured and abused in ways we can't imagine."

"You can't go there, Max. You need to let it go."

"Our entire lives have been spent upholding American values. We combat the enemy in ways they don't expect. We win, sometimes unconventionally. Our techniques, if we're honest, are more similar to the SS than some apple-pie bullshit American ideal we claim to fight for."

"I think you need a drink." Bull reached over and topped off Max's glass.

"Thanks. I think this is deeper than the bottle. You remember the rage when we went into that dacha? We didn't care if we lived or died. All we wanted was to make Sophia safe again."

Bull was silent. "That was intense."

"My rage is ten times greater than that. I want to kill, mutilate, and destroy the motherfuckers who did this to me."

"I thought you liked your life."

"I loved my life. I found a great friend, great wife, and even our job is pretty good if you can look past some of the dirtier aspects."

Bull lifted his drink slightly at the compliment and stayed quiet.

"I need to meet this Hoffa character, but I'll need your help."

"I'm in. You know that." Bull didn't hesitate. They were a team. Inseparable.

"Thanks for that. I can't walk up to Hoffa like I did to Clyde. That was stupid, I admit it. I was lucky. There should have been security. I probably don't want to know how lucky I was." Max sipped his scotch. "We need to do some recon first."

"Colonel Smith has been on the blower. We have an assignment."

"Can't it wait?"

"You know the situation. Hoffa will still be there."

"Okay. First thing when we get back."

"I'll get some staffer to prepare a file for us on him in the interim."

"You're a good friend, Bull."

"The best."

∞

*July 30, 1975*

*Bloomfield Township, Detroit*

"Are you sure he'll show up?" Bull was driving a maroon 1975 Mercury Marquis Brougham. They stole the vehicle for this exercise and planned to dispose of it later.

"We'll find out soon enough." Max was eerily calm. He always became cool and collected before an operation. It was the reason he stayed at it; he was good at it.

"The diner is up ahead. The two mob bosses are supposed to show up at two o'clock. What's he going to do when they don't?"

"I'll worry about that. I'll get him back to the car, as though Giacalone and Provenzano changed their mind about the location at the last second. I'll tell him they didn't feel safe."

"Not sure he'll believe it, but it's your call." Bull pulled into the parking lot of the Machus Red Fox Restaurant. It looked like a cross between a barn and a roadside eatery. It had a long sloping red tiled roof, with a pitched roof by the entrance. He parked near the entrance door, with his nose out so he didn't need to back out when leaving.

Max got out and looked at his watch. 2:30. "Shit. We're half an hour late." Bull stayed in the car and turned off the engine. Out of habit, he checked the fuel levels first. Full.

Max pushed the aluminum bar on the glass door and felt the swish as the weather seal brushed against the foot mat. There was a further set of wooden doors with windows inside before he smelled the smoke of cigarettes and steaks. He recognized the man on the payphone immediately. He looked aggravated, his short hair slicked back, and the call ended shortly after Max arrived.

"Mr. Hoffa?"

"Who's asking?"

"You were to meet some friends. They changed the venue. Sorry for the confusion."

Hoffa scowled. He was sixty-two years old and four years out of prison. He was the president of the largest union in America before he was forced to step down by President Nixon as part of the terms of his pardon. Max was struck by the juxtaposition of deep lines in his face while still looking as though he was thinking of a joke. *Power*, thought Max.

"Fuck the confusion. Just don't let it happen again. This is bullshit."

"Yes, sir."

"What are you waiting for? Take me to them." He pulled some money from his pocket and left a large tip on his table. He waved at the waitress as he left the restaurant. He saw Bull and the '75 Mercury. "Nice car."

Max opened the door behind Bull and Hoffa sat down. Max sat next to him.

"What the fuck? What the hell are you doing? I don't want to sit and hold hands with you. Up front." He was more annoyed than angry.

"Sorry, Mr. Hoffa. Bull, let's go." Hoffa was about to say something when Max showed him his shotgun. He had left it in readiness, assuming Hoffa wouldn't see it when he first sat down.

"You boys are making a big mistake." He showed no fear. His face looked slightly amused.

"Let me worry about that. I have a few questions and then you can go. Watch out!" Max was thrown to the side of the window as Bull cranked the steering wheel to the left. The semi-trailer honked and its driver looked out his window towards them. Both Max and Hoffa looked directly at the man in the window. They could see the recognition in his face. He knew who Hoffa was, and he had seen Max.

"You were saying?" Hoffa settled into his seat and relaxed. He had been in these types of scrapes before. It wasn't the first time a gun was pointed at him.

"Bull, watch where you're going, will you? I'd like to get there in one piece."

"Sure thing."

They pulled up to their destination, an isolated farm house an hour's drive from Detroit. There was a Quonset, probably army surplus, a hundred yards from the house. The driveway was dirt covered with stones. They heard the sound of them crunching against the tires as they came to a stop. Bull turned off the ignition and got out of the car.

"This way, Mr. Hoffa."

"Mr. Hoffa this and Mr. Hoffa that. Who the fuck are you guys?"

"Nobodies. We need to ask you a few questions."

"You've said that already. We could have done that at the restaurant."

"Would you have agreed to that?"

"I don't know. Probably." Hoffa tried to keep a straight face but then his smile was back. "Nah. I'd probably tell you both to fuck yourselves."

"We don't have a problem with you, Mr. Hoffa," Max said.

"You do now, believe me."

"You don't want to have a problem with us either," Max said. Hoffa's smile vanished. His face hardened and the vertical lines etched over six decades became visible.

"Let's get this over with, whatever it is you want."

They indicated for him to walk to the house. He did, and they followed. Max had a shotgun, Bull a pistol. The doors were open and they went to the kitchen.

"Coffee or something harder?"

"If I'm going to be offed, I'd like something harder than fucking coffee. Wouldn't you agree?"

Max smiled despite himself. He liked Hoffa. He was a real person. "Sure." He pulled a bottle of Jack Daniels from a cupboard and put out three glasses. Hoffa put back the whole of his in one shot. Max re-filled it.

"What is it you want to ask me?"

Max leaned back against the countertop, keeping ten feet between himself and Hoffa. Bull stood in one of the two doors that led to the kitchen. He was holding his pistol. Max had leaned his against the countertop, where two edges came together.

"What do you know about a family called Hildebrandt?"

"What? I don't know anyone by that name."

"Think carefully. It means a lot to me." Max watched his movements, his expressions, and his body language. The name hadn't rung any bells.

"I'm sorry, boys, but I can't remember dealing with anyone by that name."

"Maybe you didn't deal with them directly. Perhaps it was something you came across. Perhaps you used it as blackmail against a certain director of the FBI."

It took a moment before Hoffa remembered. "Yeah, I never knew them but Hoover put himself in the shit because of them."

"What do you mean?"

"He was writing to that Nazi whatshisname. Heimlich? Heimler?"

"Himmler"

"That's it. Some fucker who liked to hurt people, that's what I remember from the correspondence. Hoover wrote to him like a schoolboy with a pen pal."

"Did you get some of his letters?"

"You could say that." His smile returned to his face. "The Teamsters had people everywhere. Anything that involved people and moving things. And post is a thing that is moved."

"I thought he sent it by diplomatic post."

"It's still post. People need to pick, haul, and deliver it. My people. My members."

"That's how you heard about it?"

"Mainly rumors, but then I started getting harassed by the police and FBI. When I found the letters, I was able to get most of them off my back, but fucking Bobby Kennedy couldn't let it go." His smile disappeared and his face became redder. He shut his mouth and breathed heavily through his nose. He finished off the glass of whiskey. It was refilled.

"That's it?"

"What else was there? I was being leaned on so I leaned back. That cocksucker Hoover was so afraid of the world discovering his dirty laundry that I was able to dictate terms. We arranged a truce of sorts. I didn't piss in his porridge and he left me alone. It worked."

"You don't know anything more about the Hildebrandts?"

"Nothing. Should I? From what I understand, Hoover railroaded the whole family because he was fucking the boy at some point. Personally, I think he was in love. Sick fuck, that one. I figured if he could do that to people he never even knew, I needed good ammo to keep him at bay. Those letters did the trick." He picked up the whiskey and sipped it.

Max allowed his body to slump. He was waiting for something more definitive. Hoffa wasn't the bad guy, he was a street wise guy who did what he had to do to stay alive. Hoover was the bastard and there was nothing he could do. Max sat down at the table across from Hoffa. He drank the contents of his glass in one shot and then refilled his own and topped up Hoffa's. Bull remained where he was.

"I owe you an apology, Mr. Hoffa. I thought you were part of a cover-up."

"Why would I cover up something like that? It's in the past. Let's say we get the hell out of here?" He got up and patted Max on the shoulder. Max nodded, looking at the table. He didn't see Hoffa lunge for the shotgun or Bull react. Hoffa was turning it to Bull when the first bullet hit.

It was a body shot, a high percentage shot in the chest. When a person is moving fast in unknown directions, it is the best shot to cause damage to vital organs. Hoffa went backwards as though he was punched in the sternum. The gun remained in his hands. Bull put the second shot in his head. He was aiming between the eyes, but it struck just under the nose. His teeth and roof of his mouth were pushed aside by the oncoming bullet and out the back of his head. Hoffa's body slumped to the floor. The gun fell.

"Shit!" Max spun around to see Hoffa and then Bull. The latter was still holding the pistol aimed at Hoffa, just in case.

"I think we made a miscalculation on this one," Bull said. He wasn't smiling.

"Shit," Max repeated. He got up and kicked the chair. "Shit, shit, shit."

"It's okay, shit happens," Bull said. "Let's take a few minutes and recalibrate our situation."

Max calmed himself. *This wasn't supposed to happen*, he thought. *But when does anything go to plan in this business?*

He had to stop himself from kicking the corpse out of respect. Bull holstered his weapon.

"We need to make this mistake disappear," Bull said, breaking the silence.

"Yeah." Max couldn't engage with the reality of the situation. His training kicked in but was fought by feeling impotent about his ability to complete his mission.

"This is a safe house, so it'll have some tools and even the chemicals of a working farm. I'll check out the Quonset and see what tools are in it. It's pretty beat up but it means it's been used and not just for show."

"Okay." Max was still in a funk. "See if they have any lye. Maybe we can dissolve the bastard."

"I was thinking about a tractor. We can dig a grave and dump him in it. I don't think anyone is going to be looking for him."

"You never know," Max said. "If they do, they'll be looking for a body."

"Good thing the nurse is full time," Bull said.

"I can't think about Isabella right now."

"Sorry, but I can't stop thinking about her."

"Then maybe you should be her guardian. I'm not fit to be a father."

Bull said nothing.

"Whatever the case, we need to sort this out before the cops, or worse, our superiors, find out." Max forced himself to get up. He went to see what type of bath the house had.

"I think we'd be better off burying him. It's fast and we can get out of here. We don't want to be spending any more time here than we need to. We can focus on cleaning up the place and disappearing."

"Maybe you're right. The tub won't work. And it's unlikely they'll have the right mixture. We'll find some shitty potash or something we can cover him in. We'll need to dig deep enough so that the animals don't get to him."

"Let's hope there's a tractor of some sort."

"Amen to that." Max pulled himself out of his funk and was firmly in survival mode.

There was a tractor in the Quonset, and even a loader with bucket, but the two were not connected when they arrived.

"I really hate connecting those things," Bull said. "Either it fits like a charm the first time or you end up messing around all day getting the hydraulics connected. With our luck, we'll be here tomorrow still trying to get it connected."

"We'll give it a try and change plans if it doesn't come together. The good news is that it looks good enough for our purposes."

"It's fine. Let's hope the rust bucket starts."

It did. The deep chortle of the engine brought the 1965 John Deere to life, spewing a plume of carbon from its exhaust, filling most of the Quonset.

"At least that's the hard part done." Max went to open both doors of the curved metal structure to help clear the air. He watched Bull position the tractor and the loader so that the loader could be secured into place with thick metal pins. That done, he connected the hydraulic hoses.

"It's like magic every time I see it," Max said.

"Looks like it's our lucky day. How much land comes with this safe house?"

"No idea. I wouldn't think too much. We need to find a place where people won't notice fresh digging."

"That's not going to be possible. This isn't a backhoe. It's going to make a god-awful big hole."

"Can we dig in one of the ditches, make it like it was done by the highways department?"

"Maybe, but if someone stops, we're screwed. We don't look like a department crew."

"We need to make this bastard disappear. It can't take too long to dig. Just make sure it's deep enough so he doesn't float up when the rains come."

"And let's hope the water table isn't too high."

"Let's do it to the east of the property. I haven't seen a car since we arrived."

"Done." The old tractor began its journey to the edge of the property. The road was dirt, like the driveway, but without the small stones. The ditch was wide and shallow. The grass had been cut recently by the real highways department. As Bull put the loader into the soft earth, he saw a trail of dust behind a car going too fast down the road, away from them. "So much for being unnoticed," he said to himself.

"I found some fertilizer to cover him with. Let's use the bucket to transport the body."

"Blood?"

"We'll put the body in the hole and fire the bucket before using it to cover him up. The fire will be hidden by the dirt. Should be fine."

"Max, this is really flying by the seat of our pants. I'm starting to prefer the dissolving option."

"Not possible. We don't have the right chemicals. The weeds will cover up the earth in no time. I don't think anyone takes two looks at a ditch anyway."

"You've got the rank so I'm listening, and this is your show. For the record though, I don't like it."

"Noted. Now shut the fuck up and let's get to work."

Bull grinned. "Nice to have you back, my friend. I was missing you for a while."

Max couldn't hold a straight face either. "We're messed up, you know that? I don't know how I'm supposed to raise a girl."

They worked in silence, loading the body into the hole and covering it with fertilizer. They took some branches with leaves and placed it over the fresh earth, trying to make it greener. They returned the tractor, disconnected it, and left it as they found it. In total, three hours after Hoffa was shot, he lay decomposing six feet below the bottom of a country lane ditch. Max and Bull cleaned themselves and the house, and drove off.

James Riddle "Jimmy" Hoffa was never found, despite a nationwide manhunt and involvement by the FBI and local police offices. After seven years of active investigation, Hoffa was declared legally dead on July 30, 1982. His killers were never found.

# CHAPTER THIRTEEN

# Vera

Isabella lay in her cot, wrapped in a white and pink cotton blanket. She wore a little pink cap to keep her head warm. The cot was something Bull arranged. When Max arrived home with the nurse, it was already there.

"She's so delicate." Millions of years of evolution strained within Max to make him protective of his baby girl.

"She won't break. Pick her up." He wanted a big, homely woman as a nursemaid, but Bull had hired a sultry blonde who looked more like Ursula Andress than the nun he envisioned. Max thought that she looked familiar but was unable to put his finger on it. She picked up Isabella and handed her to him. His grief over Sophia made him feel guilty when she brushed next to him as she passed the child.

"I'm not too good with children. It was always Sophia who was going to take care of them."

"You're doing fine." She stroked Isabella's face and let her hand rest on his arm.

Max looked at Bull, who shrugged.

"I don't want to disturb her sleep. Are you able to feed the baby? Do I need to do anything?"

"I'll look after everything. You run along and do what you need to do."

Max followed Bull outside.

"Are you nuts? Of all the inconsiderate things to do."

"You're complaining about Vera?"

"That's her name?"

"She's a wet nurse. She'll be able to breast feed Isabella. I thought it was a good thing."

"That explains her massive mammaries."

"I'm sorry, Max. I can get another nurse. I didn't think she'd be a problem. I also didn't think she would look so hot." He smirked and shrugged, like the kid who broke a window by hitting a baseball further than anyone thought possible. His guilt was equally mixed with pride.

"I'm not interested. She'll be fine. I don't want her getting any ideas. I need someone to take care of Izzy. I can't do it. Smith'll take me out and shoot me with all the favors and holiday requests I've put in. At some point I need to go back to work."

"You don't need the money."

"I need the work. I can't be here. Not yet. Work will take my mind off things."

"Maybe, but it will get you killed if your mind isn't clear."

"You did it. You had a kid and survived."

"That was different. I couldn't be with my wife and I knew my son was taken care of."

"And so is mine. She's in better hands with Chesty Vera than with me."

"Hey, don't be prejudiced of a good looking woman."

"I can't stand the airheads.

"Give her a chance."

"I guess she's already here. Thanks, by the way."

"Nothing to thank. You'd do the same for me."

They sat down on the plastic chairs looking out across the barely kempt back yard. Max could see where the weeds were winning the battle against the grass and where the hedges needed trimming. He used to look forward to the few hours it took to tidy up the lawn and host a barbecue for his friends. Sophia would be darting in and out, ensuring drinks and food was plentiful. He would be burning the meat and drinking with Bull and the guys. He was rarely home for long and savored every moment.

"I hear we're being sent to the next hot spot." It was as though Bull could read his mind. They had spent more time out of the United States than in it during the last twenty-five years.

"Cambodia?"

"Old news. Australia."

"What can we do over there?"

"PM is pissing in the porridge. Wants Australia to be independent."

"Doesn't sound unreasonable," Max said. "What are we to do?"

"Not sure yet. Our man Kerr is on the ground. He's officially the governor general of the country, but he's ours. No question about that."

"And our friends from the UK? MI6?"

"Not happy either, but they are spying and they know we are too. Neither cares because of some satellite spy system in the middle of nowhere. Something Pine. Can't remember."

"Sounds like it's all in hand."

"Yes and no. Our friends in the private sector—Lockheed, I think—are building a new software system that will allow us to eavesdrop on all communications over wire. This means all telephone calls, banking details, everything."

"And?"

"And nothing. That's where we're heading. I've received the briefing papers. If you'd ever show up to your day job, you'd know what I'm talking about."

Max smirked. "Sounds boring."

"Not enough explosions and killing for you?"

"I don't know. I think you're right."

"Of course I'm right. About what?"

"About needing a break. With Sophia gone, I've lost interest in everything. I can't get motivated. I'll be a liability in the field."

Bull didn't say anything.

"Maybe you take this yourself. I know Smith'll shit himself with rage but he'll need to deal with it. I'm no good in my present condition. One moment I'm mellow, the next I'm beating an old man to death. I don't want to jeopardize any mission."

Bull nodded and looked over the back lawn.

Within a week, Bull had gone on assignment, Vera had transformed the house into a baby-nest, and Max was trying to bond with his little girl.

"I don't need to hold her all the time." Vera put Isabela in Max's arms and began cleaning the cot and room.

"You need her and she needs you." She said it matter-of-factly.

Max watched her movements. She was thorough and more serious than he thought at first. "Can I ask you a question?"

"Sure." She stopped her frenetic work.

"Why are you doing this?"

"Excuse me?"

"I mean, why are you a nurse? Why not have children of your own?"

"I need to be married first."

"But you are breastfeeding Izzy. How is that possible?"

Vera was silent for a moment before a single tear crossed her face. "I can't talk about that right now. If you'll excuse me, I need to attend to something." She left the room, leaving Isabella in Max's arms. He stared after her in surprise.

Isabella didn't make a sound. Her entire existence was sleep, feeding off Vera's oversized breasts, and having her diapers changed. She was pink with a small mouth that already had red lips. Her eyes, when open, were dark blue, but they were usually closed. Max could see her lips moving and a little milk escaped from a corner of her mouth. He sat down and placed her on his chest so he didn't need to hold her—he still feared dropping her—and she could hear his heartbeat.

Vera returned twenty minutes later. She avoided Max's eyes and went to the cot. She brought new sheets and towels. Max didn't see why it was necessary. They looked clean.

"Did I say anything to offend you?"

"No."

"Obviously, I've done something that has caused you discomfort." Max was on best behavior.

"Nothing. You've done nothing wrong."

Max watched her as she finished her work.

"Shall I take her?"

"I think she's sleeping. I'm happy with her."

"Okay. I'll prepare some lunch for you and she'll probably need something by then as well."

"You can join me if you want. We're the only two adults here. It seems awkward to eat separately."

"I'd like that, Mr. Harding. It's just that, I'd like to keep things from becoming awkward if we do eat together."

"Call me Max, please. It looks like it'll be awkward if we eat together or if we eat separately. We've tried one. Let's try the other. I promise I won't bite."

She managed a smile. *She has a nice smile and face,* Max thought. Then he felt guilt as he realized his wife was barely in the ground more than three weeks. *Am I allowed to like her smile? She looks like a Playboy model but she's breastfeeding my baby. I feel nothing for her yet I'm strangely drawn to her. Her sadness is masked by her activity. Relax, Max. If you keep talking to yourself, even in your head, you're going to go nuts.* He smiled at that.

"We'll see." This time, her smile was genuine.

Isabella gurgled and opened her eyes. Max felt a tug inside as he looked at her. *Intelligent but helpless,* he thought. *All she needs is input and a safe place to grow up.* He lifted her in his extended arms, using his fingers to keep her head from falling back. She could almost hold her head steady on her own. Her small body wiggled slightly but otherwise trusted him. *There you go, sweetheart.* She smiled and he almost wept.

∞

The days turned into weeks and then months. Max knew he had to return to the field. Vera had become more comfortable with him, and he with her.

"We're like an old married couple," Max said as she cleared their salads off the table. "Even down to not having sex." He laughed at his own joke but became quiet when he saw her face go red. "I'm sorry, that was insensitive. I didn't mean anything by it."

"That's okay. I know what people say behind our backs. They look at me and they look at you, a young widower, living together and they assume."

"They can whisper all they want. I have an infant who needs a woman. That's all."

Vera began to cry and Max became confused. "What did I say?" He got up and went to her. He didn't want to touch her but it would have been wrong not to offer comfort. He put his arms around her and let her cry. "What's wrong? Everything's going fine and then I say something wrong. You need to tell me. I won't be upset, whatever it is."

She disengaged herself from his arms and found a tissue to blow her nose. "It's nothing. Really."

"It's not nothing and I think I have a right to know." Max was tipping from sympathy to anger.

She looked at him, face flushed, unblinking. "I lost my baby and my husband the day your wife died. Car accident. I wanted to kill myself. I was in the corridor the day the doctor told you. I saw your reaction. I went to see your baby. Then I got this job."

Max's jaw would have dropped if he hadn't been so angry before. He opened his mouth to speak but thought better of it. He silently nodded and Vera continued.

"When I saw you, I wanted to hold you and let you cry like I wanted to cry. But you needed to grieve. Your baby needed to feed and I needed to give my milk. I had never thought I would need to do something so much. It was my own form of grieving. I was able to feel love and give love to the only thing that could help heal me. Izzy saved me. I know she will be able to save you."

Max sat down. Sophia was in every corner of every room. Every piece of clothing he wore had been bought be her. His baby was hers. And now a strange woman has taken the one thing most dear to him and made it her emotional crutch. He was angry and relieved and shocked. He felt a pain in his chest that opened a hole in him. Without warning, he began to cry, to bawl like a baby. This time it was Vera who came to him, comforting him in her arms.

"I'm sorry." His voice was distorted from the tears. "I don't know what hit me."

"You don't need to be sorry with me."

"Just the image of that day… when the doctor told me… It hit me like a wrecking ball. My Sophia's dead."

Vera was silent.

"I need to be alone. I'm heading out. Thanks for being here." He got up awkwardly, trying not to look like he was pushing her out of the way. As he opened the door to the outside, he turned. "Sorry to hear about your loss. Was it a girl or boy?"

Vera closed her eyes. "Girl," she whispered.

Max nodded in silence and left. The room was still except for the movement of the door. It swung slowly on its hinges, then clicked shut.

# CHAPTER FOURTEEN

# *West Berlin, Autumn 1975*

Max was glad to be on assignment again. Vera was ceasing to be a nurse and was becoming a person. He didn't like it. He didn't want another woman in his home. There was only one woman in his life and she was dead. He wouldn't let Vera become more than what she was.

"Look, Max, you don't need to buy the cow to get the milk." Bull was also glad to be out doing something. Australia's internal struggle for independence was quashed with the CIA firmly in control again.

"I'm not looking for milk or the cow. I'm just saying, it feels awkward having a woman around who isn't Sophia."

"She's a looker, that's for sure." Bull wasn't going to allow Max to wallow in grief indefinitely.

"She is a mother in search of her child and husband. Izzy isn't hers, nor am I."

"But imagine her gratitude if you pretended to be." Bull allowed himself to smile. It was harmless fun.

"I don't know why I try to talk to you, Tim. I'm pouring my heart out and all you can think about is tits and ass."

"That's because I can only dream about having what you have on the platter. Besides, look at these girls here." He extended his arm to include everything they saw as they finished their second weissbeir.

"These are hookers. I'm talking about the woman who breastfeeds Izzy."

"Take a look at some of them. They aren't too far off Vera in shape."

"I can't look at them like that."

"Now you're a monk?"

"No. I see the desperation. I don't know why men even pay for it. They can go to East Berlin and get all the sex they want. All they need is some nice stockings and chocolate."

"That's what they say. I don't believe it. No girl worth going with is going to give it up for something stupid like that."

"Too many reports to think otherwise. I'd be more concerned about picking up something from the previous platoon of men she was with."

"You know, Max. We've known each other a long time. We've seen a lot of shit together. I've never known you to be glass half empty kind of guy. You need to snap out of it."

"I can't. Everything I've ever held dear has turned to shit. Everything I relied on has failed me. I'm happy I haven't put a bullet in my head."

Bull was silent. He knew it was grief talking and he just needed to wait.

"When is your son joining us?"

"I was hoping he would have arrived by now. This location was his suggestion."

"I see he has similar tastes to his father." Max ordered another round by making a circular motion with his index finger to the waitress. She nodded and he returned his attention to Bull.

"I don't care what you say. These girls look like something out of the movies. Look at that girl there. She's got leather boots past her knees with a fur coat on. Why would she need a coat at this time of year unless there was nothing on underneath?"

"Model citizen."

"Nothing like that. She's doing what she needs to do. I admire her."

Max was silent. He had seen his share of prostitutes in their line of business, but never as a client. He felt sorry for Bull and others who felt they needed their emptiness filled that way. *Even if they fill it for you, you are still alone*, he thought. *Loneliness itself is the void for most of us.*

Neither of them noticed Tim Bull Junior arrive. They were both looking out the window at the activity on the street. They jumped when a heavy hand clasped their shoulders.

"Junior, you scared the shit out of me." Max laughed good-naturedly.

"Nice approach, son. I didn't see you coming."

"It's what I'm supposed to be good at." His white teeth gleamed. He was strong and confident and almost as proud of himself as his father was of him.

"What's your mission? I'm surprised they'd put all of us in the same place together." Max picked at some sausage between his teeth.

"Top secret, you know." He flashed his grin and Bull gave him a hug with one arm. He had sat down next to his father.

"We've been sent here to wait. Not sure for what, but I can live with that." Bull took another sip of his cloudy beer. "This wheat beer is more like a meal than the stuff we have at home."

"I think that's why they have it for breakfast," Max said.

"Breakfast of champions," Bull said. He grabbed some of the meats and put it in the heavy bread and took a bite. "Not bad for an evening snack either."

"You heard about the kidnapping of Peter Lorenz?" Junior had decided his mission wasn't so top secret.

"Yeah. He was the candidate most likely to win and lead the Berlin House of Representatives. Something similar to mayor?"

"More or less. He was kidnapped three days before the election and ransomed to the federal government. He was released two days after the election when the ransom was paid."

"Okay." Bull took another bite of his mangled sandwich.

"I'm here to infiltrate the ransom group—the Second of June Movement—and report back."

Bull put his food down and took a drink to clear his mouth. "That's pretty dangerous. Who's your backup?"

"I'm going in solo."

"I don't like it, Junior," Max said. "It doesn't make any sense."

"You need backup."

"You can be my backup, can't you? Maybe that was why you were put here."

"No."

"My contact is someone in the Red Army Faction."

"Red Army Faction is Marxist. The Second of June Movement is anarchist. Now they're buddy-buddy?" Bull knew this from his briefings. He and Max needed to know the players, even if they weren't directly involved.

"Yes," Junior said. He was sitting forward, trying to talk quietly. The restaurant bar was not particularly noisy and he was confident he could have this conversation with the two most trusted people in his life. "My contact is Brigitte Mohnhaupt. Have you heard of her?"

"She's young, mid-twenties, I think. A piece of work from what I remember." Max was not drinking anymore. He was absorbing Junior's story.

"She's going to be their leader, if not already. She's my age, more or less, and I have been chosen for the sole reason of my age and look." He struck a pose. "They think I'm her type."

"People like her don't trust easily. This doesn't smell right." Bull sat back in his chair. "I don't like it."

"I don't have a choice, Dad."

Bull and Max were silent. They took a sip of their beer.

"Okay, son. Tomorrow will take care of tomorrow. Tonight we drink."

Junior lit up and sat taller. He motioned for more beer and food and the waitress nodded. When his beer came, he lifted it in a toast. "To tomorrow."

"To today," Max and Bull said in unison.

∞

The next day, Junior went into East Berlin as planned. They agreed he would be back at the end of the day if it didn't look promising. If he wasn't back, it meant he was in. They were to worry only if he didn't make contact within three days. At that point, they were to make contact with his field officer. Max and Bull had rank on their side, but the CIA was changing and nothing was certain.

"I know I've said this a few times, but this still doesn't feel right," Bull said over breakfast. They decided to have the weissbeer and white sausage with an egg and dark bread. It created a concrete-like feeling in their stomach, but at least they weren't hungry.

"Kissinger has been stirring the waters," Max said. He enjoyed the light texture of the sausage. "Ever since the dossier came out on the CIA's internal investigation. What the hell were they thinking?"

"I'm glad we're not part of the family jewels dossier. It would mean our heads would be on the chopping block."

"Let's hope we're not. There are quite a few things we've done that I'm taking to the grave unspoken."

"Amen to that." Bull finished his beer and ordered another. His nerves were showing.

"It'll be okay, Tim. Junior's a good agent. He won't take any chances."

"I'm worried about him. He's meeting up with some real psychos. This isn't what we do best. We're supposed to find assets, squeeze them of their information, and then act on it. We're not supposed to put ourselves at risk by going undercover. There isn't enough time. We're too valuable for that."

"We are expendable. You know that."

Bull frowned but nodded. "I don't have to like it."

Evening came and went. No Junior. The next day passed with the same result.

The day after brought a message. Bull and Max received it via their usual channels.

"What are you going to do?" Max said.

"I have no choice. I have to go."

"Maybe it's a trap."

"Of course it's a trap, but I have no choice."

"They'll kill you."

"I know."

"They'll kill Junior."

"I don't think so. They want me; I'm surprised they didn't demand your head too. They won't put any more assets on this. G29 is washing its hands of me."

"There is something that doesn't sit right; none of this makes sense," Max said.

"I know. No one should have known about that operation."

"Maybe it's the dossier instead?"

"I don't see how. It wouldn't have reached general CIA clerks. This was an inside job."

"Double agent?"

"Does it matter? They're going to kill Junior unless I surrender."

Max didn't know what to say.

"I wouldn't mind if I got topped in the line of action, but not like this," Bull said.

"Your son couldn't have known."

"It smelled bad to both of us and we let him go. It's as much my fault as his."

"He didn't have a choice."

"Nor do I now. I'll make the exchange."

"Let's think on this some more."

Bull slammed his hand on the table. "This is my son, Max. Think of what you would do if they had Izzy. I'm going. Send the message."

Max called his handler and told him that his mother was ill and he couldn't make it. It was the code phrase for 'yes'.

"Now we wait."

Berlin in September is a glorious place. They had relocated from the red light district to the hotels near the embassies. The roads had cycling paths and as many bicycles were out as cars. The war was a fading memory with the only reminders a few bombed building remains that hadn't yet been redeveloped. It meant that the city was new, full of young people alongside NATO soldiers holding the island city safe from the Red Scare. The leaves had begun turning color weeks ago and were now a masterpiece of visual collage.

Neither Max nor Bull took notice. Their concentration was on the wall and the place of exchange.

"They'll probably shoot him as he crosses so I can see him die."

"If they wanted him dead, they would have done it already."

"They want me to suffer. That is one way."

"I don't know what I can say, Tim. I don't see a way out. Once you cross that checkpoint, you are at their mercy." He had dry eyes but only because he didn't have time for tears. He put his arm around Bull and hugged him.

"I'd put a bullet in my own mouth if I could. I don't want to jeopardize the exchange," Bull said. "But you can. You can shoot me as soon as Junior is free."

Max felt the bile rise to his throat. "I can't do that," he said. His voice was hoarse.

"Do you know what they are going to do to me?" He looked at Max. They both knew.

"I can't kill you. I love you, Tim. You're the brother I never had."

"We had some good times," Bull said. His voice was getting hoarse this time.

They sat in silence. The phone rang. They looked at it, both frozen to their seats. Then Bull rose and took the receiver.

"Yes? Confirmed. The bull rests with the pigs. Okay."

Max raised his eyebrows, the question left spoken.

"They want to cross at Checkpoint Charlie."

"Why there?"

"Very public, lots of traffic."

"Weird. Why would they want such a well-used crossing?"

"This exchange is as smelly as Junior infiltrating the Marxists. It doesn't follow any of the normal procedures."

Max stared at the table. There was nothing to say. He knew these were the last moments with Bull. "Do you want to get drunk or go across sober?"

Bull smiled. "Finally. You may grow a pair yet." He got up and walked to the door. Seeing Max still seated, he turned. "What are you waiting for? I've got four hours to live. Let's make the most of it."

Max got up. He had a feeling he knew where Bull was heading.

The Kitty Salon was located in one of the best districts of Berlin, at 11 Giesebrechtstrasse. The buildings all looked alike to the untrained eye. They had five floors with a red pitched roof and a square hidden to the street that was to be enjoyed by each building's residents. Number 11 was bombed during the war and rebuilt. It was a famous brothel used by the Nazis to entrap foreign and local officers and diplomats into saying what they really thought about the Nazis. There were microphones placed throughout with listeners in the basement. The prostitutes were hand selected from the wealthiest and most prominent married and unmarried women. The only criteria were their looks and their loyalty to the state.

In a twisted spoof, the new madam opened the same-named brothel for all the world to enjoy. Bull and Max had heard about it but had never visited. Max, because he wasn't interested; Bull, because it was too expensive.

"You don't need to do this for me," Bull said. He was half way up the stairs. Max could see his tongue panting, both from running there and from anticipation.

"I'm not married and you are the most important person I have in this world. I'm not letting you spend your last moments alone."

"I would be a sad bastard if I can't find someone in here to be with." Even his personality was warping. His hormones and excitement had made him impatient.

"I'll be right behind you."

"Not if I can help it." He grinned but held the door open for Max.

Inside, it looked as any affluent gentleman's home would. Chandeliers, marble, and heavy brass was off-set with muted pastel colors on the walls hung with expensive looking paintings and tapestries. Max noticed that the paintings were all set in heroic and ancient settings with most of the women in the nude. Men were portrayed with sculpted muscles, presumably to accentuate their virility.

The woman who greeted Bull looked like an aging beauty queen or a senator's wife. She was beautiful and classy with no hint of vulgarity. Her dress was formal, with just a hint of a bosom and the slightest amount of leg. Her arms were bare and her jewelry was modest, but expensive. Max figured she must be the madam in charge of the whole establishment.

"Good afternoon, gentlemen. I don't recall meeting you before." She smiled and shook their hands. She spoke in almost perfect English. She must have taken one look at the two of them and decided they were Americans.

"First time," Bull said. His voice was confident but not cocky. Max wasn't sure how many times Bull had visited a brothel, but he felt it wasn't a regular thing.

"Me too," Max said.

"Then you're in for a treat. We have some boring preliminary elements to attend to first." She led them to an antechamber with a desk and armchairs.

Max elbowed Bull and rubbed his fingers together. *Money.* Then he put his hand on Bull and indicated that it was his treat. Bull nodded in appreciation.

The financial component finalized, they were led into a large lounge. They were still on the ground floor. Girls seemed to flow seamlessly in and out of the room, as though they were mingling at a ball.

"Each one is more beautiful than the last," Bull said.

"I can't believe these girls are prostitutes. They look like such nice girls."

"Women, my friend. Women. These are full blooded, full bored women. I can't believe I've spent my entire life without experiencing this."

Max looked at his friend. He was like a man stranded in a desert looking at a waterfall. Each smile and look from a girl sent him into sensory overload.

Two women sat down, one on either side of Bull. A further two sat next to Max. They all spoke English. They talked, giggled, and got comfortable with each other. A woman would occasionally get up and bring drinks for them. They didn't drink that much at first.

The madam floated into the room like the hostess to an important soirée and noted their satisfaction. The flow of new women ceased. Neither Max nor Bull noticed. After the first drink, more followed.

The tall blonde woman next to Bull began to trace her fingers in his hair. She commented on his strength, on the way he filled his shirt. She traced along his neck and shoulders. The brunette, medium-height, woman next to Bull asked him what he did and said how he must be so stressed from working so hard, how he needed time for himself, how he must be an important man. Bull found his arms around them as they moved closer.

Max looked at Bull and felt that he had done the right thing.

Three hours later, they were woken by the same women who made sure they were washed, perfumed, and fed. The coffee was some of the best either of them had tasted. Each one was treated like a Persian prince, fed the finest foods on offer and made love to the most beautiful women. Their clothes were pressed and waiting for them as they exited the bath. The two women dressed their man and kissed him as a lover does, already calculating the time before he returns.

"My friend, thank you."

"The pleasure was all mine. Remember, you weren't the only one in there. I was educated today."

"Me too. I thought I knew a thing or two, but today I felt like the most important creature on the planet. I don't know about you, but I felt loved. I didn't think it was possible to fake it, but they did. I know it's not real. Only now do I understand a fraction of what you must feel with the loss of Sophia."

Max went quiet. It should have been long enough but his grief was still there. Today was about Bull and his sacrifice. He wouldn't tarnish his last moments. They walked until they found a taxi. They drove to Checkpoint Charlie and waited.

"Those bastards have been reinforcing the wall all year. It's bigger and nastier than ever." Bull looked to his left and right, noticing the bulk of the new asbestos concrete, dog runs, and gun towers.

"We don't need to worry about any of that. We'll get your son back and then you need to get religious and find a way out. I'll be doing everything I can from this end. Just don't give up hope."

"Abandon hope, all ye who enter here," Bull said gravely.

"Dante?"

"Above the gates of hell."

He*'s in a good mood*, thought Max. *Hard to blame him.*

The checkpoint itself was barely worth the name. It was for the use of foreigners only, mainly diplomats or people having a reason to cross. The building was the size of a garden shed. It had some sandbags around it and a handful of military in uniform.

"This is such a farce," Max said.

"If it wasn't for JFK, we would have lost even West Berlin." Bull said it before realizing the significance. He shuffled his feet, becoming impatient.

"I think I see him." Max pointed to a collection of three black sedans on the other side. Out of the last one, a figure emerged that looked vaguely like Junior.

"I can barely see. Are you sure it's him?"

"It would be one hell of a coincidence if it wasn't. Are you still sure you want to go?"

Bull responded by shaking Max's hand and then pulling him into a bear hug. They held each other for a few seconds, neither wanting to let go. Finally, Bull walked quickly towards the scrappy wooden building. He held his passport and began talking. The guards led him into the tiny booth and then out the other side. He was officially in East Berlin. He waved towards his son, who was then released, and began jogging towards his father.

They met near the middle and held each other. Junior said only one word, "Sorry." Bull held him a moment longer and kissed his neck. He began walking toward his fate. He walked slowly, ensuring Junior made it to the checkpoint. He could see the armed men in their cars holding their weapons at the ready. When he turned one last time, he saw Junior on the other side, embraced by Max. They both were waving at him. He waved back.

Then, Bull pulled something from his pocket. The men watching him began to shout and run towards him. He coughed, covered his mouth, and put his hands in the air; they stopped running, training their guns at him. He looked at each one of them in turn and then bit down on the poison he had just put in his mouth.

He died. It wasn't pleasant, but was better than the alternative. Rational suicide.

Max felt a chord ripped out of him when Bull hit the ground. It took him a moment to realize he poisoned himself. He held onto Junior. Part of him blamed him for letting this happen.

# CHAPTER FIFTEEN

# USA, 30 December, 1975

Max had the only family he knew next to him over the holiday season. Junior brought a girl, Tina, he had just started seeing. Isabella was now in a high chair, if only to see what was going on. And Vera. The five of them had spent Christmas together, opening presents, laughing, and getting drunk. They all stayed under the same roof. Junior and his girlfriend slept in the main spare bedroom, Isabella in the nursery, and Vera in her own room next to it. Max slept alone in the bed he and Sophia bought. Always alone.

Berlin was at the front of his mind. When he closed his eyes, he could see Bull cough and hit the ground. He could see the frantic movement of guards as they searched for a sniper before realizing it was poison. He could still feel the sobs from Junior as he held him tight.

He knew Bull died instead of Junior. He knew the bastards never forgot, just like his government never would. What he didn't know is who told them. It was an eyes-only security level. Whoever leaked it was part of their team. Perhaps it was Junior's stupidity that caused Bull to wind up dead. Or perhaps it was Bull's stupidity to have Junior in the first place.

He remembered the brothel he had visited with Bull. By now, it had become a dream in his head. He struggled to distinguish between his fantasy and what had really happened. He felt ashamed at his enjoyment. He told himself it was only because of Bull that he went. The soft hands, the perfumed clothing and the young, firm bodies provided a relaxation he had never felt before. It was selfish, decadent, and wonderful. He could afford it. Why not enjoy himself?

He turned on his side and looked at the space where Sophia once slept. Her warmth used to cause him to throw off the covers, preferring a single sheet and being next to her. He remembered the caresses of her growing belly where their child formed. He remembered her pure joy of watching herself become, as she said, grotesque. Everything about her gave him pleasure. A different pleasure. Not the pleasure of a warm sweater, but the warmth itself, and that always remained. It was love.

The morning was cold with a dusting of fresh snow. The house was still quiet with only the soft sound of Vera singing to Isabella. It was an adult Christmas and there was no mess to be cleaned up, apart from some cigar ash and empty bottles outside. No smoking was allowed in the house with the baby. Fresh baking was beginning to fill the house with the magic that transported every adult into childhood. Max knew that he would answer every phone call with 'Happy New Year' and would be drunk before dinner ended. He rarely made it to midnight on the best of days.

"'Morning, Vera."

She turned and beamed at him. "Good morning, Max. How was your sleep?"

"Very good, thank you. Yours?"

"Always wonderful. It's so peaceful here. And Izzy is divine." She had picked up the word from some South African friends of hers.

"Glad to hear it. How's Izzy?" He came closer to her and the baby. Isabella opened her eyes and strained her neck towards him.

"Perfect. All she wants to do is crawl. I am surprised at how fast she is getting." She looked down at the baby and then picked her up. She was always picking her up.

"She looks like she's got a fighting spirit."

"Like her father." She said it but didn't look at him. She blushed but Max didn't notice.

He didn't say anything and was looking for something to eat. He started opening the cupboard doors, knowing what was behind them but always hoping to be surprised.

"Looking for anything in particular?"

"Just something to grab and go. I wanted to walk a bit before everyone gets up."

Vera's eyelids moved and she inhaled but stopped herself. After a moment, she stood up and pulled back the tea towel that covered the freshly baked banana cake. Isabella leaned her head forward to see what was under the towel and smiled at the result. Her head bobbled as she turned to look at her father.

"Great. Mind if I take a few slices?"

"Help yourself." She backed away, bouncing the baby and watching Max.

He did, using some paper towel to wrap each piece individually. He took four pieces and put two in each of his jacket pockets. "Smells great," he said.

She smiled and watched him leave the kitchen and out the back door in his sandals. "What have I done?" She said to Isabella when he had left. "He doesn't even know I exist."

Max and Sophia purchased their home believing they would live there until they died. They had almost fifty acres of woodland and some open ground. When he wasn't on assignment, Max would walk through the woods and listen to the leaves falling or the scurry of the little animals in the underbrush. Today it was silent, leaves already fallen and the ground covered with snow. His sandals were a poor choice and he soon felt the melting snow on his toes. He was determined to ignore it.

He walked to the fallen tree he had made into a bench with his chain saw. There he sat and unwrapped the cake. He took a bite and then tore a piece off and threw it into the underbrush. "Eat, you little buggers." He could visualize them coming out later to devour it. Foxes, badgers, and the rats or mice that survived the winter still needed something to eat. He did this to each piece and shook the crumbs off the paper and himself before stretching out on the bench.

He was awoken by the urgent pushing of something wet. It pushed against his face and then licked him. He pushed Junior's dog out of the way and sat up. He didn't see Junior immediately. His eyes were developing a crusty ridge reserved for deep sleep or eye infections. He rubbed them, only making it worse.

"What's the problem, hey boy?" He rubbed Archie's head and back. The tail wagged and he put his paws on Max, trying to both hug him and lick him. Max laughed and stood up. "Down, boy. Where's your daddy? Take me to your daddy."

Not waiting, Max began retracing his steps. His sock had become soaked and then froze while he slept. He could barely feel his toes. *Hope I'm not going to regret that snooze*, he thought. *And what the hell is going on with Archie?* The dog whimpered as he trailed behind Max. It wasn't a long walk but it took them from a secluded place amongst the trees to the open area in front of his house. As he caught his first glimpse, he crouched low, out of sight.

"Shit." He barely whispered the words as he felt for his gun or knife. Nothing. Not even crumbs. He saw a single black sedan parked at an angle, as though in a hurry. The door was still open to the car. And the house.

Max crept along, just behind the edges of the tree line. The paving stones they had painstakingly put in place looked like a dead zone. There was no way for him to get from where he was to the house without exposing himself.

"Stay." He looked into Archie's eyes and the dog sat. Max then ran at full tilt to the front door of the house, stopping just outside, back to the wall. He was panting. He would wait to catch his breath before he entered. He looked back and saw the white shape of Archie still sitting at the edge of the trees. *Good dog*, he thought.

He frantically looked for something to put in his hand, anything that could be used as a weapon. *Damn Vera*, he muttered to himself. *It's so goddamn clean everywhere. So goddamn child friendly, there isn't even a safety pin out of place.*

He mentally mapped the inside of the house and the points of interest. *They aren't burglars*, he thought. *Too brazen. They aren't the best assassins. Also, too brazen. This is intimidation. A show of force. But who? And why now?*

He knew someone had come to hurt them. He felt the red rage grow inside. It threatened to cover his eyes, as it did in Khrushchev's dacha. He decided to go to the kitchen and get a weapon. He kicked off his sandals and gambled that no one would see him.

The open door led to a foyer, a landing with stairs leading to the bedrooms and a hall that opened to the lounge, study, and kitchen. He opened his stride and covered the space without seeing anyone. The kitchen was quiet. The smell of the baking had faded with the open doors and the banana cake was now half eaten. There was blood on the floor. Not a lot, but enough to see that it had been dripping heavily. Max grabbed the nearest knife.

He strained to hear something. He crept along the hallway, convinced that no one was there but needing to have visual confirmation. He confirmed that both the lounge and the dining room were clear. The same with the study. That left upstairs.

He saw the blood trail lead from the hall floor up the carpeted stairs. It was a light colored carpet and the blood showed clearly. It splattered, indicating the blood fell from a distance. The drops were close together, indicating the bleeder was walking, not running. *Or the cut was more serious*, he thought.

He willed Isabella to be safe, knowing it to be impossible. He willed the rooms to be empty, knowing that to also be impossible. *The blood led somewhere.*

On the walls at the top of the landing, the blood came faster. There were hand prints on the bannister and walls. The person must have been supporting themselves. He looked into the family bathroom and noticed only the perfectly clean tiles. There were five bedrooms but the blood trail led only to one. Isabella's. Max's body jolted with adrenaline and his mouth felt like cold steel. He didn't notice his breathing or the movement. His head was steady, hands ready, as he went to the door.

It was closed. He turned the handle and saw the leg. He drew himself flat against the door and pushed hard. It smashed against the wall as he threw himself into the room.

On the floor, carpet soaked red, lay a large man all in black. He kicked him. No response. He scanned every corner, quickly opening the wardrobe to catch anyone hiding in wait. When he determined the room was safe, he knelt beside the man and felt his pulse. Nothing. He pulled the black turtle neck back to see the Russian tattoos he knew too well.

He got up and checked all the other rooms. Everything was empty. He returned to the body.

"What the hell are you doing here?" He spoke aloud as he began searching the pockets and belongings of the man. Nothing.

He went to his room, changed his socks, and put a handgun in his jacket pocket. Downstairs, he put on proper boots and went to look at the car. The Chrysler Gran Fury was a rental. He found the papers in the glove compartment. There was nothing else in it. He put the rental papers in his pocket. He'd deal with the car later.

Max looked up and saw Archie still sitting. "Come here, boy. That's a good boy." The Labrador covered the distance in no time. "Where's Junior? Find Junior. Where's your master?" Archie looked up, not knowing what Max wanted.

"Looking for us?"

Max whipped around and saw Junior, Tina, and Vera. A second later, he saw Isabella in Vera's arms. Archie had already reached him. Max was a couple of seconds later.

"What happened?" Max took Isabella into his arms. He smelled her and kissed her until her head began trying to get away from him.

"Someone came. Luckily, Vera acted quickly and called me. I was able to disarm him and led him upstairs."

Max looked at him and then the women. He would find out the true story later. "Is everyone okay?"

They all nodded. Vera came closer to Max and held on to him. Max allowed himself to wrap his free arm around her. She was shaking.

"I think you might want to take the two of them somewhere else for a while," Junior said. His training had kicked in and saved Max and his family. "I'll take care of this." He had become very professional. Tina, his girlfriend, hadn't been crying and didn't panic. *Company girl*, Max thought.

"Are you sure?"

"I wouldn't say it if I wasn't."

"I think you're right. Vera, gather some things for yourself and Izzy. Bring enough for two weeks. I'll get the car ready as well as some supplies we may need."

Vera looked like she wanted to kiss him. Her head moved forward as he talked. Then his eyes turned their attention to his next task and she stopped herself. She took the baby and nodded. "I'll be right back." Her voice was hoarse. The baby didn't make a sound.

Max put his hand out and shook Junior's. He pulled him close for a bear hug. "I don't know how to thank you."

Junior paused, and then said "You can forgive me."

Max was silent for a moment, temporarily feeling the emotion. "I have been unfair to you. I'm sorry. There's nothing to forgive. It was me grieving."

Junior looked like his father did when Max first met him—confident bordering on cocky, yet capable. The two men looked at each other in silence and nodded.

# CHAPTER SIXTEEN

# On the Run

"Do you know where we're going?" Vera peeked into the back seat to see how Isabella was doing.

"No."

"Then why are we driving?"

"We need to keep moving."

Vera tried to keep silent but the events of earlier that day had shaken her. She had never seen a dead body like that before. She remembered identifying the bodies of her husband and little girl. It was nothing like the relief she felt at the sight of the motionless body in Isabella's room.

"How was Junior able to do that?"

Max was silent.

"The man came into the house without a sound, or at least I didn't hear him."

Max let her talk. *Junior was being kind. Vera never alerted him,* he thought.

"Junior was playing with Isabella in the kitchen when he appeared in the doorway. I was cleaning up after our late breakfast and didn't even see him. All I heard was the rustle of fabric and him shouting for me to get down."

Max was visualizing it as she spoke. Junior had already debriefed him.

"Somehow, he put his hands on the carving knife. It was still wet, sitting on the dishcloth next to me. I saw his hands grab it briefly and, the next thing I knew, he threw it at the man." She was staring out of the windshield, reliving the events, talking as much to herself as to Max.

She didn't seem to mind that Max didn't say anything.

"I felt him bang into me as he pushed off against the counter. There was no delay. He threw, then lunged after the guy. At that point, I turned around. Izzy was in her jumpy-jumpy thing. The man was holding his throat and Junior had knocked him over. The man began to crawl and the blood began to flow. I kept thinking that there wasn't as much blood as I assumed there would be."

"How did he get upstairs? That's the one thing that never made any sense to me," Max said. He could see her relief that he was responding.

"He was crawling and went up the stairs. Junior was grabbing at him and was kicked off. He crawled fast, the knife still in his throat. All I could hear was the grunting of two men. He must have been strong because Junior couldn't stop him. I could hear them banging against the wall and the rail. He reached the top of the stairs when I heard the thud of Tina against him. She didn't scream. He managed to get around the corner and went straight for Isabella's room. That's where they finished him off." She went quiet.

"You were very brave," Max said. He reached over and touched her on her shoulder. He saw her head move as if to touch his hand. He had already returned it to the steering wheel.

"I did nothing. I grabbed Izzy and ran outside. Junior and Tina showed up and took me into the woods. We stayed there for almost an hour before we saw you."

"You did well. Most people would have cracked. You didn't. You got yourself and Izzy to safety. Junior has been trained by the military, you know that. Like me."

"From Korea?"

"Yeah." She didn't know that he was CIA, and especially not G29.

"Max?"

"Yeah?"

"Why haven't you ever touched me? In all our time, you've never made a move on me."

Max felt his chest tighten. It was the last conversation he wanted to have. "I don't want to be one of those creeps who takes advantage…"

"You wouldn't be taking advantage if that is what I want." She had turned her body to face him. Her face was open, hair tied back and eyes fixed on him. She searched his face and hands.

"I… I can't."

She put her hand on his leg. He flinched, then relaxed. "I need a man, Max, and you need a woman. It's been a long time."

"It still feels like yesterday to me."

"I watch you. I can see you looking at me from time to time. It's natural. And Izzy needs a family."

"Vera, I wish I could. You are lovely and Izzy loves you, but it's too soon for me."

Vera took her hand back and slumped on her side of the car. "You don't need to let me down easy. I'm sorry."

"You never need to be sorry. Not with me." He found an exit and pulled the car over. When it was safe, he put the car in park and turned to her. "You are a beautiful woman. You know that. You see how every man looks at you."

"But not you."

"I see you, and believe me, I've thought about it many times."

"Then do something about it." She had come alive again, turning towards him. She wasn't wearing a seatbelt and had inched closer.

"Aren't you afraid of being with someone like me?"

"Why? Because you're a good father and friend?"

"Because of what happened today. It'll happen again. You must know it wasn't a random attack."

Vera was not going to have that conversation. Not now. She put her right hand on Max's leg and kissed him, slowly at first, then increasingly desperate when she felt him respond.

He wanted this as much as she did and the excitement of the day heightened both of their senses. He could feel her push her body against his as she moved from her seat. He allowed his hands to search her body and she shuddered and leaned back. In reply, the car horn blasted and continued until she untangled her body. They both laughed and kissed again. When Isabella began to cry, Vera closed her eyes and sighed in resignation. Max's breathing was heavy and the windows had begun to fog up. Her blouse had come undone and she squeezed into the back seat without going outside. Max felt her buttons across his face as she passed. She smelled good to him.

"I think I need to get us out of here," Max said. He saw Vera open her bra to let Isabella feed. He saw her smile at him through the rear view mirror.

"Okay, maybe we can stop for the night somewhere?"

"You're reading my mind." He smiled, put the car in gear, and drove.

They had recently filled the car with gas and Max didn't want to stop until they were some distance from the attack. He knew they couldn't go back. He also knew what he needed to do to keep safe. He put it out of his mind. *Tomorrow, Max. Deal with it tomorrow. Today, you're alive. Izzy's alive. And Vera. She's alive and here too.* His mind fought with his body, but his instincts would keep them all alive.

∞

The Holiday Inn was family-friendly and clean. They got two double beds and put Isabella on one, surrounding her with extra pillows.

"I want to get gas again so we can get an early start. Can you sort everything else?"

"I wouldn't mind a bite to eat." She already knew what she was having for desert.

"I'll meet you in the Ponderosa in fifteen?"

"Sounds like a plan." She kissed him. It felt natural now, and she didn't want it to stop.

The restaurant found a highchair for Isabella. Max and Vera sat on the vinyl seats, sipping at their water with crushed ice in red plastic glasses. The woodwork was heavy dark wood and the salad bar was set up prominently near the entrance. They both ordered steaks with the salad bar.

"We need to figure out what we're doing," Max said. "The more I think about this, the more I fear the worst."

"I'll do whatever you need to do."

"You won't like what we need to do."

"Try me." She put her hand on his. She was a team player, one hundred percent.

"I need to die." As he said it, he watched her face contort and she withdrew her hand.

"What?"

"Today, there was one man. Tomorrow, there will be four. The next time, there will be a small army. They will find me and kill me. If I'm not there, they'll find you or Izzy."

"Why?" Her face had drained of color and fingers of anxiety clawed at her neck from the inside.

"My work."

"Army stuff."

"Something like that. These guys want revenge for something they think I did. They killed Tim and now they want me."

She was silent, the reality of the day overcoming any doubt. "What do we need to do?"

*Damn*, Max thought. *She would have been a fine wife—and good soldier.* "First, I need to make you and Izzy disappear."

"And you?"

"I'll get to me. I want to get you out of the country. You'll need to change your names, at least your last names, and not attempt to contact me. I'll be in touch when I can."

"You're not coming with us?"

"I'll take you there, but I can't stay with you. It's too dangerous. You must believe me."

She took his hands again. Then she got up and moved around to his side of the table to be next to him.

He put his arm around her as she pushed herself close to him.

"If we are careful, this should pass, but I need to know that you are both safe first."

Vera nodded.

"I have put aside some money for situations like this. I stashed it in Winnipeg. You can live there until things are safe."

"Canada?"

"We can't make it easy for them. No one will look for you there. It's big enough to get lost in but small enough to be safe."

"Can't you come?"

"Not yet. I need to see if I can clean up this mess."

She put his arms around him and kissed him on the neck. "Let's go."

They paid the bill and returned to their room. They put Isabella in her nest. She was already asleep. As Max double locked the door, Vera stepped out of her clothes. It was the first time she had shown herself to him. Max, in turn, removed his in silence. They stood looking at each other, gently touching. They moved close and kissed before going to bed. They made love with a tenderness reserved for those who already know it is lost. Each savored the other. They wrapped themselves together and fell asleep.

# CHAPTER SEVENTEEN

# Plugging a Leak
# Hughes

Isabella was safe and would learn that her father died serving his country. She didn't need to know the truth. Her safety was the only gift Max could give her. His feelings needed to come second. Vera was collateral damage. He wished it didn't need to be like that, but he couldn't see another way.

"Colonel Smith, I have a favor to ask." He was back in Langley. Smith looked the same as the last time they had spoken.

"I'll see what I can do. What is it?"

"Bull, I mean Major Timothy Bull, died because of a leak that could only have come from here. I need your permission to find the asshole and neutralize him."

Smith sat back. "I thought Bull committed suicide."

"You know that's bullshit. He traded himself for his son. He knew what they'd do and ended it. He saved the company a lot of embarrassment. He knew secrets that neither the United States nor Russia could afford to know."

"I'll grant you that."

"His son was a decoy. Whoever put him in play is part of this. I need access to whoever tried to set up the meeting between Junior and that East German bitch."

"You want to investigate the G29?"

"I don't know. Bull's son isn't G29, is he?"

Smith paused. "Yes. We didn't want anyone to know, but I guess you were going to find out sooner or later."

"Then we need to plug a leak, sir."

Smith moved a paperweight from one part of his desk to the other. "What do you need?"

"I think this has something to do with our mission to Pitsunda, Georgia. It was botched. Khrushchev left too early and Sophia was compromised. We ended up neutralizing the entire house and escaped. No one but you should have known about the mission."

"Are you blaming me now?" Smith raised an eyebrow.

"No, sir. I'm saying someone in the chain has been compromised. Someone knew we were there. Sophia is already dead. They got to Bull through his son. They even came after me at my home. They want to neutralize all of us as payback."

"Or they have a list and are removing all of us, one by one." Smith was thoughtful.

"Have there been others?"

Smith was silent at first. Then he rose and walked around his desk. "Let's just say there have been some coincidences I am not happy with. Let me think on this and I'll get back to you."

"Thank you, sir." Max saluted and left, more concerned than when he arrived.

∞

Max was scratching ideas on a yellow pad of paper when Junior joined him. There was an awkward moment as he entered Max's office. Smith had told Junior that Max knew.

"Any headway?"

"Nothing. I can't figure it. Who else would want all of us dead?"

"You've got enemies."

"Sure, but we'd be dead by now. I would expect a little more professional courtesy. One guy to take on both of us? I assume Tina is also with the company so that would be three to one. It's insulting."

Junior didn't say anything about Tina. "I agree. I don't think it's the Russians or governmental at all."

"I'm not sure how any non-sanctioned actors could get access to this information. Hell, I didn't even know about you and you're virtually my nephew." He flipped his hands to show his palms before replacing them on the table.

"I'll take that as a compliment."

"You should. Well done." Max wanted to ask if Bull knew, but didn't want to change the direction of the conversation.

"Who's rich enough to hire this type of service?"

"Good thinking. Some Arab Sheikh? Indian Raj wishing things were better?"

"What have we done to them? Three more members of G29 were killed. Office staff. I never heard of them. A secretary and two clerks. It doesn't make sense."

"We have a leak. That is the only thing that makes sense."

"We can't get the files."

"Then we need to work with what we know. First, I still believe that this has something to do with Khrushchev. That was over twenty years ago. There were only four people in the world who knew the whole story."

"Who was the fourth?"

"Smith."

"There were other missions. Ones I can't talk about to you or even think about in my sleep. The only people who knew about the details were your father, Sophia, me, and Smith."

"What about the clerks and secretary?"

"Perhaps they stumbled across something."

"Don't say another word. Let's continue this conversation outside of this building."

Max nodded and they left. They both knew that every room was bugged. It was recorded and stored, just in case. The CIA never missed an opportunity to gather intelligence. When you are the gatekeeper, your biggest threat is another gatekeeper.

∞

"If you're thinking what I think you are, stop right now."

"Then you're thinking it, too," Max said.

"It's dangerous. It's treason. We have no proof."

"We'll never have proof. That's what makes our division so effective. We don't exist. There can't be proof. It's also why the clerks were killed. That was his mistake. He should have waited until we were gone."

"Maybe he assumed we were, so he sanctioned the hits."

"Why only one guy? He knew we would beat him."

"Did he? If I hadn't got that knife off, there was no chance. He was stronger than me. He took a beating from me and Tina like nothing I've ever seen."

"But three on one?"

"I also don't get it. It isn't consistent."

"The question for me is whether we act on our gut or wait until the next guy. If we're right, we'll be dead."

"If we're wrong, we'll be dead—by hanging or firing squad."

"Court martial will be the least of our concerns."

Junior looked at his father's most trusted friend. "I'm behind you, whatever decision you make."

∞

"Are you sure you have the right address?" Junior looked at the house from the curb. It was where the very rich and ambassadors lived. "I can't believe we're in DC."

"Welcome to Normanstone Terrace," Max said. "There are only one hundred and sixty homes, all detached. A lot of them are used by embassies."

"At least we know where he put his money."

"You can't live here if you have to earn your money," Max said. "This is wealth inherited or wealth taken. You can't earn enough in a lifetime of jobs to buy any of these houses."

"At least not an honest job."

"I think the best approach is head on. We'll ring the doorbell and see how it goes."

"Sounds risky."

"So does a court martial."

They left their car at the curbside and walked to the elevated position Colonel Smith's house commanded. It wasn't gated like some of the others, nor did it have a sweeping driveway as most did. It was a large, imposing three story brick and stone mansion.

"Nice door." Max touched the heavy oak before pressing the doorbell.

Soon the door opened. In the space stood a muscular man, around forty, in pressed jeans and a t-shirt with a black sweater thrown over. It was a V-neck and Max could see the white of the t-shirt.

"Can I help you?" His voice sounded educated and confident. His body was relaxed and he looked straight at Max, then Junior.

"Yes, we are here to see the colonel." Max tried to sound official.

"I'm not aware of any appointments. Is he expecting you?"

"No."

The man paused. "He isn't in right now, but I can tell him you called if you…" His voice was cut off as the two men pushed him back into the house and closed the door behind them.

Junior moved fast, securing the man's hands behind his back using duct tape. He wrapped his mouth and continued around the man's head. He would adjust that later.

"Are you alone?" Junior asked him. The man's eyes bulged. "Nod or shake your head."

The man nodded.

"Is the colonel expected?"

The man nodded.

"Is anyone else expected?"

The man shook his head.

"Is there a security system we need to know about?"

The man shook his head.

"I'm asking because we'll kill you the second we hear an alarm or see cops. Let me ask you the same question again. Is there a security system we need to know about?"

The man closed his eyes and then nodded slowly.

"Take me to it." They lifted him up and let him lead the way. They got to the wood paneled study and he nodded to the desk. Junior held him as Max searched it. There was a panic button positioned underneath. He followed the wire and disconnected it, careful not to break the circuit. He knew that cutting the security wires would trip the alarms as sure as if they had pressed the button.

"Good. Any weapons?"

The man shrugged and nodded. *Of course.*

"Take me to them."

The man led them to two locations in the study, one in the hallway cupboard and two in the master bed-room.

"You've been very good. I'm going to remove the tape. If you scream, I'll put it on again. If you struggle, we'll kill you. Do you understand?"

The man nodded. They noticed a wet patch in the crotch of his jeans. Junior removed the tape as gently as he could. It was holding the hair firmly on the head and he had to rip it off. The man tried not to scream but, with the amount of hair that came off, it was inev-itable. It was like he was waxing his head. The tape held a clump of hair.

"What's your name?"

"Lee."

"Okay, Lee. We're going to have a word with your boss. If everyone co-operates, everyone lives. Understand?"

"Yes, sir."

"Good. When is he expected home?"

"Anytime now."

Max was looking around the master bedroom and bathroom while Junior interrogated Lee. The room itself was three large interlocking sections. One housed the bed, which was super-king-sized, at least seven feet long. The other was a bathroom that was as large as the bedroom. It had the usual toilet and bidet but also a free-standing bathtub and a walk-in shower for at least two with a bench in it. There were two sinks with elaborate woodwork surrounding a mirror that stretched from wall to wall. There were two toothbrushes, each in their own cup next to their own sink. Max returned to Junior and Lee. Lee was now sitting in a chair in the antechamber, the third room. Max noticed two further doors that led to walk in closets. Both closets were full of men's clothing.

"Who else lives here?" Max asked. "I don't want to have to discover some girlfriend in another room or opening the door while we are talking to the colonel."

Lee began to cower. "There's no one else here."

"But I saw the two toothbrushes and the two wardrobes…" Max's voice trailed off. He was beginning to see.

Lee no longer looked at them in the eye.

"You're not saying…" Junior said. He was beginning to smile.

"I think so," Max said.

"That might explain a few things."

"I don't give a damn right now. But he is our only lead."

"And now we have some leverage." Junior looked at Lee with renewed interest.

"Stay with him as I check out the house. We need an appropriate interrogation room."

"How about that bathroom? It has all the requisite components." Junior smiled.

"I'll be right back. You get him into position."

Max left Junior with Lee and began a systematic search of the house. It had twelve bedrooms, two kitchens, three large lounges and, of course, the study. Its hallways were wide and ceilings high. There was a dry cellar with the usual garbage, Christmas decorations, and rumbling boiler. The house was heated with water radiators, each an elegant work of cast iron art with legs that made it more furniture than a functional component. The wine collection and laundry room completed the basement. He returned to see that Lee was secure and then went to the front of the house to wait for his target.

Smith arrived almost two hours later. He had been drinking and didn't manage to get the keys in the lock on the first try. When he opened the door, he called for Lee and then began to unpack his work things. First, his keys went onto the antique console table nearest the door. It had a marble top and the keys made a distant sound as they hit the stone. His briefcase was put down next to it and his jacket was hung on a hook. He didn't react to the silence until he was five steps in. He cocked his head, listening for his lover, and a worried look crept onto his face.

"Looking for someone, sir?" Max pointed the gun at his head. "Your sidearm, sir."

"What the hell is this?"

"I'm sorry, sir, but I need to ask you some questions."

"You can bloody well do so tomorrow." He began to walk.

"I wouldn't do that, sir. We have Lee upstairs. We just need to talk to you."

He paused, then sighed and nodded. "Okay, you bastards. What do you want to know?"

"Let's go upstairs and talk."

"I like it here. We can have some scotch. I've got the finest in my study."

"No need trying to trip the alarm or find your weapons. They have been collected. Lee told us everything."

Smith's shoulders dropped a little.

"I want you to walk upstairs and not to make any fast movements."

"You're making a big mistake, Max."

"That's Colonel Harding, sir. I have rank and station."

"As do I, and you may have forgotten that I outrank you."

"For now, sir. But treason is not taken lightly by any of the government institutions—secret or not."

Smith fell silent again. He walked up the stairs. He could feel the burn of Max's aim at his back. He turned right into the master bedroom. It was the only door open and he assumed that was where he would be led.

"Take off your uniform and strip to your t-shirt and boxers."

"You should know that boxers aren't good for you, soldier. Messes up the manhood."

"Sir, I appreciate the humor but spare me until after this is over."

"I hope you two know what you're doing." He noticed Junior when he walked in. He strained to find Lee.

"I hope so too, sir. I didn't make this decision lightly."

"Is this about your friend? Bull?"

"Bull, Junior, me, and others."

"I don't know anything."

"We'll see about that."

"Be careful, soldier."

"I am a soldier, and so are you. Now you find out what happens when a soldier crosses the line."

"Me or you?"

"We'll find that out soon enough."

Junior grabbed the colonel's arms and taped his hands behind his back. He tied his knees and ankles together. He was dressed only in his underwear and t-shirt. Together, they dragged him into the bathroom. He had gone silent, readying himself for what he thought was to come. In the bathroom, legs out of the bathtub, was Lee. He was on his back, alive, also taped at the knees and ankles. When he saw Smith, he had to stop himself from screaming. The tears had arrived long before.

"I can see why you live in DC and not in Langley," Max said. "You've got quite the cozy arrangement going on here." He nodded towards Lee. "We had an interesting conversation. I thought Lee was the one with the money, but he said you were. I would like to know how you can afford a place like this on a government salary."

"I got some money from my parents. I've saved my whole life…"

"Bullshit. You could save your entire life and not be able to rent one of these houses."

"It's not true. I have money." He looked pathetic. The stern omniscience of authority evaporated when the right button was pushed.

"You can tell us now or you can tell us later. You know the drill. You know what we're about to do. There's no shame in talking. Everyone talks."

They dragged him into the shower head first. His feet stuck out of the opening. On the ceiling was a large shower head, with two mobile ones on the walls. Junior sat on Smith to ensure he didn't wiggle away. They took his t-shirt and lifted it over his head to cover his face and left it there.

"Last chance, Colonel."

"Go fuck yourselves."

Max turned on the shower. They all got wet. It wasn't ideal but they needed to know the truth. The technique was five centuries old and used by the Inquisition. It was non-torture torture authorized by the CIA and used for decades by the US government. Both Junior and Max were taught the techniques as part of their training. The skill was in not killing the prisoner. By covering the breathing passages with a cloth and then applying water, the body generates an automatic gag reflex. The danger is vomit. If it's inhaled, the prisoner can die quickly.

"Shall I let you vomit, sir, before I commence? I don't want to accidently kill you."

"You'd better kill me, you motherfuckers. 'Cause you're dead after this."

"I think Colonel Smith has lost his sense of humor," Max said to Junior. He always relaxed before these missions, but never understood why. Junior remained stone-cold serious. They realized there was no going back.

Max took the hand-held showerhead and used it on the fabric covering Smith's face. He held his breath at first, but Max held it there until his body reacted, bucking and almost throwing Junior off. He held it until he heard the gurgling sound of a drowning man.

"It would be better if we had the slant board," Junior said. He glanced at Lee, who remained in the bathtub. He had experienced the same thing earlier and had no fight left in him.

Max didn't say anything. He was studying Smith's body language. He began to apply the water. Again, Smith held his breath, and again, Max held it in place until he heard the desperate sounds of frustrated inhalation. He didn't punch Smith or inflict any other bodily harm. He let nature run its course. Smith began to smell as he shit himself. He could sense the shame in that more than the improvised waterboarding.

"Do you remember anything, sir? Or shall I continue?" Max lifted the t-shirt back so that he could see the colonel and make eye contact.

Smith nodded. "You bastards are going to pay for this."

Max put the shirt back in place and continued with the water.

"How about now, sir?"

"They wouldn't give it to me."

Max removed the shirt and let Smith sit up. He turned off the water and the two of them remained in the shower. Junior checked on Lee and stood at the ready.

"Excuse me, sir?"

"All I ever wanted was to become a general. I've given my whole goddamn life for it. I've done everything for them."

"You betrayed your country for a pin and a promotion?"

"You wouldn't understand."

"Try me."

He looked at Lee through the gap. Max began to understand. "You hit a glass ceiling because they found out you were gay?"

"Some asshole, I don't know who, began a campaign to stop my rise. They couldn't prove anything, but you know how it is."

"They could have come here and figured it out in two seconds."

"People don't see what they don't want to see. You think there aren't queers in the army? Navy? Marines? No one will admit it. They'll be discharged faster than you can say cocksucker."

"Boo hoo, sir. I'm sorry that you're gay in a straight world, but that doesn't give me the answers I'm looking for. My best friend, his father, is dead. Clerks and secretaries, who have served loyally for decades, are dead. This is not something you do if you're angry at your pecker."

"You'll never understand. It's not that simple."

"Tell me who helped you. Who paid for this place? We both know there's no way you could afford it. Hell, I couldn't afford the lighting bill on my salary." Max didn't need to tell him that he could afford to buy the entire street a hundred times over. That was a secret he would take to the grave.

Smith's bravado evaporated as he visualized what he had done. "I was approached a number of years ago. I never met the guy in person. He's too powerful for that. He's untouchable. All he wanted was information."

"What kind of information?"

"Anything that might affect his airlines or contracts with foreign governments. He found out about G29 through one of my… paramours."

"Your little head betrayed your division, so you let your big head betray your country?"

"It wasn't like that." The water made him look like a refugee. He couldn't wipe his nose and his hair splayed flat and down around his head, despite its short cut.

"You took money to live with your boyfriend in exchange for lives. Patriots died because you wanted to play house with your boyfriend. My best friend died because you wanted a promotion. How is it not like that?"

Smith was silent.

"I'll tell you how it will be. I can make this fast or slow. I can make you watch Lee being subjected to the worst things Junior and I can come up with—and we're pretty sick bastards, I can assure you. Then I'll take my time on you. I will keep you alive as long as possible until you beg whatever fucked up god you pray to that you can die."

Smith was silent. He knew how this would end the moment the gun was pointed at him when he walked in the door.

"Tell me who your sugar daddy is. Who did you betray your country to?"

Smith was silent.

Max nodded to Junior, who yanked Smith's legs. His head banged against the shower floor and his shirt was put over his face again. Water was applied until he choked. Then applied again. Lee was brought over and made to stand above Smith, naked and blindfolded. On cue, Junior slit Lee's penis lengthwise in one cut while Smith watched. Lee let out a scream that surprised even Max. His manhood was splayed and bleeding profusely all over Smith. When Lee collapsed, Junior and Max held him up and let him bleed on Smith's face. One further cut opened up Lee's organs. Lee passed out, still held upright. His intestines fell out with the help of Junior and covered Smith. Smith began to scream, coughing on the blood and shock of seeing his lover disemboweled.

"Hughes," he screamed. "Howard fucking Hughes."

"Are you sure? There's a lot more twisted shit I can imagine. We're just getting started. I can stem the blood and keep your Lee alive for some time still. It won't be so pleasant for you, though."

"I'm sure. Just kill us and be done with it."

"You believe him?" Max asked Junior.

"If this doesn't get the answer out of him, nothing will."

"Okay, sir. Thank you. You're dismissed." Max used his knife to cut Smith's jugular artery in one clean motion. It was painless as he bled out.

Junior did the same to Lee and they left the two bodies to empty their blood down the shower drain.

"What are we going to do with them?"

"Torch the place. I'll get something to douse the bodies. It should destroy our presence here. There'll be a shit storm of activity when this hits the fan, but I have a feeling our investigators will hush this up once they realize that Smith died with his gay lover. It'll all come out, jokes will be made, and then the whole thing will be forgotten."

"You sound sure," Junior said.

"I'm counting on it. The CIA and military hate gays almost as much as they hate Reds. To protect themselves, they'll make this go away."

"And us?"

"We'll probably get promoted. There's a vacant office that needs filling." Max smiled.

"Payback's a bitch."

"Careful. Don't jinx it. Plenty of people will want to do the same to us. That's what makes me so pissed with this guy. We do the worst things to even worse people for our country. He betrayed all of us. It means it'll happen again."

"We can't guard against everyone."

"But we can take out the one man who is responsible for Bull's death."

"And nearly our own," Junior added.

*And the loss of my daughter*, added Max silently.

∞

Three months later, they were in Acupulco, staring at the Aztec–inspired Princess Hotel.

"Howard Hughes is no Colonel Smith," Max said. "You can't just walk up and ring the doorbell of the richest man in America."

"He doesn't have a doorbell. He has bell hops. He probably owns the damn hotel he stays in."

"From our intel, he runs everything from Las Vegas at the Desert Inns. His residence is on the ninth floor and his empire is run from the eighth. I think he's here for the drugs."

"Maybe we should hit him where it hurts, in Vegas, not here. Blow up his nerve center?"

"I want him. I don't care about his things. I want him to know that there are certain people who will fight back. We will not all be ground into dust. Every so often, a piece of grit will get in the way. It can't be ground, it can't be bought, and it won't go away."

"Yeah, yeah. Nice pep talk. I've seen True Grit as well. We're not in the movies. This man is dangerous because he doesn't appear so."

"That's why we've taken the time we have. I want to look into his eyes and know why."

"And then?"

"There is only one outcome for the man who killed Bull."

"How are we going to get near him?"

"I've got that in hand." Max had dipped into his piggy bank. He needed to get next to Hughes the way men have always gotten into places they didn't belong. It cost a small fortune, but he could spare it. *Besides*, he thought, *what was he going to spend the money on anyway?* "Just remember that he goes by John T. Conover. And, apparently, he looks weird now."

"Huh?"

"He's lost a lot of weight and has let himself go. He's nuts."

"I'm not letting it go at nuts. He killed my dad."

"Agreed. He's got a drug problem. I've arranged our cover. We're going to be Mormons. Those are the only guys he trusts right now."

"Why?"

"Who knows? He's got billions. He can trust whoever he wants."

"What do we need to do?"

"Familiarize yourself with how Mormons act. You can't smoke or drink or even have a Coke. Definitely no swearing. Your body is a temple. Remember that."

"How long will we be here?"

"As long as it takes."

"Let's do this. At least the weather is fantastic. A hell of a lot better than a DC spring."

"We deliver the codeine tomorrow. I don't know what to expect. I don't expect a high level of armed security. Just a lot of clean cut young men."

"Don't tell me he's gay," Junior said.

"Not him. He's had more women than either of us could hope for."

"Okay, nuts it is. We'll see how fate treats us tomorrow."

The weather the next day was equally glorious. Max and Junior dressed in dark pants with white shirts, open at the neck, with t-shirts underneath, and dress shoes. They carried less than twenty dollars in their pockets and no weapons. The codeine was in a small leather satchel that looked like an old-fashioned doctor's bag. It contained fifty doses and glass syringes with detachable metal needles.

"We're here to see Mr. Conover." Max stood tall and looked straight into the eyes of the first line of defense.

"Mr. Conover is not seeing anyone today."

"He'll see us."

"I'm sorry, sirs. But you'll need to leave whatever you want to give him with me. I'll send a message."

Max instinctively gripped his bag tighter. "Sorry. Call up and see if he'll let us in. If not, we'll leave. I can't give you this. It is for him only."

The man had met them as the elevator doors opened. They had made it past the foyer and into the elevators with little trouble. Max could see more men standing at ease further up the hallway.

The man lifted a temporary phone, with the cable running into the distance and around a corner past a large potted plant. When he returned the phone to the receiver, he nodded. "Please, go ahead."

Max and Junior continued walking. The next set of guards asked to search them, and they complied. They raised their hands and allowed surprisingly rough hands to pat down their arms, armpits, and groins. *Missed the ankles*, thought Max. They looked into the bag, then at each other, and handed it back to Max. They were allowed to pass.

The suite where Hughes stayed held the best view of the water and the surrounding areas. It was the most expensive and sought after room in the hotel. It had a massive bed with an en-suite bathroom that was almost as large as Colonel Smith's. Both men gasped when they saw the richest man in America.

He was lying in his bed, propped up by pillows. His hair looked like a hippy's, his fingernails were beginning to curl, as were his toenails. He wore a diaper and nothing else. The curtains were closed, leaving only artificial light. The room was hot. There were boxes that looked like empty Kleenex containers at the foot of his bed, placed the way one would place their slippers.

"Welcome, my boys. Thank you for this. You are angels."

Junior stood by the door, instinctively providing cover, as Max approached Hughes.

"We have your medication, sir. This is my first time with you. Do you want us to administer or do you?"

"Please, you do it. I really don't like needles."

"Do you want someone else to help us? There are a lot of men outside. I can call them in."

"No, no. You are okay." He was lifting his arm in the direction of the bag, willing the codeine to be put into him. He was paper thin. Max could see he was a tall man, maybe 6'4" or so, but he looked like he was in a concentration camp.

"Anyone else in your suite who can help?"

"No, I said no. Just put the needle in. I am in real pain today. The damn heat is killing me. I think my ex-wife has got them to turn off my air conditioning. And the food is inedible." Max was sitting next to him and Hughes put his arm on his to make it easier.

"I'm sorry to do this, sir. I know you are in pain, but I need to ask you a few questions." He moved quickly, taking the tape meant for bandages from his bag and placing it over Hughes' mouth. His eyes opened wide in surprise but was otherwise calm.

"Are you okay?"

He nodded. Max had performed the routine often enough to know when and how to apply pressure. They were now in the danger zone. Junior moved closer to the front door and wedged his foot against the edge. Hughes didn't make a sound.

"I need to know why you ordered Smith to kill those men."

Again Hughes' eyes grew wide and then relaxed. *His brain is fully functioning,* Max thought. He removed the bandage.

"Did they send you?"

"Who?"

"You know. It's the reason I gave the order."

"Why are they after you?"

"Too many reasons. I'm powerful. I have powerful enemies."

"But why?"

"Do I need a reason? I do what I want."

"You ordered the death of Tim Bull because of a whim?"

"What? Who's Tim Bull? I'm talking about Area 51. I've been there. They want to shut me up."

"Listen, Mr. Hughes." With the mention of his name, his eyes grew big again. "We need to know why you contacted Colonel Smith to neutralize certain people."

"Oh that." He looked almost annoyed. "It was a favor from an old friend. I couldn't refuse. You know how it is. We scratch each other's backs and all that. Smith had the added value of being petty, greedy, and ambitious. Very easy to manipulate."

"You wanted to protect your empire?"

"My empire? Dear boy, I wouldn't put my trust in a back-stabbing prick like him for anything. He wanted something and I needed to give him a reason he would understand. Like I said, it was a favor. No big deal. Now, please, let me have my medication."

Max's eyes were beginning to develop the red mist that had taken over on more than one occasion. He willed it to subside as he continued his questioning. The man was so frail, there was no resistance left.

"Tell me, sir. One more question. Who did you do the favor for?"

Hughes paused. His head began to nod, then shake, then nod. "It all comes back, doesn't it?"

"Excuse me, sir?"

"It all comes around. My new friends keep telling me how I need to save my soul. That I need to cleanse myself of my sins. And here you are. The messengers of my death. Just make it quick." He let his body go limp against the pillows.

"I'm not here to hurt you, sir. I just need answers. I can see you are not well."

"What do you want to know?"

"I need to know who you did the favor for and why."

"The why is easy. Us oil men stick together. It's hard out there. Everyone thinks it's easy to deal with the Arabs, the governments, the distributors. Everyone wants a piece of your flesh. If it were up to them, we would all be picked clean by the buzzards."

"I'm sorry, sir. I don't understand."

"The favor. I did it because, at our level, money doesn't mean anything. Favors are the currency of the truly rich."

"So now he owes you a favor."

"Exactly." Hughes' mind was as sharp as if he was still twenty-one.

"And who is the person?"

"Who else could it be? Who's as rich as me?"

"I don't know, sir. I'm not looking to guess. I need an answer."

"Getty. Jean Paul Getty."

Max was sitting close and injected the first syringe of codeine. Hughes inhaled deeply and then exhaled. He sunk into his pillow. He didn't even notice when Max left the needle in his arm, breaking off the glass from the metal where the two met.

"Thank you. Thank you for making it easy to leave this world." Hughes drifted into a daze. Max injected another syringe and broke off the glass, leaving the needle inside. Hughes drifted asleep within moments.

Max gave him three more syringes before lifting Hughes forward and delivering two percussive blows with the heel of his hand to each of Hughes' kidneys. *The shock should shut them down*, he thought. He lay him back on his pillow. It was difficult to know if he was unconscious or in a deep sleep. Max gathered up his things and got off the bed. He nodded to Junior and they left.

Howard Hughes died in his sleep. The autopsy would later declare that he died of kidney failure. All of his organs and brain were in fine working order. When his body was discovered, it was put on a plane to Houston. He was declared dead once inside United States airspace at 1:27 pm on 5 April, 1976.

# CHAPTER EIGHTEEN

# *Rogue Getty*

"I'm sorry I didn't let you do it," Max said.

"I was there. That's what matters."

"He was talking and I was in the zone. I really wanted you to give him justice."

"Don't mention it again. There's still one more. The one who is behind all of this."

"If there's one thing I've learned, you never find or kill the person who is behind everything. New ones keep popping up. It's as though the opportunity presented by the vacuum at the top forces the predator within us to evolve and step forward. As with killing a man, no one knows what his response will be until put into that position. Some can, most can't."

"I've got something going on in Russia, but when I'm back we can go to the UK and visit our friend, Mr. Getty."

"He won't be easy. I'm expecting that he'll be waiting for us."

"From what we've been able to ascertain, he's already suffering from ill health. His heart, the records say."

"These old bastards live forever. They're dying for decades and everyone is tip-toeing around them, waiting with outstretched hands. I want to see the man who killed my family and I want an answer why."

"That's the problem, isn't it? With Dad, I knew why. It was all about who betrayed him. With you, it's both. None of it makes sense."

"It will soon," Max said. "We'll know the whole story and either he'll be dead, or we will be. Either way, it ends soon."

"You'll get everything ready?"

"Yeah. You do what you need to do. Come back alive and then we'll talk."

Two months later, Max walked into the four hundred and fifty year old mansion. Sutton Hall was built in 1525 and was an impressive collection of bricks and stained glass and manicured lawns set in Surrey, a short drive from London. Getty bought it instead of living in a hotel and to foster his Middle Eastern business. It was known for its decadent parties with the most beautiful women of loose virtue entertaining sheiks, businessmen, and diplomats from every corner of the world. Getty called it home.

"Deliveries in the side," said a voice. Max looked and saw an impeccably dressed man in a suit pointing the way.

Max nodded and changed directions. He was one of five men carrying crates of champagne and fine wine. It was the most recent order from Berry Brothers and the van was parked near the deliveries entrance.

"Relax, Max," he said to himself. "Now's not the time to lose your cool."

"What's that, mate? You say something?"

"Just mumbling to myself."

"You American?"

"Canadian," Max lied. "Missus dumped me. Thought I'd start fresh as far away as possible."

"I know where you're coming from." He nodded knowingly and put another crate on his shoulder. It was a long walk and his load was heavy.

"Do you know what's happening here?"

"Who knows? Who cares? Some rich buggers having another party. Big deal."

Max nodded. He could see a marquee being set up and the caterers had just arrived. It was routine. He dropped off a few crates before beginning to mix with the other deliveries. His objective was to find a way in.

"Over here." He heard the fingers snap and another servant of the house was directing him to do something, he couldn't see what. The man was pointing to some broken bottles that were foaming on the stone.

"I'll clean that up, right away. Where are the mops stored?"

"Just over there."

"Yes, sir. I'll get it done." Max found what he took to be the garbage can and began picking up the dark glass. When the staff member saw that he was doing what was being asked, he left him to finish on his own. Max did so and then went quietly into the house.

It was easy to retrieve the house's plans from the local council's office. Listed buildings, especially one of this importance, were detailed inside and out and available for anyone to see—if they knew what to ask for. It was a simple layout set over three floors. Two levels had high ceilings and windows looking out from every perspective. The third was just the roof section, with the staff living in the eaves of the roof with no windows. His objective was to get as near to the master bedroom as possible. He used the servants' staircase to climb to the top floor. Everything was empty with all the activity going on below. *If I have to choose luck or brains, I'll choose luck*, he thought with a chuckle.

He knew where he needed to go. If there was a party, it meant Getty was doing deals. Sick or not, he was the head of his empire. He would be meeting with dignitaries and aristocrats and businessmen eager to multiply their wealth with his. The guests would drink, laugh, and possibly even dance a little. They would drift from the ancient ballroom to the marquee or the other way around. They would compare their prosperity against others. If anyone wanted to be prime minister or president or chief executive officer of a company, this was the place to be. Max made himself comfortable in a shaft he knew was located immediately next to Getty's private study. That was where the real business would take place. He had brought enough food and water along to last forty-eight hours. He also brought a bag for any waste. He hoped he didn't need to use that. Until the action began, he decided to have a nap.

Ten hours later, he heard the voices he knew would be there.

"Mr. Rock, Mr. Roth, I'm pleased that you could make it."

"The pleasure is all ours," Mr. Roth said. "How is your health? I have been hearing terrible things."

"It's fine. Just gossip. My doctor says I'll live another ten years if I give up cigars and scotch. Maybe fifteen if I give up girls as well." He laughed.

"They broke the mold when they made you," Rock said. "To your health."

"Cheers." They all took a drink.

"I don't want to raise a delicate issue so quickly, but I wanted to get your thoughts on the use of special drawing rights to ease the pain of inflation and the high oil prices." Roth was a frequent visitor and friend of Getty. They were able to dispense with the pleasantries demanded of etiquette.

"It is what our group has been working towards for decades. The dollar isn't working as well as we had hoped."

"No," said Roth. "I expected more stability. The government is not listening closely enough to us."

"Meanwhile, our products are shifting the power into the wrong hands," Rock said. "I'm happy with the money, as are you, Mr. Getty, but it doesn't help our cause."

"Not at all," Roth said. "And we need you to assist with your friends in OPEC."

"They've all gone mad," Getty said. "It's almost as bad as with Hitler. The only difference is that they're not able to work together."

"Small blessings," Roth said. "We can't afford another madman."

"It was all fine until Pearl Harbor," Getty said. "Everyone was making money. GM, Dow, Ford, IBM, and all the big banks—all of us were feeding the machine. Spain was the precursor and we were able to put our infrastructure in place. Who would have thought that Hitler would have been so untrustworthy?"

"It's the Japs. I didn't have a problem with Hitler," Rock said. "Oil and steel don't have nationalities. The Japs didn't play by the rules. We need to get a member from that part of the world if we want to deal with the world as it has evolved."

"I understand your concerns, Mr. Rock, but you know the rules."

"We lost some fine men back then," Rock said. "My father was especially fond of one of the members, I can't remember the name. At the time, the Order had decided not to get involved in the daily activities of countries or in the lives of our members' families."

"That's all ancient history," Getty said. He was agitated that they would even raise the issue. "We have moved on. We are richer and more powerful than ever. What else could we ask for?"

"Youth?" Rock said. "What I wouldn't give for another fifty years."

"True. Health is the most important," Roth said. He was solemn again as he saw his friend deteriorating in front of him.

"Forget youth or health. Give me a couple of girls of my choice and some good wine, and I'll be happy to live the weekend." Getty's eye still had the glint. The three clinked glasses and settled into the issues of finance and oil logistics facing the global economy.

When Rock and Roth left, Getty began pacing his study. Max could hear him swearing. "Those fucking bastards. They think they can run the world, just the two of them. I should have just put a bullet in their heads when I had the chance. Fucking Hitler. Another bastard who couldn't deliver his promises. And now my body decides to fail me." He stopped when he heard the knock on the door. Some sheikhs paying their respects. Max kept his ears open but couldn't understand their Arabic.

The party continued without incident and Getty went to bed. Max waited until the house was asleep before he entered Getty's bedroom. He put a wedge under the door and approached the sleeping body. It wasn't moving. Max took the tape and put it around the face, knowing that it would cover the mouth. As he applied pressure, the face looked up at him, eyes bulging. It wasn't Getty. It was a large, strong man, who grabbed Max. Two other men approached from the corners of the room and restrained him. They were professionals, and he couldn't move.

"Don't move a bloody muscle or I'll gut you stem to stern. Understood, mate?" The voice came with the bad breath of cigarettes and sleep. He was like steel and his grip didn't relent. He felt the blade next to his neck and he stopped struggling.

"Understood," Max said.

"Then let's go see the guv'nor."

They opened the door and led him to the same study. Getty was seated behind his desk. Max was put in front of him, hands and feet bound, on the Queen Anne chair beside him.

"Comfortable? That will be all, thanks."

"You were waiting for me?"

"I'm not totally stupid. It may have been a coincidence that Tolson died, but for Smith and Hughes to suddenly meet with a similar end? You really need to change the way you kill people. Both Tolson and Hughes died of kidney failure. I was able to get a copy of the autopsy report. The bruising was unmistakable. Smith and his… friend… died of symptoms my investigators felt were consistent with torture employed by the CIA."

Max said nothing. He didn't know how it was possible to come to those conclusions with a charred set of corpses.

"Don't worry. I'm not going to let you go, so we may as well talk freely."

"Why are you doing this? You have everything."

"People who have nothing always assume others have everything. It isn't true. We all have constraints on our actions."

"Why Bull? Why the clerks?"

"I had nothing to do with that. I just wanted a leak plugged."

"What is the leak?"

"You."

"What? I don't know the first thing about you."

"You opened your investigation into the Hildebrandt affair. I was simply shutting it down."

"What Hildebrandt affair?" Max wanted to keep him talking.

"Don't play dumb with me. You inherited some money and decided to spend it chasing ghosts. I'm here to tell you that the ghosts are dead. Let them rest in peace."

"I wanted to find out who killed my family. Someone pressured Himmler to keep them in the camps. I think it was Hoover. That bastard died before I could have a word with him. So I met his lover. Then my best friend was set up to die. I learned of Smith, who led me to Hughes, who led me to you."

"Very good, and in record time. You are missing things, obviously, but the connection is good enough to give you full marks. Not bad for the CIA."

"I'm a patriot."

"You're an assassin pretending to be an analysist."

"And you're an assassin pretending to be a millionaire."

"Please, a billionaire. If you're going to insult me, at least be accurate." He smiled and took a drink of water.

"Enough of this. You're going to kill me, fair enough. But tell me why."

"Why is always a simple question with a simple answer. Life is about power and love. The answer is also about power and love. I had all the sex I could hope for—that is really just about money—and I am still chasing love. Power was my aphrodisiac. I wanted more."

"How does this connect to my family?"

"There was a group of us who met to try to work together, you know, to make things better for ourselves. The other members talked about things like a new world order and grand social plans, but I never took much notice of it. I looked at their power relationships and realized there were two men who controlled it and, in turn, most of the world. It was a simple hostile takeover."

"I don't know what the hell you're talking about."

"Then shut up and let me talk. Or would you rather I put a bullet in your head?" Getty was agitated but wanted to tell Max. "We were all supporting Hitler. He knew how to treat businessmen, not like Roosevelt and the liberals in the US. Russia was becoming a force and we needed a stalwart to hold the line for us industrialists. Then came bloody Pearl Harbor. The Americans made it illegal to trade with Germany and most companies pulled out. I didn't. I doubled down and made unimaginable riches. My father felt I would destroy the company, but I made it great. You don't achieve greatness unless you take chances."

"What does that have to do with my family?"

"Your great grandfather was also a member of our Order. Before my time, naturally, but he made more money than most of us. Then he hid it. No one cared. But I learned about it and I wanted to leverage my own efforts with it. The family never knew about it. They wouldn't miss it."

"Then let them live."

"Someone knew about it. I would hazard a guess that you now know about it. It's the only reason I'm still talking to you. It must have grown to quite the sum by now without all those greedy hands taking pieces over time."

Max said nothing. He had no intention of telling this sociopath anything.

"I backed Hitler with everything I had and I used Hoover to achieve that goal. I was able to protect and promote him—in exchange for information that helped me. I'm not a charity, you know. I was able to end the Hildebrandt line and then scoop up the money. The only problem was that Hitler lost and you disappeared. I assumed you were dead. I had no reason not to believe the stories. Besides, I had better things to think about—rebuilding Germany and Europe, for one."

"So everything you did was to outmaneuver Rock and Roth?"

"Rock and I are in the same industry. His control of the Order with Roth made him the biggest. Roth and his family controlled the world with finance before I was born. If I didn't get rid of him, he would eventually crush me."

"Why not just kill them?"

"You don't know the Order. They would find out and kill me. That's why I went to such lengths to distance myself from the dissolution of you and your friends."

"This whole thing sounds ridiculous. I don't believe you."

"You don't need to believe me. I wanted to achieve my ends, but they turned on you just the same. Roth and Rock voted to abandon your family in the camps despite having full knowledge of the event. You should be angry at them."

"They may be guilty, but it is from not doing anything. You actively hunted my family."

"You have no idea of the type of people we are talking about. You have your CIA but our group was around a century before it was formed and will be around after Langley is in cinders. When it looked like the Nazis were going to lose, I even had Himmler killed—and he was in Allied custody. They say he committed suicide but you know I'm telling the truth. Everyone associated with that fiasco had to be terminated."

Max looked at Getty and saw a different glint. It was the power of taking life. He was a predator who had developed a new taste. "And you were able to keep your seat at the magic table."

"Exactly. As though nothing had happened. If anything arose that caused concern, it could be dismissed as wartime hubris or folly."

Max had heard enough. "Okay. You've answered my questions. Now kill me and finish the job."

"You'll die, but you need to tell me some things as well. It would be a waste to kill someone with as many secrets as you have. I'm sure I will be able to put them to better use than you can."

Max's innards went liquid involuntarily. No man could withstand torture for long, and he had a feeling

Getty was particularly imaginative in getting people to talk.

"It's only fair. I told you everything you wanted to know. Now, it's your turn to tell me everything I want to know."

"And that would be?"

Getty paused. He had been readying himself to move to the second basement he had dug for such purposes, when sound became an issue. "I would like to know who your employers are, for a start."

"You already know. You had my CO in your pocket."

"I didn't know him. He was Hughes' stooge. You don't seem to understand. My structure is not that dissimilar to yours. I can only know things people report to me—or where I initiate a report to dig further. Hughes was the insulation between Smith and me. I didn't need to know about him so I didn't. All I knew was that he was CIA."

"Then you know who my employer was."

"Not quite. There is something different about your group. I can't find out anything about it other than its existence. There seems to be little to no paperwork and even fewer tongues to wag. In many ways, it is an institutionalized version of my group."

"You keep talking about your order as though it's something special," Max said. "It sounds like any other handful of investment clubs that dot the world. You're delusional."

Getty ignored him. He couldn't understand—or he was trying to distract him. He pushed a button and the three men appeared again. "Take him to the room."

Max didn't struggle as his legs were freed. They decided they could trust him to walk. He did so and went to the basement, past the state-of-the-art heating and cooling and humidity system, past the locked cellar containing the fine wines delivered the day before. Past the downstairs kitchen to a locked door which, when opened, led to a recently dug lower level. It was not on the plans and had been made to Getty's specifications and requirements for privacy.

Max was put into a room with padded walls, measuring fifteen feet by fifteen feet. Its ceiling was also relatively high at nine feet. Max noticed the hanging devices before anything. In the middle of the room was a dental chair with straps for his arms and legs. He sat down without a fight and watched as they tightened the straps to the point of pain.

Getty appeared after Max had been put into place. A chair was brought for him and placed four feet from Max. A man in a white lab coat arrived and opened a small black bag. A table was brought in and the bag was placed on it. He didn't speak.

"I'm sorry for the elaborate arrangements, but I use this room for multiple purposes. You see, I have guests with vivid imaginations who have the need to enact their fantasies. These rooms allow them to play." He extended his arm towards the door. Max took it to mean there were many more such rooms.

"So you can stick things up each other's asses?" Max said.

Getty laughed. "Again, you don't know what you are talking about. This is consensual sex. The women and men need to be matched to their needs and wants. It would be boring, wouldn't it, to eat vanilla ice cream your entire life?"

"Perhaps, but I don't stick it up my ass for a change. I simply try chocolate."

"Why the fascination with the ass, Max? Is this something you fear the most?"

"You have the most beautiful women on the planet with bodies that grace the silver screen. Why subject them to whips and chains and whatever else you do here?"

"I'm not here to discuss sexual preferences with a dead man. Anton, you may begin."

The man in the white coat pulled out his instruments. The three men were summoned and strapped Max's head firmly to the chair's headrest. Then, he was forced to open his mouth and a device was put inside to spread his lips and hold his mouth open. Immediately, he could feel the saliva begin to choke him.

"I hope you're not comfortable, Max. Anton is an amateur dentist and I try to assist in his education where I can."

Max felt the metal of a dental plier grab one of his front teeth. Intellectually, he was ready for what they were about to do. He understood that he would be subjected to pain, but feeling the metal changed the experience. He could feel Anton's bony body as he leaned against him to find the necessary leverage. There was a sheen of sweat on his forearm as it rubbed against Max. He smelled of disinfectant and Max found that ironic, almost funny. The firm grasp of his front tooth extended into the plier and Anton's forearm. There was little movement as he felt the force being applied. When it didn't come out easily, Anton repositioned himself and began again.

The pain was blinding. It went straight into the brain and caused him to think of things he thought he had made himself forget. The day at the book depository. Khrushchev's dacha. Tehran. Istanbul and Manilla. All became vivid again. His mind fooled him into thinking that Korea and Vietnam were happening in the present. He felt the tooth begin to release and tears began to flow. It was a natural reaction. He felt Anton remove himself and present the tooth like a trophy in front of his eyes and then Getty's.

"Interesting, isn't it?" Getty began. He had to say it twice before Max realized he was talking to him.

Max closed his eyes. He focused on not drowning on his own saliva, and now blood.

"Take that thing off him," Getty instructed. "Good. I've heard about this technique but never used it until now. It is supposed to activate the memory. No real torture necessary. No threats. No beatings. Simple biology."

Max's head restraint was removed and he leaned forward, coughing. He spit the blood onto his shirt and allowed himself a few deep breaths. "I have never heard of this technique," Max began, trying to ignore the pain or the situation. "But I do see the results."

"Good. Now perhaps you are ready to be more reasonable and begin answering some of my questions. We're both reasonable men. I can see that in the way you have handled yourself. Part of me is regretting this."

There were three muffled bangs and the three occupants of the room turned their attention to the padded door. Another two muffled bangs, then silence. "Expecting someone?" Max said.

The door began to open. "I told you, we were not to be disturbed!" Getty was aggravated and began to rise from his chair. He sat when he saw the strange man enter. It was Junior.

"I thought you weren't coming," Max said. He no longer felt any pain.

"You, over there. Next to the old man." Junior indicated by waving the muzzle of his gun.

"Who the hell are you?" Getty said. He wasn't afraid, merely curious.

"The son of the man you murdered. Tim Bull."

"How many sons of bitches am I to be dealing with?" He said it as much to himself as Max and Junior. "I told you, I had nothing to do with that. That was Smith, your CO, covering his own ass. I can't help it if he cocked it up."

Junior put a bullet into Anton's head. He undid Max's straps.

"One of us needs to get those bodies inside," Junior said. "I have a feeling you have a splitting headache. I'll do it. You cover that bastard." He handed Max the gun.

Max took it and didn't say a word. He spat blood every few seconds instead.

"The wheel has turned," Getty said with a smile. "This is the type of thing I was trying to do all those years ago. The prey becomes the predator. Rock and Roth are the worst people to be ruling the world. You have no idea. You think I'm cruel? This is kid's play compared to what they would have done to me."

"I'm not interested in your stories or your lies." Max heard Junior dragging the large bodies inside. "I don't care about your little club or the bullshit that you carry out. I care that you killed my best friend. I care that you killed my family. I care that I grew up as an orphan, thinking I was unloved and unwanted. You are the one who doesn't understand. You made me alone in this world. Even now, I am alone. It's too late for me. No person can make me feel complete. I place that at your feet."

"Very dramatic, Max. Well done. Sorry about the tooth. I was only trying to…"

"Shut up or I'll put a bullet in you now."

"You'll never get away with this. I'm not some street thug who can be murdered and discarded. You'll be hunted to the ends of the Earth."

"Let me worry about that. Junior, that's it? Good. Put the gun with them. It'll look like some messed up arrangement gone wrong. Who knows, maybe the family estate will hush this whole thing up. Frankly, I don't give a shit." The blood shot through his missing front tooth.

"And what about me?" Getty was looking amused.

"We have something specifically for you. Junior? You can do the honors."

Getty looked afraid for the first time. Junior pulled out a syringe with a long needle. He approached the frail man, stuck it in his heart, and pushed the contents inside. Jean Paul Getty died instantly of a heart attack. Junior and Max carried him to his master bedroom and left him in his bed. It was not yet dawn on June 6, 1976. The bodies were found and the story covered up, as Max had hoped. The only concern of the estate, the government, and the Order was the continuity of operations of the Getty Oil Company and his other two hundred enterprises. No one missed him.

# CHAPTER NINETEEN

# A New Beginning

Max enjoyed the crescent in the morning with its ever-present river. There was a path for the joggers and their dogs, for cyclists, and for people like him. He walked with Isabella and Vera, the crisp morning air threatening the winter that would be there in a couple of months.

"How is school?"

"Fine." She was dressed in her school uniform and a little shy.

"How have you been keeping?" he asked Vera. He held her hand, but only in friendship. She had since married.

"Better than expected. Sean has been a godsend and I feel like a local here."

"Ten years will do that to a person."

"You still look the same. I can't get used to your new name."

"It is part of my retirement. I'll never be allowed to leave entirely. They always have strings on you. But so far, I can't complain."

"Small town life. Don't you miss the excitement? The guns and all that?" She tried to sound casual but it still hurt her when she saw him. The pain of losing him was greater than the fear of that day.

He smiled and kissed her on the cheek. "That's all in the past. I'm just a retiree living on a pension. I play around in my garage, make some things. Nothing more."

"Doesn't your mind need more?"

"Sometimes."

"Don't you get lonely?"

"Always."

His reply made her stomach tighten. "Don't you want to do something about it?"

"The ones I love die. I can't have that anymore. It is the price I need to pay."

"You've paid enough."

"You don't know the sins I have committed."

"You were a soldier. These things happen."

Max didn't respond. He squeezed her hand and she turned and smiled. She held Isabella's hand.

"It's here, sweetheart. Do you want us to walk you to the school or are we allowed only to the gates?"

"To the gates, Mom. I told you. I'm a big girl and the other girls are watching."

Vera kissed her on the cheek and laid her hand on her head. "Are you going to say goodbye to Uncle Joe?"

"Goodbye, Uncle Joe." She said it in the awkward way children do when they want to be quiet but know they need to say something. The words had to battle to get past her lips.

"Will you give me a hug?" Max bent down to her level. When she did, he held her tight. He had to turn away when he released her. He watched her disappear behind the steel bars of St. Mary's.

"Will I be seeing you much?" Vera's eyes glistened with unfallen tears.

"It may be best that I visit only occasionally."

"If I didn't say thank you before, please remember that I would not be here if it wasn't for you. Our home on Wellington Crescent, a beautiful daughter." She wanted to continue, but feared what she would say. Her heart cried when he was near her. When he was gone, she could still feel his body all those years ago. It was as though with the thought of him, the idea and the flesh became one. Time ceased in memory. The past and the future became confused with emotion. The present became overwhelming for her.

"You need to think of her as yours. I will always be around. If you need anything, you only need to call. I will be there. You can count on it."

"Max, I mean Joe, walk with me some more."

She linked her arm in his. She never wanted to let go.

## Genealogy: The Hildebrandts

The Patriarch:   Meyer Hildebrandt, Industrialist
      Born 1830      Died 1913
First Wife:      Siegrun Hildebrandt
      Born 1854      Died 1883
Son:   Joseph Adel Hildebrandt
      Born 1880      Died 1945
Grandson:      Otto Hildebrandt
      Born 1905      Died 1941
Second Wife:   Anna (nee Voigt)
      Born 1858      Died 1939
Daughter:      Elizabeth Hildebrandt
      Born 1883      Died 1941
Grandson:      Theodore Shultz
      [changed names after WWII]
      Born 1899      Died 1973
Great-Grandson:       Max Harding
      (Born Joseph Hildebrandt-Shultz)
      Born 1931
Great-Great-Grand daughter:    Isabella Harding
      Born 1975
Great-Great-Grandson:  Jack Harding
      Born 1992

# ABOUT THE AUTHOR

Baron was born in Canada.
He currently lives in South East England,
somewhere near the Surry/Sussex borders.
Sightings vary.

If you'd like to follow Baron and receive free samples
of his future writing before it is published, please visit
www.baronalexanderbooks.com